I Only Have Lies for You

A Rat Pack Mystery

Books by Robert J. Randisi
(J.R. Roberts)

Rat Pack mysteries

Talbot Roper novels

The Gunsmith series

Lady Gunsmith series

Angel Eyes series

Tracker series

Mountain Jack Pike series

For more information visit:
www.SpeakingVolumes.us

I Only Have Lies for You

A Rat Pack Mystery

Robert J. Randisi

SPEAKING VOLUMES
NAPLES, FLORIDA
2020

I Only Have Lies for You

ISBN 978-1-64540-192-6

To Marthayn,
I Only Have Love for You—
As always.

"Are the stars out tonight?
I don't know if it's cloudy or bright
'Cause I only have eyes for you, dear."

Song by Harry Warren, lyrics by Al Dubin, 1934

Prologue: 2009

"I'm not advocating that everyone should drink. It just worked for me."

The speaker was Jackie Gleason. I was watching him doing the Tonight Show with Johnny Carson on YouTube. I'd had a computer for some time, but had only recently discovered YouTube. I started watching clips of the guys: Dino, Frank and Sammy, either together as the Rat Pack, or individually. It was a real pleasure to see them all again.

Although I was still in good condition for a guy in his 80's with diabetes, and I was able to live and get around on my own, I had started spending more and more time in my apartment. I had a computer, a large screen T.V., and a DVD player. They were all hooked up together, so I could actually watch my clips on the big screen.

After watching the same clips over and over again, though, I had started looking for others or performers from that era. I watched Jerry Lewis, Don Rickles, Buddy Hackett, Bob Newhart, Red Skelton, Nat King Cole, Julie London, Steve and Eydie, Keely Smith . . . all people I knew over the years I worked in Vegas. Tonight, I had found clips of Jackie Gleason, and the one on the screen at the moment was from 1985. I had watched a few episodes of the Honeymooners, and some clips from his American Scene Magazine variety show, and then came to this one.

Jackie was sitting with Johnny and Ed, talking about his career and his new movie—which would be his last—called "Nothing in Common," with Tom Hanks. I had seen the movie years ago, but I made a note to pick up the video next time I was out, so I could watch it again.

Jackie was 69 in 1985, when he did the Tonight Show, and had never been on before. He'd never be on again, because he died 2 years later. I attended his funeral in 1987, saw a lot of my old buddies there.

I paused the video, got up from the sofa and poured myself a small bourbon. It was Jackie's drink; and he had introduced Frank Sinatra to bourbon. So, I decided to have a short one in their memory.

I brought it back to the sofa with me, sat down, and started the clip up again. Jackie had a habit that was very evident. While he spoke with Johnny, he'd reach into his jacket pocket and come out with a cigarette. Not a pack, just a single cigarette. Then, from the same pocket, he'd take a lighter and light it. As they talked, he smoked it down, put it out in an ash tray, then reached into his pocket and did it again, coming out with a single cigarette. I remembered that habit from years ago.

As the clip ended, I thought back to a time when I first met Jackie in Miami, and then later, when he came to Vegas to see me because he had a problem that Frank told him I could help him with.

It was 1965 . . .

Chapter One

Miami Beach, Florida, February 1965

I flew into Miami with Frank on his private plane. He was going to be performing at the Fontainebleau Hotel for a few dates and had invited me to fly over with him from Vegas. I had some time off coming to me, so I accepted.

It helped that Dean and Sammy were going to be in Florida, as well.

We were the only two passengers on the plane. His valet, George Jacobs, had not made the trip with us. As we landed, Frank looked over at me and said, "Sammy's already at the Eden Roc, did his first show last night."

"And Dean?" I asked. "You said Dean was gonna be here, too?"

"Yeah," Frank said, "like old home week. The Summit back together, only not in Vegas."

Frank never referred to him and the guys as the Rat Pack. That came from the newspapers. He always referred to their meetings in Vegas, their shows at the Sands, as the Summit.

"Dean's here," Frank assured me. "He's doin' Jackie's show."

"Gleason?" I said. "You mean that American Scene Magazine he does?"

"That's it," Frank said. "He moved the show here last year. He wanted to be able to play golf all year round. And probably look at girls in bikinis every day."

"Are you gonna see him?"

"Gleason? Well, sure, he's a buddy of mine. Actually, he's more of a mentor. He introduced me to one of my best friends."

"Who was that?'

Frank smiled and said, "Bourbon."

***

We deplaned and got into a limo the hotel had sent for Frank to take him over to Miami Beach. Since Frank was playing the Fontainebleau, that was where he was going to be staying—most likely in one of their best suites.

"I'll have to get a hotel room somewhere—"

"Forget it, Pally," Frank said, cutting me off. "You're with me. I got you a room at the Fontainebleau. Not a suite, but a nice room—on me—so don't worry about it."

"Thanks, Frank," I said, "but I coulda got a room somewhere else—"

"Hey, I invited ya, didn't I?" Frank asked.

"Yeah, you did," I said. "Thanks."

"No worries, Clyde."

Frank was always very generous with his friends, and this was just another example of that. I decided to accept as gracefully as I could. The Fontainebleau was way above my pay grade, so this was going to be interesting.

The limo took us along Collins Avenue, which ran parallel to the beach, and before long the hotel loomed ahead of us. It also fronted the beach and was the most lavish hotel in Miami Beach.

Frank had filmed a scene from the movie *A Hole in the Head* at the hotel in '59, and in '60 he shot a television special during which he welcomed Elvis Presley back from his military service in Germany. In 1960 it was also the setting for Jerry Lewis' movie *The Bellboy*. It had been prominently featured in the short run of the T.V. show Surfside 6. And, most recently, had appeared in last year's James Bond blockbuster movie *Goldfinger*. It's the hotel where the girl is murdered and painted gold—or was it the other way around?

The limo pulled up in front of the hotel, and immediately there was a bellman with a cart, and a man in an expensive suit grabbing for Frank's hand, pumping it enthusiastically.

"Take it easy, Jack," Frank said, reclaiming his hand. "I've only got two of those."

"I'm sorry, Mr. Sinatra," the man said. "We're just so pleased to have you here with us at the Fontainebleau. I'm the assistant manager."

"Did you say assistant manager?"

"Yes, sir."

"Don't I even rate the manager?"

The man paled immediately and began to stammer.

"Oh, sir, let me assure you our manager will be with you shortly, he's just, uh—"

"Hey, I'm kiddin' with you, Charlie," Frank said. "Take it easy."

"Oh, yes," the man said, "of course, Mr. Sinatra—"

"Now listen to me," Frank said. "Have my luggage taken to my suite. I do have a suite, don't I?"

"Oh, of course, sir."

"Okay, good," Frank said, "have my luggage taken to my suite, and have my friend's bag taken to his room."

"Your friend?"

"This is Eddie Gianelli. I told you I was bringing a friend."

"Oh yes, of course," the assistant manager said. "Mr. Eddie G., correct?"

"That's right," Frank said, "everybody knows him as Eddie G. Put his bag in his room and bring the keys to us in the bar. We're gonna get a drink."

"Yes, sir," the man said. "Anything you want. It's on the house."

"Of course it is." Frank grabbed my arm. "Come on, Clyde. We're gettin' a drink."

I looked at the assistant manager, shrugged and followed Frank inside.

Frank led me to the Bleau Bar, on the lobby level of the hotel.

"Two bourbons," Frank told the bartender. "Jack Daniels and water, on the rocks."

"Comin' up, Mr. Sinatra."

We managed to find two seats at the busy bar and settled in.

"When's your first show?" I asked.

"Tomorrow night."

"What are you gonna do until then?"

"I thought we'd go see Sammy at the Eden Roc tonight," Frank said. "Then I'm gonna have lunch with Jackie tomorrow. You wanna come and meet him?"

"Ah, I can stay here and look at girls on the beach," I said. "I don't wanna butt in."

"You ain't buttin' in," Frank said. "I'm invitin' you. You'll like meetin' Jackie. He's one of a kind."

"I would like to meet him," I admitted.

"Good," Frank said, "if it makes you feel better, I'll call ahead and let him know you're comin'."

"Okay," I said, as the bartender set the drinks in front of us. "What about Dino?"

"He'll be here tomorrow for Sammy's openin'," Frank said. "He's gonna do Jackie's show, and you know how he hates to rehearse, so he's not comin' early."

Frank finished his drink and put the empty glass down on the bar. As if by design, the assistant manager appeared.

"Here are your keys, gentlemen," he said, handing us each a key. Frank's room was on a much higher floor than mine.

"You both have a view of the beach," the man said.

"Very good . . . what's your name again?" Frank asked.

"Oh," the man said looking alarmed, "I never gave it to you. Allow me to introduce myself. I am Arthur Korson."

"You weren't here the other times I stayed, were you, Artie?"

"Oh, no, sir" Korson said. "I just came to town for this job—"

"Well," Frank said, slapping him on the shoulder, "you're doin' a bang-up job, ain't he, Eddie?"

"Bang-up," I agreed.

"I'm gonna freshen up," Frank said to me, ignoring Korson now, who sort of slunk away. "How about we meet down here for dinner in a coupla hours?"

"Suits me," I said.

We left the bar and walked to the elevators, each ready for a little alone time.

Chapter Two

I was satisfied with my room. Why wouldn't I be? I was in the Fontainebleau, wasn't paying, and I had a view of Miami Beach. The room was lush—as lush as any I had stayed in at the Sands, in Vegas. Only this was better. The phone wasn't going to ring any minute with some problem or other that required my attention. I wasn't going to hear from my boss, Jack Entratter, to come down to his office right away, either for a job, or a balling out.

I unpacked, since I've never liked living out of a suitcase. I wasn't sure how long we'd be there, but we'd be flying back the same way we came, on Frank's plane. It wasn't like we had to check out on a certain day.

Once I was unpacked, I decided to take a shower before meeting Frank for dinner. As I was drying off, the phone rang. I had an immediate fear that it was Entratter, telling me to get back to Vegas right away. But I was wrong. It was Frank.

"Hey, Pally, you mind if we don't eat dinner in the hotel?" he asked. "I mean, I know it's on the house, but I sorta wanna get out for the night. Whataya think?"

"Suits me, Frank," I said. "I'm in your hands. Like I told you, I've never been to Miami Beach before."

"Awright!" he said. "See you out front in fifteen minutes. The same car."

"See you there."

***

With all the wonderful restaurants in Miami Beach—many of them Cuban—Frank naturally had the driver take us to an Italian place. It was right on Collins Avenue, and was called Fellini's.

"I discovered this place when we shot 'Hole in the Head' here," he told me, as we got out.

They remembered Frank—or simply recognized him—and showed us to a table ahead of a lot of people who were in line, but because it was Frank, nobody seemed to mind.

As usual, Frank ordered spaghetti and meatballs. I opted for the chicken parmesan, and we both had a martini—Beefeater Gin with just a shade of Vermouth, the way Frank liked them. Strictly speaking, I wasn't a martini man, but I drank them with Frank.

"I called Jackie as soon as I got to my room," he told me, after we'd ordered. "He insisted I bring you to lunch tomorrow."

"That's great," I said. "Maybe there'll be some June Taylor dancers there too, huh?"

"Actually," Frank said, "Jackie's latest is June's sister, Marilyn."

"You're kiddin'," I said. "Isn't he still married?"

"Oh yeah," Frank said, "but that's not gonna end any time soon. Even though Genevieve filed for legal separation in fifty-four, when she first found out about Marilyn, she ain't givin' him a divorce. She's a real devout Catholic."

"That's a tough situation, for both of them. Where does she live?"

"I don't know," Frank said, "but not in either one of Jackie's houses."

"How many does he have?"

He's got one here, a party house with a great view of the Miami Beach Country Club, where he plays golf. And he just had a new one built outside of Hialeah. But his favorite golf course is Inverrary Country Club in Lauderhill."

"So he really likes it here, huh?"

"He loves Florida," Frank said. "I don't think anythin' will ever pry him away from this place."

The waiter came with our martinis and Frank quickly ordered two more, even before we took a sip.

"And his show is goin' great guns," Frank added. "Good for him."

"Tell me something about him," I said. "I mean, since I'm gonna meet him tomorrow."

"You know who dubbed him 'The Great One?'"

"No, who?"

"Orson Welles."

"Because he's so funny?"

"Naw," Frank said, "it's got nothin' to do with that. He and Welles went drink-for-drink one night and he drank Welles under the table. The next day Welles called him 'The Great One.' Jackie loved it!"

"I never heard that story," I said.

"I'll tell you another thing," Frank said. "He comes from the same background as you and me. More you, since you both grew up in Brooklyn."

Frank was from New Jersey which, to his mind, was in the same ballpark as Brooklyn—but that was only because he wasn't from Brooklyn. I knew Gleason would feel the same way about New Jersey as I did.

"You guys are gonna get along."

"Do I have to play golf with him?" I asked. I was not a golfer.

Frank laughed. "You can leave that part to me and Dino."

Relieved, I sat back and allowed the waiter to set down our plates, and fuss with our silverware and nap-

14

kins. When he had everything to his liking, he stood up straight.

"Anything else, gents?"

"Just keep those martinis comin', Pally," Frank said, "and make sure they stay dry."

Chapter Three

I woke the next morning with my mouth feeling stale from all the martinis Frank and I drank. No sooner had I opened my eyes when there was a knock on the door and a voice calling, "Room service."

"I didn't order room service," I called back.

"Compliments of Mr. Sinatra."

I crawled out of bed and staggered to the door. When I opened it, a smiling bellboy wheeled in a cart and asked, "On the balcony, sir?"

"Sure," I said, "the balcony's fine."

He wheeled it out there, then headed for the door.

"Hold on, I'll give you—"

"I've already been taken care of, sir," the bellboy said. "Have a good day."

After he left, I went to the bathroom to wash my face and hands, try to wake myself up, and rinse out my mouth. Then I went out to the balcony to see what Frank had sent me. The odd thing was, aside from the taste in my mouth, I was fine. I didn't even have a hangover.

I lifted the cloche on the table, expecting to see bacon-and-eggs, or pancakes. Instead, what I saw was a perfect martini sitting there. Next to it was a card, and on the card was written: "Hair of the dog."

Very funny.

Thankfully, next to the cloche was a pitcher of ice cold orange juice. I poured myself a tall glass, drank half of it down. It was the best cure for what ailed the inside of my mouth.

I carried the rest of the glass to the rail and looked down at the beach. The bunnies were already out in their bikinis, pursued by males of varying sizes, shapes and ages. They could have their pick. This was their jungle, and many of them came down to Miami Beach for this very hunt. But the game was capture and release, nobody was looking for anything permanent. It was the same for the men, but they weren't as well armed.

And when the time was right, they all left the beach and came to Vegas. The games were different there, so were the rules, and the ammunition was money.

But I wasn't hunting. I was just along for the ride, and to get away from dice, roulette wheels and cards for a while. Not that I would mind a little catch and release, myself, if it came along.

I finished my juice and went back inside, leaving the martini to sit where it was, like a little time bomb.

Frank and I agreed not to meet for breakfast, because we'd be having lunch with Jackie Gleason—who, Frank assured me, could eat or drink both of us under the table.

I decided to shower and go downstairs for a little breakfast by myself. Just something light that wouldn't interfere with my lunch, but that would assure I wouldn't have to start drinking on an empty stomach. Because, having lunch with Frank and Jackie Gleason, I knew there would be a lot of drinking.

***

The same car was waiting in front of the hotel. I got there before Frank. The driver was leaning against the car, and, when he saw me, he opened the back door.

"Thanks," I said.

"Yes, sir."

He remained outside until, moments later, Frank came rushing out. He spoke briefly with the driver about whether or not he knew where a certain restaurant was, and then the driver opened the door for him to climb in next to me. Funny, it didn't matter that I'd known him personally now for about five years, and that we were friends, there were times I was still intimidated in his presence. On this morning I had to pinch myself. I'm in a limo in Miami Beach with Frank-fucking-Sinatra!

"Hey, Clyde," he greeted me.

"'mornin', Frank."

"Sleep well?"

"Pretty good," I said. "This place has mattresses as good as the Sands."

The driver got in and we were off.

"Jackie's lookin' forward to meetin' another Brook-lynite" Frank told me.

"I hope I don't disappoint him."

"Believe me," Frank said, "you're still more Brooklyn than anythin' else. After all, I'm still Frank from Jersey."

Yeah, right, I thought.

***

When we entered the restaurant, we were greeted expansively by a maître d', who showed us to a table where Jackie Gleason was waiting. Jackie stood and opened his arms wide for Frank to rush into. The two friends greeted each other enthusiastically, and then Frank introduced me.

"Jackie, this is my buddy, Eddie G."

"Eddie G.," Jackie said, sticking his hand out. "I've heard a lot about you, pal!"

We shook hands. Jackie's handshake was firm, and he didn't put his weight behind it. He looked just the way he looked in "The Hustler," when he played Minnesota Fats to Paul Newman's Fast Eddie Felson, 4 years ago. Those were two of the most riveting performances I'd ever seen on the screen at one time. Throw in George C. Scott, and

19

you had a film that was a tour de force. At least, that's what some of the critics said. I always said it was a helluva flick.

"Glad to meet you, Jackie," I said. "I've heard lots of stories about you, too."

"I bet you have. Come on, fellas, siddown, siddown."

We all sat. I'm not going to name the restaurant because it was never well known that Jackie ate there, but it was a Chinese place. A waiter came over and Jackie ordered for the table.

"I hope you fellas don't mind me orderin', but I've got a helluva hangover, and this is the best cure for it!" I'd never heard of Chinese food for a hangover, but it was okay with me. I had spent most of my early life growing up in Bensonhurst and Bay Ridge. Bensonhurst had huge populations of both Italians and Chinese.

"Whatever you say, Jackie," Frank said, and I just nodded in agreement.

I was seated at a table with two of the biggest personalities in Hollywood. I didn't expect to get a word in, edgewise. But I was wrong, and it was only because they made sure I was included.

"Frank tells me you're from Brooklyn, Eddie."

"That's right," I said, "but not the Brooklyn you're from, Jackie. Bensonhurst and Bay Ridge are a long way from growing up in Bed-Stuy." Bed-Stuy was predominantly a black neighborhood and known to be a rough one.

"Bedford-Stuyvesant was a tough neighborhood, all right," Jackie said. "But I knew since I was six that I wanted to be on stage, so although I hung out a lot in schoolyards and pool halls, I spent most of my time on stage, not in the streets." Jackie actually grew up at 328 Chauncey Street, which was the same address as the Kramdens on *The Honeymooners*.

Since Jackie was apparently a regular at the restaurant, food came fast and furious. Before long, the entire surface of the table was covered with platters and we dug in.

Frank and Jackie caught up, but were sure to keep me involved in the conversation.

"We still gotta get you on the show, Frankie," Jackie said, at one point.

"You don't need me, Jackie," Frank said. "You got Dino this week, and with him you got two great crooners on the show."

I knew Frank was referring to Frank Fontaine, who played "Crazy Guggenheim" on Jackie's show, during the "Joe the Bartender" skit, and was a fine singer.

"Fontaine's great," Jackie said, "but he ain't you, Frank."

"We'll just have to work it out with our schedules, Jackie," Frank said. "It'll happen."

"Yeah, yeah, that's what you always say."

"Hey," Frank said, "didn't I do you a favor last time I was here? Remember?"

"Sure, throw that in my face," Jackie said, with good humor.

Frank looked at me. "I'm at the Fontainebleau last year, and Jackie calls me and says he wants me to do him a favor. He wants me to appear on a radio talk show with this kid, Larry King."

I'd never heard of Larry King, but I didn't interrupt.

"The kid's got it," Jackie said. "Larry's a good interviewer."

"That's the thing," Frank said. "He was a good interviewer, but I did that show for you, Jackie, so don't say I don't pay my debts or do favors for my friends."

I didn't know if it was payback or a favor, but I knew that in spite of the fact that Jackie was a year younger than Frank, he had been something of a mentor to Frank. He had also helped Frank get through the whole Ava Gardner fiasco when Frank's career was at a low in '50 and '51, before "From Here To Eternity" brought him all the way back.

I Only Have Lies for You

Jackie and Frank stopped arguing about Frank being on Jackie's show, and then Jackie and I started telling Brooklyn stories for the rest of lunch.

Chapter Four

Jackie and Frank were both a few years older than I was, but the Brooklyn Jackie and I grew up in was still pretty much the same. We had some old hangouts in common, both had spent time at Coney Island (for Nathan's Hot Dogs), Sheepshead Bay (for Seafood) and Jones Beach (for bathing beauties). The oddest thing was, we both had fond memories of a girl from Rockaway. Luckily, it wasn't the same girl. His was named Lola Marie Dennehy, and mine was Pepper O'Brien.

"Is that where Mr. Dennehy comes from in your Joe the Bartender skit?" I asked.

"You know," he said, "maybe it is. A lot of my characters are right outta my younger years in Brooklyn."

Frank told us about some of his Jersey hangouts, like Atlantic City and the Jersey shore, and then Jackie said he had to leave.

"They're rehearsing for the show," he said.

"You hate to rehearse," Frank said.

"Like the plague, but I gotta stop in and watch. They usually have a stand-in read my part, but I pretty much ad lib and throw them completely off during the show. It's a riot. I used to do it on *The Honeymooners*. Drove everybody crazy, especially the broad who played Trixie, Joyce

Randolph." He started to laugh. "Every once in a while, she'd just stand there with her mouth open, dumbfounded, and Art Carney would have to step in and deliver her line. Now there's an actor. Carney's aces,"

"You guys had some chemistry on that show," Frank pointed out.

"No different from the chemistry you, Dino and Sammy have on stage, pal."

"Speaking of Dino," Frank said, "you're gonna have a great time with him. He works the same way you do. No rehearsal."

"Should be a ball, then."

Jackie insisted on paying the bill, saying we were his guests, and then we all stood up. We walked out front together, where two limos were waiting. Jackie and Frank embraced warmly again, and then the Great One turned and shook my hand again, but this time with more warmth.

"It was a pleasure to meet ya, Eddie. Nice to see somebody who remembers the old days in Brooklyn."

"The pleasure was mine, Jackie," I told him. "And thanks for a great lunch—both the food, and the conversation."

"Sure thing, pal." He turned to Frank and poked him in the chest with a stubby forefinger. "You're gonna do my show, right?"

"We'll set it up."

His driver opened the back door and Jackie got in, giving us one more wave. We watched as the limo drove off.

"He's a helluva guy, right?" Frank asked.

"You got that right," I said. "A funny guy, and watching him pack away the food and the drinks, I can see why Orson Welles named him 'The Great One.'"

"Oh, there are a lot more reasons than that, let me tell you," Frank said. "He was like a rock back when I was in the pits, while I was tryin' to get the part in '*From Here To Eternity.*'"

We got into the back seat of the limo and the driver ran around, got in and pulled out.

"Speaking of '*From Here To Eternity,*'" I said, "whataya got comin' out next, Frank?"

"I got two war pictures in the can. '*None but the Brave*' is bein' released this month. I did that with Clint Walker. Jesus, he's a big sonofabitch—almost as big as your buddy, Jerry. The other one is called '*Von Ryan's Express,*' comin' out in June. I shot that with Trevor Howard and my buddy, Brad Dexter."

"What about that book you were readin'—was it last year?"

"Oh yeah, that private eye thing," Frank said. "I'm gonna shoot that next year, with Nick Conte." Richard

Conte's friends referred to him as "Nick." "Get this, I'm playin' a private eye named Tony Rome."

"Sounds good."

"I don't know if it'll be any good, but it'll be fun," Frank said. "We're shootin' it down here, that babe Jill St. John's in it, and my kid's gonna sing the title song."

"Frank Junior?"

"Nancy. She's gonna be hot, that little lady. She's got lots of projects comin' up, including a spot in a film called The Oscar next year. Hey, get this, we're gonna play ourselves."

"Wow, you're both busy."

"That's the name of the game, buddy boy. What about you?"

So we talked a bit about my new job as something called "A Casino Host." It was Jack Entratter's idea to give me that job last year, since so many people were coming to me to solve their problems it was interfering with my work as a pit boss.

"Sounds good to me," Frank said. "You know you're our go to guy for trouble, and we get ourselves into a lot of trouble."

"We goin' to the Eden Roc tonight?" I asked.

"You know it," Frank said. "Smokey's openin' tonight, so you better get some rest because it's gonna be a hot night on stage, and after."

"I'll go back to my room and take a nap," I promised.

"Good," Frank said, "I don't want you draggin' us down. This trip is all about havin' a blast."

Chapter Five

Sammy killed it.

The Eden Roc was not as luxurious and over the top as the Fontainebleau, but it was close, having been designed by the same architect, Morris Lapidus. It was located right down the street at 4525 Collins Avenue (The Fontainebleau was at 4441). He designed it in 1954 for Harry Mufson, after Mufson and his partner in the Fontainebleau, Ben Novack, had a falling out.

Sammy sang, played instruments, did impressions, and then introduced Frank and Dino, both of whom I was sitting with. He called them both up on stage for a little impromptu Summit action (which the *Miami Herald* the next day referred to as a mini "Rat Pack" reunion).

Sammy also took the time to introduce Jackie, who simply stood and waved, graciously refusing to join Sammy on stage. He was sitting to my right, with Marilyn Taylor on his left. He introduced us when Frank and I got to the Eden Roc. She was stunning. Her sister, June, was credited by Jackie as the one who helped him overcome his stage fright, so when he got his own show, he hired her and her dance troupe to appear on the show. June won an Emmy in 1955 for doing just that; Marilyn was one of the dancers.

After the show we went backstage. Sammy hugged Frank and Dino, slapped me on the back and shook hands with Jackie. He was also very gracious to Marilyn. It was a mob scene, with visitors, columnists and photographers, so we agreed to meet Sammy out front and all go to dinner.

Jackie supplied a stretch limo to accommodate all of us, and when Sammy managed to get away, he joined us and we drove to a night club that Jackie frequented. There was a table waiting, and we ate, drank and laughed all night, with nobody able to keep up with "The Great One's" consumption of food and booze. But we all tried.

***

The next day Frank stayed in all day, working with his band for that night's opening at the Fontainebleau. Dino and Jackie played golf. They invited me, but I declined. I had played in the past, but it really wasn't my game. Sammy was at the Eden Roc, working with the band, smoothing out what he thought were some bumps in his opening night. I hadn't seen any, but he would know much better than I would.

So I spent the day alone, but Frank, Dino, Sammy and I had all agreed to meet for Frank's show, and then dinner. I was not a beach person—although I had spent many summer days in the sand at Jones Beach in Brooklyn with friends—but there were too many beautiful women out there not to want to get a closer look. So I put on my swimming trunks and sat in a lounge chair for a few hours, under an umbrella, girl watching.

I met a pretty divorcee named Fiona Harpe, who was in a lounge chair to my right. While ogling all the young beach bunnies bouncing and jiggling up and down the sand, I would steal glances over at this beautiful redhead in her 30's. Finally, I sent a drink over once I was sure I recognized what she was drinking—margaritas.

She smiled and waved a thank you. We ended up moving our chairs closer together.

"I'm here just trying to get my bearings after a brutal divorce," she said, "and trying to decide if I want to go back to Chicago or not. Why are you here?"

"Time off from my job in Vegas," I said.

"Oh, what do you do there?"

"I used to be a pit boss at the Sands, but now I'm what's called a 'host.'"

"The Sands?" she asked, her eyes getting brighter. "Isn't that where Frank Sinatra and Dean Martin play?"

"Yes, it is," I said. "I'm actually here with them for Sammy's opening at the Eden Roc, which was last night, and Frank's opening tonight."

"Omigod!"she said. "I'd love to see that show to-night." Then she put her hand over her mouth. "Oh! I'm sorry, that was incredibly tacky of me."

"Not at all," I said. "I'd love to take you, if you'll have me as an escort."

"Oh, God," she said, "would you, really?"

After that I thought we might end up spending a pleasant, exhausting afternoon in her room or mine, but it didn't happen. But who knew what would occur after Frank's show that night?

I promised to pick her up at her door for a pre-show drink later that evening, and we parted ways there on the sand. Not even a lunch together. I watched her walk away, much more enamored of her mature body than with those of the jiggly co-eds on the beach. They were pleasant to watch, but this was the kind of woman you wanted to be in bed with. More "cushiony" than "jiggly."

***

When I got back to the hotel, there was a message waiting for me at the desk.

"A lady, sir," the clerk said. "She came in about an hour ago, said she'd be in the bar for some time, waiting."

"Did she leave a name?"

"No, sir."

"Okay, thanks."

It couldn't be my divorcee, Fiona, since she'd been with me on the beach. I decided to see who it was even before going to my room to shower and change. After all, she'd already been waiting a long time. It would be rude to keep her any longer.

I entered the Bleau Bar and saw her immediately. I was surprised. At first I thought it was Marilyn Taylor, but then I realized it had to be June. When she spotted me she waved and I walked over.

"Mr. Gianelli?" she said, standing. "I'm June Taylor."

"I know who you are, Miss Taylor," I said. "Please, sit."

"How did you know?" she asked.

I seated myself across from her. "Well, let's say I guessed. I met your sister last night, and I can see the resemblance."

"Marilyn's the beautiful one," she said. I could tell she meant it, and wasn't being modest, but I thought she was quite pretty, as well.

"I'm sure that's not the case," I said, "but I don't think that's the subject you came here to discuss."

"No, it's not. Would you like a drink?" she asked, as a waiter came over.

She had what looked like a Manhattan in front of her, which I would never touch with a ten foot pole. "A gin martini," I told him, completely unmindful at that moment that I'd consumed several Margarita's with my new divorcee friend.

"Right away, sir."

She smiled across the table at me and said, "This is odd."

"Is it? Why?"

"I've heard a lot about you."

"From who?"

"Through the grapevine," she said. "The celebrity grapevine. People who have been on Jackie's show, some have been to Vegas and met you. A little from Frank. A little here and there. Eddie G. is the guy to go to in Vegas if you have trouble."

"The 'go to guy,'" I said, quoting Frank.

"Exactly!"

"And is that why you're here, June?" I asked. "You need the go to guy?"

"I need somebody," she said, sipping her drink.

"And you don't want to go to the police?" In my experience, very few celebrities want to go to the police with their personal matters.

"I'm not really sure it's a police matter, to tell you the truth."

I was not only a 'go to' guy in my view, but a 'Vegas' guy. I didn't know what I could do for June in Miami, but I thought I ought to at least listen to what she had to say.

"Well then," I said, "I'm all ears. Let's see if I can help."

Chapter Six

She toyed with her glass, making interlocking wet circles on the table.

"I'm not sure where to start, or how to say it," she said.

"The beginning usually works."

"It's about my sister," June said. "I think she may be in trouble."

"What kind of trouble?"

"See, that's where I lose credibility," she said. "I'm not sure."

"Not sure she's in trouble, or not sure what kind it is?" I asked. I was trying to be helpful, but maybe I was just making the situation worse. I decided to sip my drink and just listen.

"I suppose you know that she and Jackie are . . . seeing each other?" she asked.

"I'd heard that."

"And you know he's still married?"

"Heard that, too."

"Genevieve is such a devout Catholic, she refuses to grant Jackie a divorce, even though they legally separated in nineteen fifty-four."

This time I just nodded, to indicate I was listening.

"My sister has told me that lately she feels like she's being followed."

"When?"

"Whenever she leaves rehearsal," June said.

"Do you leave rehearsals together?"

"No," June said. "When the dancers are done, I stay behind to work on routines, do paperwork. They are, after all, the June Taylor Dancers. I have a lot more work to do when they're finished."

"Have you ever left rehearsal together?"

"Oh, yes, on occasion."

"And on those occasions, did you ever feel you and Marilyn were being followed?"

"No."

"So she's only mentioned that she's being followed when she's alone," I concluded.

"Yes."

"Has she told the police?"

"Oh, no," June said, "mostly Marilyn feels she's being silly. She doesn't want to involve the police. Besides, that might be embarrassing for Jackie, if it's got something to do with Genevieve."

"So does Marilyn think it's Genevieve who's having her followed?"

"She can't imagine who else it would be."

"And has she told Jackie?"

37

"No," June said, "just me. And she has sworn me to secrecy."

"And yet you're telling me."

"Well," she said, hedging, "she's made me swear not to tell Jackie."

"So what would you like me to do?"

She sat back in her chair, dropped her hands away from her drink, and shrugged helplessly.

"Oh, I don't know," she said. "I suppose I just wanted to talk to somebody."

I thought it was odd she'd want to talk to a stranger, a man she hadn't even met yet, but had only heard about from the "celebrity grapevine." I always knew there was a grapevine, but I didn't realize that I was on it. Apparently, my efforts on behalf of Dino, Frank and the guys over the past few years had afforded me a reputation that stretched even beyond Vegas. After all, I *had* also gone to Chicago to talk with Sam Giancana, and to L.A. on behalf of both Ava Gardner and Marilyn Monroe. Not to mention Graceland in Memphis to see Elvis. So maybe it wasn't so odd in June's mind for her to ask me to help with a Miami Beach problem.

"When's your next rehearsal?" I asked.

"This evening."

"When do you shoot the show that Dino's doing?"

"Tomorrow."

38

"So this is the final rehearsal before the actual show?"

"Yes."

"Has Marilyn had this feeling before, or has it only been during rehearsals for this show?"

"She's only mentioned it to me since we started rehearsing for the Dino episode."

Now it was my turn to sit back, which pulled her forward in her chair.

"Are you thinking this has to do with Mr. Martin being on the show?"

"I don't know," I said. "I'm just trying to connect the dots you're giving me."

"I'm not giving you all that many."

"That's the problem."

She sat back again.

"I'm sorry to bother you with this," she said. "I just didn't know what to do."

"Well," I said, "you could start by inviting me to rehearsal tonight."

Chapter Seven

Okay, so I had managed to get myself in a bind.

We didn't have lunch. June said she had to get to rehearsal, which would be going on most of the afternoon. The bind was that I had just promised to come to rehearsal, but I was also supposed to go to Frank's opening.

I was going to have to figure this out.

I paid the bill—I insisted and she finally relented—and then walked out to the lobby with her. June's dancers attracted a lot of male glances along the way.

"I'll see you at rehearsal," I said, "I just don't know what time."

"Shall I tell Marilyn you're coming?"

"No," I said, "don't say anything to her just yet. If it comes up, just say that Jackie told me I could come and watch the famous June Taylor Dancers rehearse."

"All right." She touched my arm. "Thank you so much, Eddie."

"You can thank me if I decide I can do something, June."

The doorman got her a cab and I heard her give the driver the address of the theater.

The first thing I had to do was apologize to my new divorcee friend that I wouldn't be able to take her to Frank's show, after all. I went to my room and called her from there.

"Eddie, is this because we didn't end up spending the afternoon in bed?" Fiona asked. "You could've just said something, you know."

"No, this isn't because of that," I told her, "but that's good to know."

I told her I'd still leave her a ticket for the show, and a backstage pass, and that I might show up later on. Either way, I'd let Frank know she was my friend, and he'd look after her.

Next, I called Frank to tell him what I'd be doing that night, possibly instead of coming to his show.

"I'll try to make it if I can, of course, but—"

"Don't worry about it, Pally," he said, cutting me off. "You go and help June, if you can. Jackie would want you to do that. And take the car and driver."

I told him about Fiona, that she'd be at his show if he left her a ticket, and a backstage pass.

"I'll take care of your lady, Eddie," he promised. "You take care of whatever June's dealin' with."

"Okay, Frank. Thanks."

I hung up and went to take a shower.

41

***

The Jackie Gleason Show broadcasted from the Miami Beach Theater of Performing Arts at 17th and Washington Streets. June said she'd leave my name at the door so they'd allow me to enter during rehearsals. True to her word, I told the guard who I was, and he waved me inside.

June must have been watching for me, because she came running over and took hold of my arm.

"Thanks for coming, Eddie."

"Sure," I said. "Have you told anyone?"

"Yes," she said, "but I only told them you were coming to watch rehearsals, that Frank had gotten Jackie to okay it."

"Is Jackie here?"

"No," she said. "Neither Jackie nor Dean are here. We have stand-ins for them. But there's somebody who is here."

I turned, saw a pleasant looking man in his mid-40's approaching us with a half-smile on his face.

"Who's that?" I asked, before he reached us.

"That's Frank Fontaine."

"Crazy Guggenheim?" I asked. "He doesn't look anything like him."

"I know," she said, "it's the hat, and then he screws up his face . . ."

At that point Fontaine reached us and she stopped talking.

"Hey, June," he said.

"Frank," she greeted him. "I want you to meet a friend of . . . of Jackie's. This is Eddie Gianelli."

"Mr. Gianelli," he said, extending his hand. I took it and we shook briefly. "How do you know Jackie?"

"Through Frank Sinatra," I said.

"Ah, how is Frank?"

"He's good," I said. "He's in town to perform at the Fontainebleau."

"Good, good," Fontaine said. "I know he and Jackie are close. So, if you have any questions, just let me know if I can help."

"Sure thing," I said. "Thanks, Mr. Fontaine."

"Frank," he said, "just call me Frank." Suddenly, he screwed up his face and he was somebody else, entirely. "Or call me Crazy!" he said, in Guggenheim's voice. Then he gave that crazy laugh, slapped me on the shoulder and moved on.

"Come on," she said, "I'll show you where you can watch rehearsals from."

She led me to a place down front in the theater from where I could watch all the action.

43

"I'll want to walk around a bit backstage, too," I said. "Is that okay?"

"Everybody's been told you're a good friend of Jackie's," she informed me. "That means you've pretty much got the run of the place."

"Okay, June, thanks," I said. And where's your sister? Where's Marilyn?"

"She's with the other girls," June said. "We'll be rehearsing a number any minute. She may be my sister, but she has to toe the line like all the other dancers."

That sounded fair enough, to me.

"And can anybody else get in here the way I did?" I asked her.

"No," she said, "nobody else's name has been left at the door."

"I'll keep an eye out, anyway. Have a good rehearsal, June, and try not to worry about anything," I said. "Let me know when Marilyn is ready to leave."

"What about Frank's opening?" she asked.

"I've been to plenty of Frank's openings," I said. "I'll go and see him tomorrow night. Tonight, I'm here."

She squeezed my arm again. "Thank you, Eddie!"

She hurried away to work.

Chapter Eight

I sat in the front row and watched June put her dancers through their routine, several times. She knew what she wanted and rehearsed until she got it. Then I watched as Jackie's stand-in went through his paces. They did this to get the lighting right, the timing, as well as the marks that everyone else would have to hit around him.

After I watched them work with Dino's stand-in, I got up and moved backstage. I saw June, Marilyn and a few of the other dancers huddled together, still working on aspects of their routine. The Gleason stand-in was sitting in a chair, smoking a cigarette. And Frank Fontaine was walking around in his Crazy Guggenheim persona. I glanced back to where Marilyn and her sister were, then looked around to see if anyone was paying attention to them. That was silly. It was a dress rehearsal, and they were all in costume, with lots of flesh showing. Most of the crew was staring at them, and some of the staff. Even the catering guy.

"Finding it interestin'?"

I turned, saw Guggenheim, but Fontaine's voice was coming out of his mouth.

"Very," I said, "and a little disconcerting. It's hard to reconcile that you're two men."

He laughed. "I get that a lot. Mostly, it's the hat." He took the hat off to illustrate his point, and I got it. Without it, he was Frank Fontaine. When he put it back on—boom, Guggenheim.

"Weird," I said, "but interesting."

"Where you from, Eddie?" he asked.

"New York, originally," I said, "but I'm in Vegas, now."

"Ah, Vegas," Fontaine said. "Which casino?"

"The Sands."

"I've played Vegas," Fontaine said, "but never the Sands. I usually played nightclubs rather than hotel/casino showrooms."

I didn't remember ever seeing Fontaine's name on a marquee, but I kept that to myself.

"I don't do too many dates like that, though," Fontaine added. "I've got nine kids." Nine at that point, I remember, but he ended up with eleven, eventually.

"Nine? Jesus. How many wives?"

Fontaine laughed. "Just the one." He stuck the hat back on his head and, in his Guggenheim voice, said, "I gotta go and do my number."

"Break a leg," I said.

Fontaine walked over to the Joe the Bartender set, where Gleason's stand-in was standing behind the bar.

I decided to take a walk around, see what the Taylor sisters were up to, and look for any uninvited prying eyes.

The Taylors and the other dancers had dispersed. I figured the sisters might be in their dressing rooms—if, indeed, they had dressing rooms. At least June must have had her own. Marilyn probably shared space with the other girls.

I popped my head into a few doors, and in one I caught the dancers in various stages of dress and undress. It reminded me of being in a showgirl dressing room at one of the casinos.

"Hey, handsome," one half-dressed girl greeted me. She was tall, dark haired, showing off a long, lean, lovely frame in a bra and panties. "Come on in,"

"Don't listen to her," cried a thin blonde, who was holding a robe up in front of her, "get out of here!"

"Handsome men are always welcome," another semi-clad girl, this one a redhead, said.

"Sorry, cowboy," one woman said, approaching the door, "no peeking allowed." As she pushed me out and closed the door, I realized it was Marilyn Taylor. At least I knew where she was, and that she was safe.

I could hear the last echoes of Frank Fontaine's song from the Joe the Bartender set, and wondered how much longer rehearsals would go on?

Returning to the front of the house I listened to Dino's stand-in going through the motions for Dean's spots—a song, and a skit—and then rehearsals seemed to be coming to a close. I checked my watch and saw that I might actually be able to make it to Frank's opening, depending on when Marilyn Taylor decided to leave the theater.

After determining that the cast would all be leaving by the same door, I decided to go outside, get back into the car and watch from there. If anyone was loitering, waiting to follow Marilyn Taylor, I'd be able to catch sight of them.

"Have you driven Frank before?" I asked the driver, as he opened the door for me.

"Yes, sir," he said. "I drive Mr. Sinatra every time he comes to Miami."

That was good. Frank's driver was so used to asking no questions, and he just got into the driver's seat, and waited with me.

It was getting dark when cast members and crew began filing out the door. June had said Marilyn felt that one man was following her. I watched other doorways, corners where the shadows were beginning to form, anywhere a man might lie in wait. I also kept an eye on nearby parked cars. Finally, June and Marilyn came out together. I hoped they wouldn't both get in the same car, because that might have dissuaded anyone from following. But they kissed, embraced, and walked to two different cars.

I didn't see what June was driving because I watched Marilyn walk to a late model Chevy and get in.

"I'm gonna want to follow that blue Chevy," I told the driver.

"Yes sir." He started the motor.

"But first I want to see if anyone else follows."

"I got you, Mr. G."

That was the first indication that Frank had told the driver who I was.

"Nobody else pulled out, Mr. G.," he said.

"What's your name?"

"Paul, sir."

"Okay, Paul, let's follow her at a respectable distance so she doesn't see us."

"Don't worry, Mr. G.," he said. "I've been drivin' for a long time."

I sat back in my seat and let Paul do all the work. Checking my watch, I resigned myself to the fact that I wouldn't see Frank open, but maybe I'd get there a little later and fill the empty seat next to Fiona.

Chapter Nine

"She's pullin' in, Mr. G." Paul said, breaking into my reverie.

"Where?"

"It's an apartment building, up on the right," he said, pointing with one hand and keeping the other on the steering wheel. "It's got an underground parking lot."

I sat forward to take a look.

"Are we still in Miami Beach?"

"Yep."

"You know the building?"

"Yes, I do," he said, "I've driven some people here, before."

"Can we follow her in without giving ourselves away?" I asked.

"Yes, sir."

"Do it, then."

He drove down a ramp into the underground parking structure.

"Where is she?" I asked.

"Brake lights to the right," he said, pointing again.

I looked out the right passenger window and saw what he meant.

"Can you stop here?"

"Yup. But if I have to move," he said, "I'll come back around."

"Okay, Paul. Thanks."

I got out, walked between some parked cars toward where we had seen the brake lights, hoping they were indeed hers. If they weren't, then I'd lost her.

But there she was, walking across the parking lot to the apartment elevators. There was no way I could get into the elevator with her, because she had seen me around the studio, but I could make sure no one else got in there, with her.

As I watched, she reached the elevator, pressed the button for it. The doors opened, she stepped in and no one else came along. When the doors closed, I rushed to them to check the indicator and see what floor she went to. Lucky for me it was 4. I found the stairwell and hotfooted it up to 4. Earlier, June had given me Marilyn's address, and apartment number. I made my way along the hall to apartment 4K. There was no one else around, so I pressed my ear to the door. I heard music, as if Marilyn had put on a record or turned on the radio.

I was tempted to knock and ask her if she was all right, but June had said she didn't want Marilyn to know I was there. So I gave it up, figuring she was safely home for the night, and went back down, this time taking the elevator.

As I stepped out at the parking lot level, something hit me in the back of my head, and everything went black.

Chapter Ten

I woke up to somebody shaking me and saying my name.

"Mr. G.!"

I looked up and saw Paul crouching over me.

"What happened?"

"I got worried, so I came lookin' for you, found you lying here in front of the elevator."

He helped me sit up, and I put my hand to the back of my head.

"Somebody hit me," I said, feeling the lump. "Did you see anybody?"

"I didn't see a thing," he said. "Nobody pulled in after us."

"Did somebody pull in right before her?"

"I don't think so."

"Help me up, will you?"

"Sure thing."

He put his hand beneath my arm and yanked me to my feet.

"Whoa," I said, feeling dizzy.

"Hang onto me," he said, and I did, gratefully.

"Did you go up?" he asked.

"I did," I said. "She took the elevator, and I took the stairs."

"See anybody up there?"

"Not a soul. I went to the door, listened in, heard some music, figured she was safe. When I came back down, I used the elevator and when I walked out . . . boom."

"You still got your wallet?" he asked. "Maybe it was just a mugger."

I released my hold on him, remained upright, checked for my wallet and found it.

"Nope," I said, "still got it, and my watch."

"So what do you figure?" he asked.

"He must've been here all along, waitin' for her," I said. "When he saw me, he couldn't follow her to the elevator."

"So he waited for you to come down and blasted you."

"Sounds right."

"Then whataya wanna do, get outta here or go up and check on her?"

"I guess we better make sure she's safe," I said. "Her sister's not gonna like it, but what else can we do."

I pressed the button for the elevator. As the doors opened, we both froze and stared at the body inside. It was a man in a suit. He'd been stabbed, and the floor of the elevator was pooled with his blood.

"I guess we gotta call the cops," he said.

But I heard sirens, and they were getting closer.

"I think somebody already did."

Chapter Eleven

Before we could do a thing—like get to the car and hustle out of there—a police car came down the ramp with its lights still going. As the siren wound down and stopped, two cops got out. We could have run up the stairs, but why? We hadn't done anything except follow Marilyn to make sure she got home safely. So we stayed right where we were and waited for the cops to reach us.

Miami's finest—one older, one younger—stared at us and the older one asked, "You guys call in?"

"Not us," I said, "but I'm guessing this is what they called you about."

Paul and I stepped apart so they could see into the elevator.

"Jesus!" the older one said.

The younger one had a different reaction. He drew his gun and pointed it at us.

"Just stand still and don't move," he commanded.

"We're not movin'," I promised him.

"Put that away, Peters," the older cop said.

"But—"

"But nothin'," the more experienced man said, "they ain't goin' nowhere."

Peters holstered his regulation revolver, but kept his eyes on us, and his hand on the butt.

"Is this guy as dead as he looks?" the older one asked.

"We haven't had time to check," I said.

"You guys found him?"

"Well," I said, "the doors opened and there he was, so I guess you could say we found him."

"But you didn't call it in?"

"We would've," I said, "but here you are. Obviously, somebody else called."

"Who?"

"The killer?" I asked.

"How do you know he was killed?" Peters asked.

"Because," I said, looking at him, "I don't think he cut himself shaving, and bled to death in the elevator."

"What're you, some kinda wise guy—" Peters started, but the older cop cut him off.

"Simmer down, Peters," he said. "Go to the car and call this in. Get everybody: the sergeant, a meat wagon, and the detectives." As Peters walked away, still eyeing us warily, the other cop said, "You guys relax, we're all gonna be here a while."

***

While we waited for the entire crew to arrive, Paul and I were able to stand off to one side and talk.

"I think we can keep Marilyn out of this," I said, keeping my voice low.

"Is that her name?" he asked.

"Yeah, Marilyn Taylor. She's June Taylor's sister."

"The dancer chick on Gleason?" Paul asked. "My wife loves that stuff!"

"We'd be doin' Gleason and June a favor by keepin' them out of this," I said. "Bad publicity, and all."

"Yeah, but they're gonna ask us what we're doin' here," Paul said. "What do we say?"

"Good point. But if we say we came to see her, they're gonna drag her down here."

Paul shrugged. "Maybe she knows the guy."

"Maybe . . ."

In the end I decided to go ahead and tell them who we were there to see. When they brought Marilyn down, I'd have to leave it to her if she wanted to keep Gleason and her sister out of it.

"Okay," the older cop said. We never did find out his name. "The detectives are here. Time for you guys to cough up."

"Sure," I said. "We're ready."

Chapter Twelve

They questioned us right there in the parking lot, but eventually all of us—Paul, Marilyn and I—ended up being taken to police headquarters.

I didn't have a chance to talk with Marilyn before they hustled us into three police cars, keeping us apart so—presumably—we couldn't coordinate our stories. At police headquarters, I was put into an interview room that looked much like the ones I'd been in before, in Las Vegas—grey walls, grey table and chairs. I assumed Paul and Marilyn were in similar rooms. After about a half-an-hour—probably long enough for them to move the body, maybe even find out who he was—the door opened, and the two detectives entered.

"Can we get you anything, Mr. Gianelli," they asked. "Coffee, tea . . . water?"

"Some coffee would be fine," I said. "Black, no sugar."

"Easy," said the detective who made the offer. He looked at the other man, who left the room. He walked to the table and sat in one of the chairs across from me.

"I'm Detective Eisman, that was my partner, Detective Winter. He'll be back with your coffee."

"What about my driver, and Miss Taylor?"

"He took coffee," Eisman said, "she asked for tea."

"I meant—"

"I know what you meant," the detective said, chuckling. "You gotta excuse me. My wife says I think I'm funny when I'm not."

Winter came back in, carrying a white mug. He put it down on the table where I could reach it, then sat next to his partner. They were both in their late thirties, suntanned and fit, Eisman taller and Winter heavier. Eisman's hair was thinning, though, while Winter had a full, bushy head of healthy locks.

"Okay," Eisman said, "we're ready."

"For what?"

"To hear your story."

I wondered if Paul had already told his story and, if so, what had he said? If our stories didn't match, we were going to be there a lot longer than we should.

"Okay," I said, "I came here to see Miss Taylor."

"Marilyn Taylor?"

"That's right."

"Why?"

"She works on the Jackie Gleason show," I said. "Her sister is June Taylor—"

"Hey," Winter said, "the June Taylor dancers, right?" These were his first words.

"That's right."

"My mother loves them."

"Well, I was watching them rehearse today, and I saw Marilyn—"

"Whoa, whoa," Eisman said, "back up. Who are you, and why do you get to watch them rehearse the Jackie Gleason Show?"

"My name's Eddie Gianelli," I said, "I worked at the Sands Hotel and Casino in Las Vegas—"

"Doin' what?" Eisman asked, opening a small notebook and taking a pen from his pocket.

"I used to be a pit boss, but now I'm sort of a . . . a casino host."

"What's that?" Eisman asked. "A casino host."

"If a guest in the hotel, or a player in the casino, has a problem, or something special they want, they ask for me. I try to satisfy them."

"You mean like gettin' them a prostitute?" Winter asked.

"No, not like that," I said. "Mostly, I see to it that people—celebrities who come to play the Sands—have a good time."

"But no whores," Winter said, sounding disappointed.

"No whores."

"Happy now?" Eisman asked his partner. He looked at me. "Go on. You work in Vegas, so what are you doin' here?"

"Frank Sinatra is opening at the Fontainebleau—well, he opened tonight," I corrected. "He asked me to come with him to Miami Beach—"

"Wait, wait," Eisman said, interrupting me again. At the rate we were going I was going to be there all night. "You know Frank Sinatra?"

"I do, yeah," I said. "We're friends."

"And Dean Martin?" Winter asked.

"Him, too."

"Get outta here," Winter said.

"I told you," I said, "when celebrities need somethin', they ask me. That's how I met Frank and Dean, and Sammy—"

"Sammy Davis, Jr.?" Eisman asked.

"Yes, him, too," I said.

"What," Winter said, "no Joey Bishop?"

"I know Joey, too."

"And Lawford?" Eisman asked. They both seemed starstruck.

"I know Peter, but I wouldn't say we're friends."

"But you're friends with the other members of the Rat Pack," Winter said.

"Yes, but they don't like to be called that. The newspapers call them that."

"What do they call themselves?" Winter asked.

"Frank likes to call them the Summit."

"The Summit?" Eisman repeated.

"That's terrible," Winter said. "I like 'the Rat Pack.'"

"Fine," I said, "we'll call them the Rat Pack. Can I finish my story?"

"Sure, sure," Eisman said, "go ahead. Finish your story. We'll try not to interrupt so much."

"Okay," I said, "so Frank asked me to come with him . . ."

Chapter Thirteen

I told my story. They interrupted, but only once or twice more. Eventually, I got it all out.

"Okay," Eisman said. "Sit tight."

"Have you talked to my driver, yet? Or Marilyn? You're gonna compare our stories, aren't you?"

"Like he said," Winter spoke up, "just sit tight. I'll bring you some more coffee."

They both left the room. I pushed away the half a cup of cold coffee that was left. My story was that I found out where Marilyn lived, had Frank's driver take me there so I could talk to her, maybe ask her out. If that didn't match what Paul told them, we'd be in trouble. I had no idea what Marilyn was going to say, but it wasn't as important. It was only Paul's and my story that had to match . . . sort of.

I waited another half hour, and then the door opened and Eisman entered without Winter.

"What, no more coffee?"

"You don't need it," he said. "You're free to go."

I stood up.

"I guess our stories matched."

"Enough," Eisman said.

"Can I leave town?"

"You in a hurry to do that?"

"Actually, no," I said. "Frank's playing three nights at the hotel, so I guess we'll be here a couple of more days, at least."

"That should be enough."

He opened the door for me.

"Your driver's waitin' outside."

"And Miss Taylor?"

"I don't know," he said. "We let her go."

"Alone? At night?"

"We offered her a ride home, but she said no, she'd get a cab."

"Right after somebody in her buildin' got killed?" I asked. "You should've given her an escort home."

"If you're that worried," he said, "maybe you can catch her."

"Yeah, maybe I can."

I made my own way to the front of the building and out the door. Not only was Paul waiting for me there, but he had the car.

He got out to open the door for me.

"Glad you got the car."

"I went back and got it," he said. "They let me out way before you."

65

"Well, let's get movin'," I said. "We've got to see if we can catch up to Marilyn Taylor. She's all alone, lookin' for a cab."

"Oh, I don't really think we have to worry about her," he said.

"Why not?"

"You'll see."

And I did.

As I climbed into the back seat, Marilyn was sitting there, smiling at me.

"Oh," I said, as Paul closed the door behind me.

"Hello, Eddie," she said.

"Miss Taylor."

"Oh, I think since we've been in jail together you can call me Marilyn."

"Okay, Marilyn." For someone who had spent some time in jail, she looked pretty damn good. She still had some of the make-up on that she'd worn to rehearsal. She was a very lovely woman.

Paul got behind the wheel. "Where to, boss?"

"Let's take Marilyn home."

"Right."

Chapter Fourteen

"So," Marilyn said, "who put you on my tail, Jackie or my sister?"

I considered not telling her, but I finally said, "June asked me look after you."

"For how long?"

"Well," I said, "I'll only be here a few more days. I told her I'd see what I could do about finding out who's been following you."

"Oh," she said, "I can tell you that."

"Can you?"

"Yes. The dead man in the elevator."

"You recognized him?"

"The police made me look. It was him."

"Did you tell them that?"

"I did," she said. "They asked me if I knew anybody who'd want to kill him."

"What'd you tell 'em?"

"I'd never seen the man before he started following me," she said. "We never spoke, so I don't know his name. How would I know who wanted to kill him?"

"Did you tell the police that you know Jackie?"

"I had to tell them I worked on his show, but that was all," she said.

"Then there's no reason for them to suspect him or question him."

"What about you, and Paul?"

"I'm pretty sure they suspected us, all right, but I think our stories matched," I said. "What'd you tell 'em, Paul?"

"That we were there to see Miss Taylor, just waitin' for the elevator, and saw the body when it opened."

"They ask you what you were doin' drivin' me?"

"I told them I work for Mr. Sinatra, and you're his friend." He looked at me in the rear view mirror. "Was that okay, Mr. G.?"

"That was perfect, Paul," I said. "That's why they let us go."

"Why did you tell them you were coming to see me?" she asked.

"I told them I was watching the rehearsal, noticed you, thought you were beautiful and wanted to ask you out."

"They believed that?" she asked.

"Why not? They saw you, didn't they? It's a believable story."

She actually looked away, shyly, and I almost expected her to blush. Which was a surprise for someone who danced in those June Taylor costumes.

Paul pulled into the underground parking structure again, and this time I walked Marilyn to the elevator and up to her apartment while he waited downstairs.

"Keep an eye out," I said, "see if anybody follows us."

As we stepped into the elevator, she moved all the way to one side to avoid the bloody floor. I did the same, going the opposite way.

"Have you told Jackie any of this?" I asked. "I mean, about being followed."

"No," she said. "If he knew he'd wrap me in plastic. Besides, he's got enough on his mind."

"Like what?"

"His life, his marriage, his show . . . he doesn't need to take on my problems."

"But you know he'd want to."

"Oh yes," she said, "definitely."

The elevator stopped and the doors opened. I put my hand up to stop Marilyn from getting out, so I could exit first and make sure the way was clear.

"All right," I said, and she came out.

We walked down the hall and entered her apartment. Again, I went in first, turned on some lights, determined it was safe for her to enter.

"Do you want a drink, Eddie?" she asked.

"I do, but I don't want to make Paul wait downstairs."

"What should I do, Eddie?" she asked. "Do you think I should tell Jackie?"

"I think you have to, Marilyn," I said. "because you work for him, the cops might want to talk to him, ask some questions, maybe even see if he knows the man."

"I suppose I should call him and June tonight," she said. "No matter how late it is."

I looked at my watch. "It's after eleven p.m."

"He'll be awake," she said. "He's probably been trying to call me. June, too. We usually talk in the evening."

"Then call 'em," I said. "Maybe one of them will come over and keep you company."

She came toward me and put her hand on my arm.

"Thank you, Eddie."

"For what?"

"Who knows what might have happened if you weren't here?" she asked. "If you hadn't followed me home. You got me to my door safely."

"Well, then, thank June. She's the one who sent me."

She walked me to the door.

"Will I see you tomorrow?" she asked.

"I'm bettin' yes," I said. "Jackie's probably gonna want to talk to me."

"Don't worry," she said. "I'll tell him you did all you could."

"I hope that's true," I said, and left.

Chapter Fifteen

I didn't find out the dead man's name until the next day, when I read the *Miami Herald*.

When Paul drove me back to the hotel the night before, I went directly to my room and to bed. I rose early, ordered a room service breakfast, which came with a copy of the newspaper.

His name was Philip Rossi. He had an address further north, in Orlando. That was all they printed, all the police had released, in case someone would come forward and claim the body. Nothing about what he did for a living, what he was doing in that building in Miami Beach.

I was halfway through my breakfast when someone knocked on my door. When I opened it, I found Frank standing in the hall, a big smile on his face. He was wearing a loud, Hawaiian shirt and a big smile.

"'mornin', Pally," he said, breezing past me. "I smell bacon. Got any coffee?"

"Help yourself, Frank."

He walked across the room to the terrace and my breakfast cart then poured himself a cup of coffee.

"I had a helluva show last night," he said. "I was fabulous. You missed it. But your friend, she had a good time."

"Fiona?" I said. "Frank, you didn't—"

"Naw, naw, Clyde, I'd never do that to you," Frank said. "So, what happened to you last night?"

"Have a seat," I said, "I've got a story to tell you."

***

By the time I was done with my story we had both eaten all my bacon and gotten to the bottom of the coffee pot.

"Holy shit, whatta night you had!" Frank exclaimed. "And the cops let you go?"

"I've got no connection with this fella Rossi. Neither does Paul."

"But what about Marilyn?"

"All she knows is that he's been followin' her for a while," I said.

"So who do they think killed him?"

"They have no idea," I said. "I'm hopin' it's not just another admirer of hers."

"Jesus, is she gonna tell Jackie about this?"

"I think so," I said. "I'm pretty sure she called him and June last night."

"Pally," he said, rubbing his chin, "I think Jackie might be callin' you today."

"If he does, I can't tell him anymore than I already told the cops."

"Well, he still might wanna hear it from you," Frank said.

"If he does, I'll be around."

"Well, I gotta go down and rehearse with the guys," Frank said, getting to his feet. "There were a coupla blips last night."

"I thought you said it was fabulous?"

He spread his arms. "I was fabulous, but the band needs some work. In fact, I might be firing somebody today."

"Riddle?"

"Nelson's not here," Frank said. "He and I are sort of . . . driftin'. I've got a new guy I'm tryin' out because Don Costa wasn't available. Will you be there tonight?"

"I promise," I said, then added, "if nobody else gets murdered."

"If it ain't you, you better be there, Pally." He slapped me on the back and was gone.

***

After Frank left, I got dressed, intending to head out to find Fiona the divorcee and try to make amends, but before I could leave my room the phone rang. When I discovered who was on the other end, I thought Frank might have been psychic.

"Eddie G.? It's Jackie G."

I knew from his voice that it was, and nobody was trying to play a joke on me.

"Hardy har har," he said, "I just got that. Hey, pal, I wanna buy you lunch."

"Well, that's nice, but—"

"No," he said, cutting me off, "I mean *I am* buyin' you lunch. Meet me out front."

"Now?"

"It's an early lunch," he said, and hung up.

***

Out in front of the Fontainebleau I found a limo waiting. As I approached it, the driver got out and opened the back door for me. As he did, a cloud of smoke escaped. I looked in and Jackie Gleason smiled at me.

"Come on, get in, pal," he said. "We got lots to talk about."

"We do?"

"Yup."

I got in, sat next to him as the driver closed the door. When he got into the driver's seat Jackie said, "Louie, take us to that Chinese place I like."

"I dunno if they're open this early, Boss," Louie said.

"I called 'em and told 'em we're comin'," Jackie said. "They'll be open."

Jackie lit a new cigarette from the one he'd been holding, then stubbed that one out in an ash tray.

"Eddie, I heard what happened last night," he said. "Boy, did I hear about it."

"From Marilyn?"

"From Marilyn, from June, from the cops. Those detectives came to see me early."

"I thought they might . . . just as Marilyn's employer."

"Yeah, well they ain't stupid," he said, "but that's the way the sisters and I played it."

"Jackie listen, I didn't—"

"Now relax," he said, holding up his hand, "I ain't mad at ya. You did a favor for June, and you were there for Marilyn last night. I appreciate that. I thank you for it."

"You're welcome."

"I wanna talk about it all," he said, "in detail, but let's wait until we get to the Chink's—what the hell's the name of that place, Louie?"

I thought Louie said Ah Choo, but I wasn't sure.

"Yeah, that's it," Jackie said. "Some fried rice, some chow mein, and then we can talk."

"It's your show," I said.

"It's always my show, kid," Jackie said. Louie hadn't started the car yet, so Jackie sat forward, slapped his palm on the divider. "And away we go!"

Chapter Sixteen

Over another Chinese meal with Jackie, I went through the events of the previous night. By this time, I believed that both Marilyn and June Taylor had already told him everything. And I figured by pumping me, he was finding out for himself if they had left anything out.

The restaurant was empty except for us, and the two waiters who kept bringing food and drinks. Louie, the driver, was outside. I had no idea if Gleason was sending food out to him.

"The cops talked to me early this morning," he said, when I was done. "Showed me a picture of the bum who got killed, the one who was following Marilyn. I didn't know him, but if she had told *me* about him . . ."

I waited for him to go on, but he didn't.

"It was just as well she didn't," I said. "You're legit when you tell the cops you weren't involved."

"Yeah, but you ain't," Jackie said, "that's what worries me. What if they think you—or worse, Marilyn—had somethin' to do with it?"

"I don't think they do," I said. "I've been questioned by cops before, and I think they bought everythin' we told them . . . mostly because it was the truth—sort of. The only thing I didn't tell them was that I was following Marilyn because June asked me to."

"And that kept June out of it," he said, "and my show. If both sisters were involved, they'd have to think it had somethin' to do with the show—and me." He picked up his glass of bourbon and held it up to me. "I salute you, Eddie. You kept us all out of it."

"Well, they're still gonna be interested in anybody who's interested in Marilyn," I warned him. "If I was you guys, I'd keep a low profile, for a while, til things die down."

"Or until they find out who killed him," Jackie said. "It's probably got somethin' to do with him and his life, and nothin' to do with ours."

"Just a coincidence that it happened in Marilyn's buildin', on the night I was there?" I shook my head. "I don't know if even I buy that."

"What're you sayin'?" he asked. "That they're gonna be after Marilyn?"

"I think they'll probably watch Marilyn to see if any-body else is watchin' or followin' her," I said. "So, like I said, keep a low profile."

"That's hard for me, you know?" he said. "I'm pretty much a high profile kinda guy."

"Well," I said, "keep bein' Jackie Gleason, the Great One. Just don't be seen with Marilyn for a while."

"That'll be kinda hard," he said. "I was sorta figurin' to keep her under my thumb, for a while. You know, watch out for her. I was gonna have her move into my house, temporarily."

"I wouldn't do that. If you want to keep an eye on her, have somebody do it for you," I suggested.

"You mean, hire a bodyguard for her?"

"Why not?" I said. "Even if the cops spot him and suss him out, it'll make sense to them."

"You know anybody?"

I thought about my buddy, Danny Bardini, but he was a P.I. in Vegas and wasn't licensed to work in Florida. Then something else occurred to me.

"Make it somebody local," I said. "That way the cops'll recognize him and know he's a legit bodyguard. They might even think Marilyn hired him, herself. In fact—"

"I getcha," he said, cutting me off. "Have her do it."

"Right."

"She can hire him, but I'll be givin' her the money to foot the bill."

"That's between you and her," I said. "Nobody else has to know that."

"June'll know," Jackie said, "and you, but that's it."

"That's enough."

"Eddie," Jackie said, toasting me again, "now I know why Frank calls you 'the guy.'"

I returned the toast with my green bottle of Tsingtao beer.

***

When we got back to the limo, Louie the driver was working on his teeth with a toothpick, so I assumed he'd eaten, probably almost as well as we had.

"We'll drop you back at the hotel, Eddie," Jackie said, as we got in, "then I gotta go to the theater and meet with Dino. He should be landin' just about now."

"It should be a hell of a show, Jackie," I said. "What I saw in rehearsal was real good—and it'll be even better with you and Dino playin' your own parts."

"Oh yeah," he said, "Dean and me, we'll work good together. Neither one of us likes rehearsin'. But we'll both know our lines."

As we drove back down Collins Avenue I said, "You know, Jackie, you were incredible in "the Hustler." Why haven't you made more movies?"

"The right part's gotta come along," he said, "and I tend to want to be in charge. Lots of directors don't like that."

"I know that from watchin' Frank work on some sets," I said. I'd seen how Frank ran the show on "Oceans 11" and "Robin and the 7 Hoods." He'd even flexed his muscles on the latter enough to give me a small role.

"Well yeah," Jackie said, "but he's Frank."

He sat back, with his hands clasped in front of him, as if to say "'nuff said."

Chapter Seventeen

I couldn't attend Jackie's show that night because I had to go to Frank's. After all, it was what he'd flown me to Miami to do. But I had a conversation with Dean on the phone.

"I understand why you choose Frank over me, Pally," Dino said. "After all, he's the Leader."

Dean was kidding.

I thought.

I knew for a fact that Dean only referred to Frank as the Leader because he knew Frank liked it. It was no skin off Dino's nose if people thought so. Dean Martin's ego needed no massaging—not ever. Frank's was a little different story.

I spent some time looking for my divorcee friend, Fiona, and she wasn't on the beach, she wasn't in the lobby, and she wasn't in any of the restaurants or shops. Of course, I wasn't paranoid enough to think she was avoiding me after knowing me only one day. She was simply never where I was.

I did spend most of the day around the hotel, so that if anyone was looking for me—Jackie, the Taylor sisters, even the police—they'd be able to find me, easily. Fortunately, nobody seemed to need me in relation to the

murder. Maybe I was in the clear. I would've hated it if
the police kept me from leaving Miami and going back to
Vegas. But I was still expecting to hear from Detective
Eisman before leaving town.

In any case, I made it to Frank's second show that
night. If there were any kinks the first night, it seemed
like he'd managed to work them out.

When the show was over and he had done a couple of
encores, he shouted to the crowd, "Come on back tomorrow night, my pal Dino's gonna be here!" and the crowd
went crazy. I thought that was a sure way to get people to
come back a second time.

I went backstage to congratulate Frank, found him
mobbed by critics and friends, and some special attendees
whose ticket price included a stop backstage. At one point
he waved at me and shrugged, so we sort of wordlessly
agreed to meet up later on, and I left.

I went to the lounge for an after dinner, after show
drink. As I sat at the bar and worked on a bourbon rocks,
a man came over and sat next to me.

"I'll have what he's havin'," he said to the bartender.

It took me a moment to realize he was talking about
me.

"Hey," he said.

"Hello." I barely looked at him, at that point.

The bartender brought him his drink. "Thanks. Put it on my friend's tab."

Now I knew he was talking to me, and I started to turn toward him, an objection on my lips.

"No, don't turn," he said, putting his hand on my arm. "I have a gun and I'm not afraid to use it here."

I froze. There was a mirror behind the bar, but there were also shelves of bottles there, blocking my view of him—which suited me, at that moment.

"What's goin' on?" I asked.

"You're payin' for my drink, right?"

"You got it," I said. "Have two."

"No, one's enough, but thank you."

He had an educated way of speaking, yet I had the feeling he was from the street, like me.

"We missed each other last night," he said, "which was lucky for you bud."

"I guess so," I said. "So that was you?"

"It was," he said. "Rossi was a bit of business for me. You would have just been in the way, and I wouldn't have had much of a choice. I'm glad I didn't have to."

"So am I," I said, with feeling. "So, why are you here now?"

"Well," he said, "first of all, I had a ticket for Frank's show. Wasn't he great?"

"Terrific," I said, "as always." I was going to agree with everything this guy had to say.

"And on the other hand, I wanted to have a nice talk with you."

"Well, that's what we're doin'," I said, "havin' a nice talk." I sipped my drink. Mostly to wet my dry mouth. I figured as long as we were talking, he wasn't killing me.

"Yes, we are," he said. "Look, I know who you are, and I know where you live. You might think that once you're back in Vegas I won't be able to get to you, but I will. It doesn't matter where you go."

"And why would you want to get to me?" I asked. "I don't know anything. I haven't even seen your face."

"And that's lucky," he said. "That's very lucky for you. And the only reason I'm lettin' you go home."

I sipped my drink again, waiting for the other shoe to drop.

"But let me tell you somethhin'."

"I knew there was gonna be a but."

"If you come back, I won't be so forgiving. If you try to help the police, same thing. I want you to go home, Eddie G., go home to Vegas and live your life."

"I don't get it," I said, not believing the words coming out of my mouth, "wouldn't it just be easier for you to kill me?"

"Maybe it would," he said, "but I'm not getting paid to do that. Now, finish your drink, enjoy the rest of your stay, and when Frank's plane takes off, be on it."

"Okay, but—"

"Keep staring into your drink for the next ten seconds."

"You got it."

I stared into my drink and counted to twenty, just for good measure. When I turned my head, the stool beside me was empty.

I waved at the bartender.

"Another one?"

"Yeah," I said, "and this time make it a double."

Chapter Eighteen

I'm not a fool.

I called Detective Eisman right away. And not from my room. I had the bartender bring me a phone right then and there. And I arranged to meet him somewhere.

Normally, my next step would have been to call Frank and get his driver to take me, but I decided against that. Instead I went right out to the front of the hotel and had the doorman get me a cab. I thought if I didn't stop to think, I wouldn't change my mind.

"Where to, pal?" the cabbie asked.

I gave him the address the detective had given me, but added, "And I need to make sure I'm not being followed."

"Really?" the cabbie asked. "Not 'follow that cab?'"

"Twenty bucks over the meter if you make sure I'm not followed."

"Hang on, bub," he said, and pulled away.

***

"We're here," the cabbie said.

I leaned forward and looked.

"Where?"

"The far end of Collins Avenue. It ain't the best neighborhood, lemme tell ya."

I remembered a few blocks back we passed a motel that looked a little rundown. It was called the Pink Grotto. That must have been what he meant. Kind of tacky.

"Were we followed?"

"Impossible."

I gave him two twenties and got out.

"You want me to wait, Mac?"

"No, that's okay," I said, through the open passenger window. I turned, then whirled back around. "Wait! Is there a bar around here?"

"Down by the beach," he said. "Follow that path. Booze, beer and burgers, not much more."

This end of Collins Avenue was not in keeping with the rest of it. The buildings were burnt out and boarded up, there were homeless inside and in the doorways. But as I walked further along the path to the beach, the homeless faded away, and I could hear music.

On the beach was a small, square box of a place with lights strung all over the outside. The music was coming from there. But when I got through the front door, the lights were gone, and it was cool and dark.

There was a long bar with a few people seated at it, some four top tables, and booths. Sitting in one of the booths, with a drink in front of him, was Detective

Eisman. The bartender gave me a glance as I walked by, but never stopped cleaning the glass he was holding.

I walked over to the booth and slid in across from him.

"Mr. Gianelli."

"Detective," I said. "I'm taking a big chance coming here."

"How's that?"

"I don't know who this button man is workin' for."

"Button man?"

"Maybe I better start from the beginning," I said, as the bartender came over. "Beer, on tap."

"What kind?'

"Anything."

"Comin' up."

"So," Eisman said, "from the beginning."

I stared at his drink. It was green. "Is that a grasshopper?"

"A stinger."

"What makes it green?"

"The crème de menthe."

"You're supposed to use white."

"Don't judge," he said, "talk."

So I talked . . .

"Let me get this straight," Eisman said, when I was finished. "A guy just sat down next to you in a bar and said he was the hitter who killed our vic? And that you should go home to Vegas and not say anything else about it?"

"That's it."

Eisman raised his hand to the bartender and asked just loudly enough, "Hey Vince, two more."

"Comin' up, Boss."

The bartender carried two more drinks to us and set them down.

"Boss?" I said. "You own this place?"

"I've got a piece. I don't want to be a cop forever. This was all I could afford with a Collins Avenue address, but things are lookin' up. They're going to clean up this end of the avenue. Or so they say. Anyway, back to your story."

"It's not a story," I said. "Check it out with the bartender at the hotel. I was just sittin' there mindin' my own business."

"You from Brooklyn?" he asked.

"Yeah, why?"

"Your accent shows every once in a while," he said.

"Yeah, well, usually when I'm nervous, or agitated."

"Which one are you now?"

"Both."

"Why?"

"Because I did just what he told me not to do. I called a cop."

"Yeah, why'd you do that, Eddie?"

"Maybe because I don't like being told what to do," I answered.

"Well, you might just need a bodyguard for a while when you go back," he said. "I mean, until we watch him."

"I had the same thought," I said, "and I've got somebody in mind."

"Good," Eisman said, "'cause I'd kinda like you to stay alive. Think you can i.d. this guy by his voice?"

"Oh yeah," I said. "I'd know it anywhere."

"And you're sure you never got a look at him?"

"Not even a glimpse," I said. "He said don't look, so I didn't."

"Probably a smart move," Eisman said. "We don't need to have the bar at the Fontainebleau get all shot up."

"So what's your plan now?" I asked.

"That's easy," he said. "You go home, we catch the guy, you come back and help us i.d. him."

"You're gonna let me go home?"

"I'm pretty sure you didn't kill the guy in the elevator, Eddie," he said "Did you?"

"No!"

"I'm also pretty sure you didn't tell us everything." He held up a hand to keep me from protesting. "But I think we've got enough of the truth to go on."

"That's real understanding of you, Detective."

"Mind you," Eisman added, "if I find out you actually lied to me, I'll come to Vegas and get you."

"Call ahead," I said, "I'll make sure you have a suite at the Sands."

Chapter Nineteen

That night was our last one in Miami Beach.

Frank, Dean and I went to the Eden Roc Hotel to see Sammy Davis Jr. open. Naturally, Sammy called Frank and Dino up on stage with him, and they had a mini reunion of the Summit. It was hilarious. Afterward, we all went out to dinner. I had tried to invite my divorcee friend, Fiona Harpe, but I was told she had checked out and gone home. Might have been a missed opportunity, there.

After dinner Sammy went back to his hotel, Frank, Dean and I went back to the Fontainebleau. We had a drink in the bar, and I told them about the hitman, and my conversation with Detective Eisman.

"So what are you gonna do?" Dean asked. "You can't stay here?"

"We ain't," Frank said. "We fly back tomorrow."

"And I go home tomorrow," Dean said. "So we've done Miami—again."

"Are you gonna be safe in Vegas?" Frank asked. "I mean, what if the button man changes his mind and decides you might have seen something you shouldn't have?"

"You need a bodyguard," Dino said.

"The detective said the same thing," I told them, "and I have somebody in mind."

"So do I," Frank said. "That private eye friend of yours, whatsisname, Bardini?"

"No, not Danny," I said. "I was thinking more of Jerry."

"Big Jerry!" Frank exploded. "Of course. Why didn't I think of that."

"He'll be perfect," Dino said. "He'd take a bullet for you, any day."

"Well," I said, "hopefully it won't come to that. I'll give him a call as soon as I get back."

"And do what?" Frank asked. "Get him on a commercial flight? By the time he gets to Vegas you could be dead. No, no, as soon as we're back in Vegas, I'll send my plane for him. I've got to go and spend some time at Cal-Neva, anyway. You know, bookkeeping."

Cal-Neva was a casino hotel in Lake Tahoe that Frank owned a piece of—Dean, too, at one time, but he had since divested himself of the property. I don't think Dean appreciated having to do business with "the boys." He was much too easy going to have to put up with that kind of nonsense.

"Okay, thanks, Frank," I said. "I'll take you up on that. I'll give him a call when we get back to the Sands."

"I've got a phone in the car," Frank said. "You can call him on the way to the airport tomorrow."

"You're just full of good ideas today, ain't you, Frank?" Dean said, with a slow grin.

"It's just how I do business, Pally," Frank said.

"That's why they call you the Chairman of the Board," Dino commented.

***

We all hit the sack after that and I met Frank by the car the next morning, with a bellman packing our suitcases into the trunk. Frank shook hands all around—bellman, doorman, assistant manager—leaving a $50 bill in each hand. That was also how he did business. I had no idea how much our driver, Paul, would be getting, but if I had my way, it'd be a bundle.

I tried calling Jerry from Frank's car phone, but the big guy wasn't picking up.

"He's probably out breakin' some legs, kid," Frank said, as I hung up.

"There's a lot more to Jerry than that, Frank."

"Hey, take it easy, pal," Frank said. "I didn't mean nothin' by it. Jerry's a great guy."

"Yeah, he is," I said. "Sorry. It's just that, when I first met him, that's what I thought. He was just a big leg breaker."

"But now he's your friend," Frank said. "I get it. You don't want anybody badmouthing your friend. I feel that way, too."

I knew he probably felt that way about Dino. Dean Martin was about the only person who could do no wrong in Frank Sinatra's eyes.

When we got to the airport, our luggage was loaded onto Frank's plane, and we were off, headed for Las Vegas.

Once we were seated and on our way with drinks in our hands—martinis, natch—Frank said, "Jackie had a lot of good things to say about you."

"Is that right?"

"He really appreciated what you did for Marilyn."

"I didn't do much, beyond finding a dead body."

"Well, don't tell that to Jackie," Frank suggested. "It can't hurt to have one of the most powerful men in television feel indebted to you."

"Why do the most powerful men in television seem to be funny men?" I asked. "Sid Caesar and Milton Berle in the fifties, and now Jackie."

"Don't think I haven't asked myself the same question," Frank replied, drolly.

Chapter Twenty

When we got to McCarron Airport, Frank took a helicopter to Lake Tahoe to the Cal-Neva Casino. We parted on the tarmac and I went to the parking lot to get my Caddy.

Miami Beach was nice—or it would have been, without murder—but it was a pleasure to be back in Vegas. Driving down the street, even during the day when the marquees weren't lit up, was exciting. When you see names like Nat King Cole, Louis Armstrong, Keeley Smith and Louie Prima, Alan King, Buddy Hackett playing at the Riviera, the Flamingo, the Stardust, Sahara and Frontier, you can't help but have your heart beat a little faster. At least, I can't. And the Sands marquee, as I pulled in, said, as usual, "a place in the sun," announcing Dionne Warwick and Charlie Callas playing the Copa Room. My boss, Jack Entratter, was making an attempt to attract the younger generation by booking acts like Warwick, Wayne Newton and Bobby Darin.

Back inside the Sands—more my home than my own house was—I checked in with my boss, Jack Entratter. He had another new girl working in his outer office. Since the death of his longtime assistant, he'd been having trouble finding a reliable replacement. This one was in her 20's, pleasant-looking, not a knockout. Maybe the fact that she hadn't been hired for her looks was a good sign.

She had been hired a few weeks before I left, so she knew who I was when I walked in.

"How was Miami, Mr. G.?" she asked.

"Hot, Wendy," I said. "Hot. Is he in?"

"He is," she said. "You can go on in."

"Thanks."

As I entered Jack's office, he looked up from his desk, sat back and smiled. He had a big cigar stuck in the middle of his face, as usual. His jacket—which was usually stretched to the limits by his shoulders—was hanging on the back of his chair.

"Finally back, huh?" he asked. "You ready to do some real work?"

I dropped myself into the chair opposite him and said, "I'm ready to work, all right."

"Why does that sound like Miami wasn't such a good idea? Didn't you get to meet the Great One and compare notes about your Brooklyn upbringings?"

"I met him," I said, "but there were other things happening."

So I filled him in on the Taylor sisters, the body in the elevator, and the hitman at the bar. It took a few minutes and he listened patiently.

"You want a belt?" he asked, when I was done.

"Yeah, I do."

He got up, walked to a sideboard he'd had installed, with a few bottles and decanters on it. He poured two glasses of bourbon, handed me one and sat back down.

"That's quite a story," he said, then. "We gonna have hitmen comin' to the Sands lookin' for you? 'Cause if we are, I gotta tell somebody."

"Somebody" meant he had to report to his mob bosses, who owned the casino. Texas tycoon Jake Friedman had built the hotel and was the owner of record, but it was generally known—or suspected—that people like Meyer Lansky and Frank Costello owned a share. Those were the people Jack Entratter worked for.

"Well," I said, "I did talk to the detective in charge of the investigation before I left, but we met at a pretty out of the way place."

The smile had long since faded from his face and now, as he chewed on his cigar, he was looking less and less happy.

"And I'm thinking of, maybe, bringing in a bodyguard for a while."

"A bodyguard?" he asked. "Like who? Your pal Bardini?"

"No," I said, "I'm gonna give Jerry Epstein a call."

"Huh," he said, rotating the cigar in his mouth. "I guess that's better. At least he's connected."

99

"In fact, I'm gonna give him a call as soon as I'm done here."

"Well," he said, sitting forward, "finish your drink and you're done. You can work things out with him, and then start back to work tomorrow."

"Okay."

"There's one more thing, though," Entratter said.

"What's that?"

"While you were away—in fact, you might've still been on Frank's plane—Nat King Cole died."

"Oh my God," I said. "I know he collapsed here last year—December, wasn't it?"

"Yeah," he said, "and they found a tumor on his lung. The doctors told him to stop working, but he didn't listen. He died in San Francisco. He was forty-five."

"When's the funeral?"

"It might've been today," Jack said, "but I wouldn't be able to spare you again so soon, anyway."

"Yeah, yeah, I know." I knew Nat King Cole from his play dates at the Sands, but I wouldn't say we were friends. It was a pity, though, to have that voice silenced so young.

I'd only taken a few sips of the bourbon, so I downed the drink and I set the glass down on his desk. "Thanks for the drink."

I Only Have Lies for You

As I left the office, he was pouring himself another drink.

***

I staked out an empty desk in the office next to Jack's and used the phone to dial Jerry's number. This time he answered on the third ring.

"Hey, Mr. G.," he said, when I identified myself. "How's it goin'?"

"Not so good, Jerry," I said. "I think I may need you. The problem is—"

"I know all I need to know, Mr. G.," he said, cutting me off. "You need me, I'm on my way."

"Mr. Sinatra is sending his plane for you, Jerry. It'll pick you up at LaGuardia."

"Wow," the big guy said, "this *is* serious. I guess I'll see you soon."

"Yeah and try to bring your cannon with you."

***

I decided to meet Jerry at McCarron Airport later that night. Usually, you had to declare a weapon and show a license. Since he didn't have to fly commercial, I figured he'd have a way to get the gun on and off Frank's plane with no trouble.

I don't know how Frank did it, but we didn't have to stand in any lines when we were in the Miami Airport, and now Jerry came out a separate door from the rest of the passengers, carrying a single bag.

"Hey, Mr. G.," he said, as we shook hands.

"What gives, big guy?" I asked. "You lose some weight?"

"Yeah," he said, glumly, "I'm on a diet. Dropped nearly twelve pounds, so far."

"Why?"

"Doc's orders," he said. "Somethin' about bein' borderline diabetic?"

"Jesus," I said, as we walked through the concourse to get to the parking lot, "I don't know much about diabetes."

"Me, neither," he admitted, "but the doc told me if I lose some weight, I might be able to head it off."

I shook my head. "I can't imagine you on a diet."

"*You* can't imagine it," he said. "Oh, sorry I snapped at you. This diet's got me on edge."

It didn't seem like he'd snapped at me, but I let it go. He did seem tense, though maybe because of the weight loss, he was sounding different.

When we got to my Caddy, he tossed his bag into the back seat and assumed the driver's position, as he usually did. Just sitting behind the wheel, it seemed to me that he'd relaxed a bit. His houndstooth jacket wasn't straining at the seams, as it usually did.

As we pulled out onto the street Jerry said, "Okay, that's enough about my weight. Why don't you tell me what's goin' on?"

The drive to the Sands from the airport wasn't long, but there was enough time for me to lay it all out for him.

"So you think this guy's gonna come for you?" he asked, as we pulled into the Sands parking lot.

"He'll either come if he has second thoughts about letting me go," I said, "or because he knows I went to the cops before I left. Either way, he'll kill—"

"Not while I'm around," he said, pulling into a parking spot.

We got out of the Caddy, but before we went inside, he opened his suitcase, took out his .45 and stuck it in his belt.

"Okay," he said, grabbing the suitcase, "let's go."

Chapter Twenty-One

I got Jerry into a room where he could clean up and stow his gear, and then we went to get something to eat. Down in the Garden Room, where Jerry and I had shared many meals over the past 5 years or so, he agonized over the menu.

"No French fries, no French fries . . ." he kept chanting like it was a new mantra for him.

I realized I was starving. A burger and fries sounded great, but I didn't want to order it in front of him.

"You order whatever you want," he said, without looking up from the menu, as if reading my mind. "I'll find somethin'."

When the waitress came over, it was a girl I knew slightly, but who had never seen Jerry before.

"Lisa, this is my friend, Jerry."

"Hi, Jerry. You're a big one."

He looked up at her. "Not as big as I used to be." He seemed sad when he said it.

"Lisa, I'll have a burger and fries," I said. "Oh, and a Coke."

"And you, big fella?"

Jerry closed the menu and put it down with finality. "Pancakes!"

"A big stack?"

He winced and said, "A small stack."

"Okay," she said. "I hope that does it for you."

"So do I."

As she walked away, I said to him, "Pancakes?"

"Smaller portions," he said. "That's not somethin' I ever thought I'd be worried about."

"What about the syrup?" I asked. "I mean, diabetes, that's about sweets, right?"

"I'll just have a little dab," he said. "What are we gonna do after we eat?"

"Get a drink. Tomorrow, I'll start workin' like normal, and you'll have to shadow me."

"What about the dick, Bardini?"

"What about him?"

"Ain't he gonna help?"

"I don't know," I said. "I haven't talked to him since I got back."

"Well, maybe you better," he said. "He's gonna be pissed if ya don't."

"You're probably right," I said. "Okay, I'll go and see him tomorrow before I start my shift. If he's in town."

"You goin' home tonight?" Jerry asked.

"I was gonna, yeah."

"I'll have to go with ya, sleep on your sofa."

"No," I said, "we'll go to my house and I'll pack a bag. Until we know I'm in the clear, I'll stay here."

"In my room? Gonna be crowded."

"We'll get a suite," I said. "With two bedrooms."

"So we'll be roomies."

"If you want to look at it that way."

"I dunno how to look at it," he said. "I ain't never had a roommate before. But you and me, we split hotel rooms before."

"Yes, we have." For short periods of time. Who knew how long this would take, though.

Lisa came with the plates and put them down. I watched Jerry spread butter on his pancakes, and then pour a dollop of syrup about the size of a half dollar on top. After that, he used a knife to spread and spread and spread it, until it disappeared. Then he cut into them and started eating. I picked up my burger and took a big, not-so-guilt-free bite.

"You know," he said, while chewing, "I do got some connections. Maybe I can make some calls and find out who this hitter is."

"That would be helpful," I said.

"Hopefully, he ain't a freelancer, or too much of a loner," he went on. "If he was sent to Miami to do a job, maybe we can find out who sent him. How did he do it?"

"A knife."

"That's a specialist. You got the name of the guy he stabbed?"

"I do. But it was just some man who was stalking Marilyn Taylor."

"Maybe," Jerry said, "that's just what he happened to be doin' when the button man found him."

"That's pretty smart, Jerry."

"Yeah?" he asked. "I don't feel so smart since I been eatin' less."

"I don't think there's a connection, there."

"I hope not," he said. "I always been kind of a dope. I don't wanna turn into a damn idiot! Sorry."

I guess he thought he had snapped, again.

"You don't have to keep doin' that."

"What?"

"Apologizing."

"Oh," he said, "sorr—uh, okay."

We both went back to our meals. When he was done, he used the last forkful to soak up whatever syrup and/or butter was left on his plate, which wasn't much.

"You gonna finish that?" he asked.

"What?"

"That." He pointed with his index finger, which was still as big as a sausage.

I looked down. I hadn't even realized I'd left some fries on my plate, and a pickle.

"No," I said, "go ahead."

He switched plates with me, put another half dollar sized dollop—this time of ketchup—on the plate, then finished the few potatoes I'd left there, dipping each one. The last thing he ate was that pickle, which he held in his hand like he wanted it to last forever.

"I'll start makin' calls tomorrow," he said, gesturing with the pickle. "I'll start with the victim, find out who or what he was. Maybe that'll tell us who wanted him dead, and we can find out who hired the hitter."

"You're talkin' like a real detective, big guy," I said.

He laughed. "That comes from hangin' out too much with you and the dick."

"Well," I said, "as far as I can see, losing weight hasn't killed any of your brain cells."

He bit into the pickle and said, "Yeah . . . not yet."

Chapter Twenty-Two

We drove to my house. Jerry watched and waited while I packed a bag. We were in and out in fifteen minutes, and on our way back to the Sands.

"If this guy's specialty is a knife," Jerry said, on the way, "then he's gonna have to get close to do the deed." He looked at me, then back at the road. "I ain't gonna let him get that close."

"Glad to hear it."

He kept one eye on the road and one on the rearview mirror, just in case.

"I don't think he'd be here now," I said. "After all, I just got back. He'll need time to decide whether or not he made a mistake. Or to find out I talked with the detective in charge."

"Hopefully," Jerry said, "nobody'll tell him that part."

"Yeah."

When we got to the Sands, I arranged with one of the clerks to get a two-room suite for us and we dropped off our bags.

Since Jack Entratter had taken me out of the pits, my job was basically to be on the casino floor, available to anyone who had a problem, or a special request. That meant Jerry was going to have to be on the floor with me.

"How about you sit at the bar and watch?" I suggested.

"No can do, Mr. G.," he said. "If this jerk is a knife guy, he's gonna wanna get up close. That means I gotta be close enough to stop him."

The year before, there had actually been a hit out on me and Jerry stayed right by my side the whole time. I knew how committed he was to keeping me safe. And, truth be told, I would have put my own life at risk to save his, so I knew how he felt. This wasn't just a job.

"Okay," I said, "but let's start out sittin' at the bar, anyway."

We went into the Silver Queen Lounge, grabbed two stools and ordered beers. Jerry frowned and digested while we waited.

"What's the matter?"

"The stools feel different from the last time I was here," he complained.

"It ain't the stools, you mook, it's your butt that's different. That weight you lost must've been from your keester."

"Oh yeah!" He looked pleased as the bartender set down two beers.

"Are you supposed to drink that?" I asked, as he picked up the bottle.

"I'll just drink half," he promised.

As I picked mine up and turned to look at the room, one of the cashiers from the cage came in, looked around, spotted me and came running over with a nervous look on his face. I had a feeling I knew what he wanted.

"Eddie, it's Mr. Skelton," he said. "He wants to raise his limit, but Mr. Entratter said—"

"It's okay, Louie." I took the slip he was holding, checked the amount, and signed it. "let him have it."

"Sure thing, Eddie."

"Red Skelton still gamblin' here?" Jerry asked. "Seems like everytime I'm here he's askin' for his limit to be raised."

"He's a good customer and a good friend," I said. "He promotes us whenever he can."

Jerry turned around on his stool as well and leaned back against the bar.

"I love this place," he said.

"The Silver Queen?"

"The whole package," he said. "Vegas."

"What about Brooklyn?"

"Ah," he said, "it ain't what it used to be, what it was when we were kids."

"You know, I met Jackie Gleason in Miami," I said. "He talked a lot about Brooklyn."

111

"Hey, that's right," Jerry said, "he's from there. You know, he actually lived in that building where the Honeymooners lived."

I was always surprised at the scope of Jerry's knowledge when it came to T.V. shows, but I had always thought it was limited to shows like *77 Sunset Strip* and *Maverick*, not comedies.

"Three twenty-eight Chauncey Street, in Bed-Stuy," he said.

"Have you ever been by there" I asked.

He had once made me take him to the location of 77 Sunset Strip when we were in L.A., even though the address was actually 8524 Sunset Boulevard, as there are no two digit addresses on that strip.

"Naw, never," he said, "but I ain't never been to the Statue of Liberty, either."

I didn't know what the Kramden's apartment and Miss Liberty had in common, but I didn't ask. Sometimes Jerry's logic boggled my mind. So far, though, he'd been having good ideas since he got off the plane.

"Hey, Mr. G., I gotta make some calls. Can I do it from here?"

"Yeah, sure," I said. I signaled the bartender that I needed a phone. He nodded and brought one over. "There you go."

"Thanks," Jerry said. "Okay if I call Chicago?"

"Be my guest."

He turned around and started dialing furiously, apparently from memory.

Chapter Twenty-Three

Jerry made several calls, speaking in low tones so no one else in the lounge could hear him—except once or twice when he got excited, or agitated and decided to threaten somebody. Several times I tried to get off my stool and walk away, but he reached over, grabbed my arm in a vice-like grip and pulled me back onto my seat. He was serious about sticking to me.

He finally put the receiver down for the last time and shoved the phone away.

"No luck?"

"Nobody knows nothin' about a blade man bein' in Miami Beach," he said, mournfully.

"Did you ask firm enough?"

"I threatened to break a few heads if they didn't talk, but it didn't help. I got squat."

"Well, it wasn't because you didn't try."

"I'm still waitin' for a couple of calls back," he said. "Maybe somethin'll turn up."

"Jerry," I said, "my butt's numb. I've gotta get off this stool and walk."

"Sure thing, Mr. G.," he said. "Let's go."

We both eased off our stools and walked out onto the casino floor. It was February, but this was Vegas. Miami

Beach had been full of bikinis, but here it was high heels and mini-skirts. The men were in sports jackets, with loud shirts underneath.

"This place looks like it's full of tourists," Jerry commented.

"It's winter," I said. "Lots of folks come lookin' for the heat, as well as the gambling."

"Is that Julius LaRosa at the craps table?" he asked.

I had been spoiled by singers like Frank, Dean and Tony Bennett, so others like Al Martino, Julius LaRosa and Buddy Greco tended to blend together for me. But since I knew LaRosa had been performing at the Desert Inn, I nodded.

"Yep, that's him. Singin' at the D.I., but gamblin' here."

"Whatayou think of him?"

"Well," I said, "he's no Jack Jones."

"Who?"

"You know, 'Wives and Lovers?'," I said.

He shook his head.

"He's a friend of Nancy Sinatra's, had a big hit earlier this year with a song called 'The Race is On'."

"Oh, that guy," Jerry said "Yeah, he's okay. He's pretty young, ain't he?"

"I guess, still under thirty."

115

"Well, he ain't as good as that Donkey-shane kid, Wayne Newton."

I was digesting that when a bellboy from the hotel came running over.

"Mr. G., Mr. Entatter's lookin' for you. Says it's important."

"Yeah, okay, thanks, Willy." I gave him a buck. "I gotta go to Jack's office. You comin'?"

"I guess," Jerry said. "I can't read that guy. I don't think he likes me."

"I'm not even sure he likes me," I assured him.

***

In a week I'll get called up to Jack's office at least once a day. It usually has something to do with a high roller who's coming to town and wants a certain kind of entertainment, or a celebrity who needs special treatment.

This time it was the high roller.

As I entered his office with Jerry behind me, Jack looked at us and scowled. That wasn't going to help Jerry's feeling that Entratter didn't like him.

"Lew Ordway's comin' to town," he barked at me, which explained his scowl.

"Okay," I said, "I'll call Lily and warn her."

Lily Grant ran a high-priced call girl operation in Vegas that we used a lot for high rollers.

"She's gotta have at least one girl left who hasn't been beaten up by him," Entratter said.

"I'll check."

"Yeah, lemme know," he said. "How ya doin', there, Jerry?"

"Good, Mr. E.," Jerry said. "Thanks for askin'."

"Thanks for comin' out on such short notice."

"Sure thing," Jerry said. "Anything for the Sands, you know that."

"And we appreciate it," Jack said. "You got a good room?"

"We got a suite, Mr. E."

Jack looked at me.

"I thought I ought to stay around here for a while, so we got one of the two bedroom suites."

"Yeah, okay," Jack said, "probably a good idea. Any word on who the mechanic was in Miami?"

"I can't get a peep outta nobody, Mr. E.," Jerry admitted. "And I called Chicago."

"I can make some calls," Jack said. "What do we know?"

"Just that he's a blade man," Jerry said.

"Okay," Jack said, "I'll give it a try." He looked at me. "Keep that asshole Ordway happy. I want him to drop a million!"

Jerry and I went out, passed the new girl, who nodded, and then he grabbed my arm in the hallway to stop me.

"Do people come here and drop a million?" he asked.

"Every day."

Chapter Twenty-Four

We had four more high rollers that week, and three celebrities. One of the high rollers—or "whales"—was a politician, so I really had to make him look clean while he was getting dirty as hell.

We were eating in the Garden Room one night—Jerry chomping on a salad, of all things, and eyeing my plate to see if I was going to leave any fries—when he asked, "So this is what you do every day?"

"This is it," I said. "I get people what they want or help them decide what they want."

"It's exhaustin', ain't it?"

"Yes," I said, "a lot of the time. But then there are the times it's enjoyable."

"Like when Mr. S. and Dino come to town?"

"Exactly." I had given up trying to figure out why Dino could be Dino, but I had to be Mr. G. and Frank had to be Mr. S.

"Also people like Sammy, Joey, Nat King Cole, Julie London—"

"Julie London?" he exclaimed. "Man, she's gorgeous. You know her?"

"She plays Vegas every so often," I said. "I've met her."

"Met her?" he asked. "The way you 'met' Miss A. and Miss M.?"

He was talking about Ava Gardner and Marilyn Monroe, both of whom we had helped out of some sticky situations. Jerry had always thought I slept with both of them. But I only had sex with Ava. Marilyn, she was like a child. I just wanted to protect her. She called me the night she died, but by the time I got there she was gone. I think about that often. And Ava pops into my mind on more than one or two occasions.

"No," I said, "not like that. She comes to town with her husband, Bobby Troupe."

"Ain't he a drummer?"

"That's right."

"Musicians," he said, shaking his head. "They get lots of pussy, don't they? Drummers, guitar players . . ."

". . . and singers."

"Yeah," Jerry said, "especially them."

He finished his salad—every leaf and nut in the bowl—and then hungrily eyed my plate.

"You gonna eat those?"

"I looked down at the small pile of French fries that were still on my plate, next to the meatless T-bone.

"No," I said, pushing the plate to him, "go ahead."

He grabbed it, did his thing with the ketchup, and started dipping and eating.

So far, during the first week, no one had come close to trying to kill me. A few men, strangers, had *come* close to me, but Jerry had quickly stepped in and determined that they were innocents.

"How's your love life, Mr. G.?" he asked, as he bit a particularly long fry in half.

"Why do you ask?"

"Well, I ain't even seen you talk to a woman all week unless she was a waitress, a dealer, a hotel clerk or a cigarette girl."

"How do you know I'm not sleepin' with a waitress, a desk clerk, or even a hat check girl?"

"You ain't even made a call," Jerry said. "You ain't seein' nobody, these days?"

"Nope," I said, "nobody. I almost made it with a divorcee in Miami when I was there, but it didn't happen."

"Why not?"

"A guy got killed in an elevator," I said. "That kind of put a crimp in my plans."

"It always does," he said, and I wasn't sure whether or not he was kidding. Death had been more a part of his life than mine.

Suddenly, he looked past me and said, "Oh, this can't be good."

I turned and saw Jack Entratter coming toward us. For Jack to leave his office and come looking for me rather than call me up there—yeah, Jerry was right. Not good.

"Shove over," he told me, and slid into the booth next to me. Sharing a booth with both him and Jerry was not only cramped, but humbling. I felt like a small boy.

The waitress, a middle-aged woman who had been working there for years, came rushing over when she saw Jack.

"Mr. Entratter, we're not used to seein' you down here."

"Hello, Molly."

"Can I get you somethin'?"

"Just some coffee, thanks."

"Right away, sir."

She rushed off, came back immediately not only with a cup, but a fresh pot.

"You gonna eat those?" Jack asked Jerry, and reached onto my former plate for a fry. I thought Jerry was going to cry.

"What brings you down here among the unwashed, Jack?" I asked.

"I got a call from Frank. He's been tryin' to call you at your house. Since you weren't answering, he figured he'd call here and leave you a message."

"Must've been some message to take you out of your office to deliver it," I said.

"To tell you the truth, I don't know what kind of message it is. From what I understand, he wants you to know as soon as possible." He drank some coffee.

"About what?"

"Gleason."

"Jackie? What about him?"

"He's comin' here."

"To Vegas?" Jerry asked, excited. "When? Why? Is he playing here?"

"No," Jack said. He looked at the plate again, but since he took one, Jerry had scarfed down the rest of the fries. "He's comin' specifically to see you, Eddie. He'll be here tomorrow. Have a suite ready for him."

"Sure, but what's he comin' to see me for?"

"I don't know," he said, "and if Frank knows, he didn't tell me."

"This has got to have something to do with what happened last week," I said, "otherwise I have no idea. Maybe I should call Frank."

"He's still at Cal-Neva," Jack said. "They got some problems there he's tryin' to clear up. He said he just wanted to give you a heads-up, but that Jackie would fill you in when he gets here."

"That's it?"

"That's it," Jack said, finishing his coffee. "I've got to get back. Bein' a goddamned errand boy for you ain't in my job description, damn it!"

He got up and left before I could say anything.

I looked at Jerry.

"Can't be about anything else, that I can think of," I said.

"I guess you'll find out when he gets here," Jerry said. "Hey, I get to meet 'im."

"Yeah, you do," I said. "He'll like meetin' another Brooklyn boy."

Jerry poured himself some coffee from the pot Molly had brought to Entratter.

"Mr. E. took a French fry from me," he muttered.

"I saw. I admire you for not removin' his arm and beatin' him to death with it."

"I don't like people eatin' from my plate."

I refrained from reminding him that it was *my* plate he had gotten the fries from.

Chapter Twenty-Five

"Are we gonna pick up Mr. Gleason at the airport?" Jerry asked, as we left the café.

"No," I said. "I'm gonna do my job until I hear from Jackie that he's here, then I'll arrange a time and place to see him. Besides, he'll be coming in on Frank's plane. So it could be any time."

"What are we gonna do now?" he asked.

"I'm—we're going to our suite so I can call Frank at the Cal-Neva and see if he knows anything."

"Right."

On the way across the hotel lobby floor to the elevators, it looked for a moment as if a man there was going to approach me. Jerry instantly moved to get between the two of us, but the man kept moving.

"He's nobody," I said.

"We don't know that," Jerry said. "Maybe he kept goin' because he saw me." He looked after the man, who kept walking out the door. "I'm gonna be on the lookout for him."

"Listen," I said, "I'm just going up to the suite. Why don't you see if the valets know anything about him? Or the hotel staff. And then meet me up there."

"I should stay with you—"

"Go!" I said, "I'll be fine in the room until you get back."

He turned to head toward the lobby, but pointed at me and said, "Don't leave the room!"

I watched him lumber across the lobby floor, then got into the elevator and went up.

***

I had to wait for somebody to find Frank and bring him to the phone. I chose to wait on the line rather than leave a message for him to call me back, because who knew when that would be?

He came on the line. "Eddie? What's up, pal?"

"Frank, I just got word that Jackie is comin' here to Vegas to see me."

"Gleason? In Vegas? Not one of his usual haunts."

"Do you know anything about this?" I asked.

"Well . . . I know he wants to talk to you, but I ain't sure what it's about."

"All I can think of is the stuff that went on with the murder, and Marilyn."

"Maybe . . ." he said, trailing off. I had the feeling he knew more than he was saying, and why not? He'd been friends with Gleason a lot longer than we'd even known each other. If the Great One had told him not to say anything, he wouldn't.

It still made me mad, though.

"Yeah, okay," I said. "Thanks for nothin'."

"Hey, kid," he said, "don't get sore."

"S'long, Frank," I said, and hung up.

On Frank Sinatra.

Me.

Frank had a temper. It had been well documented in the trades many times. However, I had never been on the receiving end of it, and I had never really seen it, except during the whole Peter Lawford/Kennedy thing. When Jack chose to stay at Bing Crosby's house instead of at Frank's in Palm beach—after Frank had built him a wing and a helipad—Frank destroyed the helipad with a sledgehammer, and almost did the same to Lawford. Peter had been cut off since then. Oddly, Frank's anger was never directed at Der Bingle. He figured the fault was with Lawford and the Kennedys, not Bing.

Now I'd hung up on him. Was he going to get mad at me? I've got to say, at that moment I wasn't too worried about it.

***

"You did what?" Jerry asked, after I'd let him in and told him the story. "Hung up? On Mr. S.?"

"Well," I told him, defensively, "he wasn't very helpful, and I got mad."

"Why?"

"He knows Jackie," I said. "He probably knows why he's comin' here."

"Maybe Mr. Gleason asked him not to say."

I sulked a few seconds.

"I thought we were friends," I said, finally.

"You are," Jerry assured me, "but he knows Mr. Gleason a helluva lot longer."

"Yeah, yeah, I know all that," I said, waving my hands at him. "I'm just wondering if this is gonna have to do with that murder. I really don't wanna have anything to do with that, anymore."

"I can't blame ya for that," he said. "Nobody likes murder."

Then I remembered why he hadn't come up in the elevator with me.

"You find out anything about that guy?"

"Naw," he said, "nobody in the hotel even knew who I was talkin' about. And the valets just said he was a good tipper, but he didn't give them any idea what he was doin' here."

"Then like you said, he could've been lookin for me, saw you and changed his mind."

"Maybe."

"Well, that guy's probably nobody, but you're right in the middle of my bullseye," I said. "Maybe you should go home, Jerry."

"Too late for that, Mr. E."

"I know, he's seen you. I'm sorry—"

"No, I mean, it's too late because now I'm here and I ain't leavin' you. Nobody's gonna take you out as long as I got somethin' ta say about it."

I was touched. "Thanks, Jerry."

"We could probably use some backup, though," he admitted. "Or just another pair of eyes."

"I know," I said. "Danny."

"The dick's got a big opinion of himself," Jerry said, "but ya can count on him."

"I'll give him a call," I said. "And I'm sure he'll like to know your opinion of him."

"You tell 'im what I said," Jerry replied, "and I'll call ya a liar."

I laughed and went to the phone. For the moment I wasn't mad, anymore.

Chapter Twenty-Six

Since Frank had called Jack Entratter about Jackie Gleason coming to Vegas, Jack didn't mind me leaving the property during working hours. Not as long as I was doing something for "the guys."

Jerry and I met Danny at the Horseshoe casino coffee shop, down on Fremont Street. It was one of Jerry's favorite places to eat in town, but I didn't know how he was going to do on this new diet.

The coffee shops in Vegas were not high-class dining. Mostly you either ate breakfast there—best bacon'n'eggs in town at a cheap price—or just a burger platter.

Danny was already in one of the red leather booths when we got there.

"I ordered three burgers," he said, as I slid into the seat across from him.

Jerry sat next to me on the end.

"Hey," he said, "usually I got one cheek hangin' outta here." He wiggled a bit.

"What?" Danny asked.

"He's on a diet."

"Oh, ho!" Danny said. "You got a girl, Jerry?"

"I got diabetes." His delivery was absolutely dead pan.

"Oh," Danny said. "Uh, sorry to hear that, big guy."

"It's okay," Jerry said. "I just gotta watch what I eat."

"Well, I'm sure you can do it," Danny said. He looked at me for rescue. "What's on your mind?"

"There might be a hitman after me," I said.

"Didn't we go through this already? Last year? The year before?"

"Well, as far as I know there's no hit out on me, officially," I said, "but I got involved in something when I went to Miami with Frank."

He listened while I told him everything that happened.

"Leave it to you to go to Miami Beach and find a body that's not wearin' a bikini," Danny said, sitting back to let the waitress put down our plates. "Plus, you blew your chance with a sexy divorcee."

"That's what you got out of that?" I asked.

"No, no," Danny said, "I get it. The killer let you walk, but he might decide he's made a mistake. I assume that's why Jerry's here."

"Yeah," Jerry said, picking up his burger, "but I can't be with him every minute."

"So you want me to . . . what? Be the backup?"

"Yeah," I said. "It was Jerry's idea."

"Is that right?"

"No," Jerry lied, "it ain't."

"Well," Danny said, picking up his own burger, "whoever's idea it was, I'm in. We can't have our pal Eddie ending up toes up in a morgue, can we?"

"No, we can't," Jerry said.

***

Over the course of the meal, we tried to figure out the best way to use Danny.

"You're gonna see Gleason tomorrow?" Danny asked, eating his last French fry.

"That's right."

"When?"

"Whenever he arrives," I said. "Frank's flyin' him in."

"Frank didn't tell you when?"

"Frank didn't tell me anything," I replied. "He was no help."

"Whoa," Danny said, "trouble in paradise with the Chairman?"

"Never mind," I said. "I'll take Jerry with me to see Gleason, so maybe you can stay on the perimeter and watch our backs."

"No problem," Danny said. "I can do that."

He sat back in his seat, pushed his plate away.

"You gonna eat that last piece of bacon?" Jerry asked him.

"I thought you were on a diet?"

"I ain't finishin' my fries," Jerry argued, "but I can eat bacon."

Danny didn't think that was right, but since he knew very little about diabetes he said, "No, man, go ahead, have it."

Jerry picked the piece of crisp bacon up from Danny's plate and popped it into his mouth.

"How long do you think this is gonna go on?" the detective asked.

"I don't know," I said, "at least until the Miami Beach police solve their case."

"You think they're gonna catch the guy?"

"Probably not," Jerry said. "Not unless they find out who hired him."

"And that means they've gotta find out who wanted the dead guy dead," I added.

"So you think maybe Gleason's comin' to town with some information?"

"I've got no idea why he's comin' to town," I said. "Tomorrow we'll know more."

I pushed my plate away, purposely leaving a piece of bacon for Jerry.

"Mr. G.," he said, "are you gonna—"

"Go ahead, Jerry, "I said. "It's yours."

Chapter Twenty-Seven

Jerry and I returned back to the Sands and I went to work. He hovered. People who would normally come over and talk to me seemed to hold back because of his slightly less than usual hulking presence.

"Jerry," I said, at one point, "you've gotta give me a little more space. You're scarin' my regular customers."

"Sorry, Mr. G.," Jerry said, "but I got to be close enough to do my job."

"Your job?"

"That's how I'm approacin' this," he said. "I wanna do it right."

"You're doin' great," I said, "but let's see if you can do it from a little further back."

"Okay, Mr. G.," he said, "I'll back off . . . a little."

He backed off a bit, but not much. At one point I just decided to sit in the bar with him and wait to hear from Gleason. People could find me there if they needed me, and approach if they so desired, under Jerry's watchful eye.

Finally, just when I could hear Jerry's stomach start growling for lunch, there was a phone call for me.

"Thanks," I said, as the bartender handed me the phone.

"Sure, Mr. G."

"Hello?"

"Eddie? Pal? It's Jackie!" Each line was like an explosion in my ear.

"Jackie," I said, looking at Jerry and pointing at the receiver as I held it to my ear, "where are you?"

"I'm here, in your hotel," Jackie said. "I got a nice suite. That you're doin'? Or Frank's?"

"Probably Frank's, since I didn't know you were comin' until yesterday."

"Ah, well, I'm glad he told ya we were comin'," Jackie said.

"We?"

"Yeah, Marilyn's with me. We both came to see you, pal. You got time for us?"

"I've got all the time in the world for you, Jackie," I said. "Why don't I come on up?"

"Nah, nah," Jackie said, "you know how women are. Marilyn's gotta, ya know, clean up. Why don't we meet ya somewhere in, say, two hours?"

"Sure, Jackie," I said, "that'll be just in time for an early dinner. I'll have a limo out front for you."

"Yeah," Jackie said, "that's good. Take us someplace nice, kid. You know, let's do it up for Marilyn. And don't worry, it don't have to be Chink's."

"Okay, Jackie, I know just the place."

135

"And bring somebody," Jackie said. "Ya know, a date."

I looked at Jerry and said, "I know just the person."

I hung up and looked at Jerry.

"Well?" he said.

"They're here," I said, "him and Marilyn. We're havin' dinner in two hours."

"Me, too?" he asked.

"Yeah, you, too," Eddie said. I slapped him on the shoulder. "You're my date."

Chapter Twenty-Eight

The Bootlegger was an Italian restaurant off the strip, one of Frank's favorites.

Jerry and I were standing at the limo when Jackie came out with Marilyn. He was resplendent in a fitted tux, and she wore a beautiful blue dress that showed her figure off.

"Hey, pal!" Jackie yelled. He shook my hand and pounded me on the back.

Marilyn leaned in, kissed me and said, "It's good to see you again, Eddie."

"This is Jerry," I said, as Jackie looked him up and down.

"Your date?" he asked.

"My bodyguard," I said, "and my good friend, who also happens to be from Brooklyn."

"Hey, good to meet somebody from home," Jackie said, shaking Jerry's hand. "Bed Stuy."

"Sheepshead Bay," Jerry said.

"Yeah? I used to fish there all the time."

We three gentlemen allowed Marilyn to get into the car first, then followed Jackie and me in the back, and Jerry in front with the driver.

"Where we headed, pal?" Jackie asked. As usual, he had a cigarette in his right hand.

"The Bootlegger," I said. "One of Frank's favorites."

"Italian," he laughed. "That figures. Frank loves his spaghetti."

The limo driver dropped us directly in front of the restaurant. As we entered, a maître d' met us at the door with a big smile. Any friend of Mr. Sinatra, and all that. I hadn't called ahead, so it must have been Frank. He showed us to Frank's booth.

"Anything you need," he assured us, "just tell Carlo, here, and he'll get it for you."

Carlo, an experienced Bootlegger waiter, nodded and assured us that was correct. We ordered drinks and Jackie told him to bring them "chop-chop."

When we all had drinks I asked, "Jackie, what's goin' on? Why are you and Marilyn here?"

"Well, Eddie, ol' pal," Jackie said, "one reason we're here is that we wanna stay alive."

"He's being a little dramatic," Marilyn said.

"That's not true," Jackie said, looking me in the eyes. "I'm bein' dead serious."

"Does this have to do with the dead guy in the elevator?" I asked.

"Oh yeah," Jackie said, "that's exactly what it has to do with."

"I thought the cops were on that."

"They were," Jackie said, "they are, but they ain't gettin' no place fast. They got his name. After that, they're stumped."

"That ain't unusual," Jerry said. "Cops are usually stumped, especially when they're dealing with a professional hitter. He came to town, did the job, and left."

"See," Jackie said to me, pointing at Jerry, "he sounds like he knows what he's talkin' about."

"Okay, so the cops are stumped," I said. "That doesn't explain what you're doin' here, the two of you. Don't you have a show to put on?"

"June is workin' the dancers," Jackie said, "and everybody else is still on the job."

"And since Jackie doesn't rehearse, he's not being missed—yet," Marilyn laughed.

The waiter came back and we all ordered dinners— spaghetti and meat balls, just to make it simple.

"So why the comment about wantin' to stay alive?" I asked Jackie.

He pointed at Jerry again. "He says the hitman came and went. I ain't so sure."

"Why not?"

"Because someone is still watching me," Marilyn said.

139

"It's gotta be him," Jackie said. "Who else could it be?"

"Why would the hitter be watchin' this pretty lady?" Jerry asked. "He did his job."

"Well, look at her," Jackie said. "Wouldn't you wanna watch her?"

"Well . . . yeah," Jerry said, blushing.

"You're sweet," she said to him, making him blush even more.

"Wait a minute," I said. "You're tellin' me that a hit-man came to town to do a job, killed the guy who was watching Marilyn, and now he's got a thing for Marilyn and is watchin' her?"

"That's what I think," Jackie said.

"So okay," I said, "let's say that's true. Where do I come in?"

"You're the guy!" Jackie exclaimed happily.

"What guy" I asked.

"Frank says you're the guy who solves all the problems," Jackie said. "Him, Dino, Sammy, they got problems, you solve 'em. Ava had a problem, Judy, you helped them, too. So now I've got a problem, and Eddie G. . . . you're the guy!"

Chapter Twenty-Nine

We ate.

Jerry ate with gusto. He was considering this a free pass, meeting Jackie, and all.

Gleason ate with even more gusto than Jerry, if that's possible.

Marilyn picked at her food.

I sulked, ate a bite or two.

Frank had stuck me right in the middle of this little drama, and I was pissed.

But when you get pissed at the Chairman of the Board, what do you do? Do I say, hey Frank, what the hell? I'm ticked off at you. In trying to do his friend and mentor, Jackie Gleason, a favor, he stuck me.

Hey Frank, ain't we friends?

"You know," Jackie said, gesturing with his fork, "this ain't Chinks, but it ain't half bad. I can see why Frank likes this place."

Marilyn looked at me. She sensed my mood, and I could tell she felt bad for me.

I decided to get over it and started eating in earnest. Jerry and Jackie were almost done.

"You gonna finish that?" Jackie asked Marilyn.

She looked down at her plate, which was half full, and said, "No, you can have it."

"Just some of it," he said, and switched plates with her.

Jerry looked at my plate and I said, "Don't even think about it."

We decided against dessert, even though Jackie didn't look happy about it.

"We can get coffee, tea and something from room service," Marilyn told him.

"Sure," Jackie said, "room service."

I didn't tell him that the Sands had nothing like the Bootlegger's tiramisu, but I did know they had some good cheese and chocolate cakes.

The Bootlegger must have been used to taking care of Frank's driver. The man was wiping his mouth with a napkin when we walked out to the car.

"Right," he said, stuffing the napkin into his pocket, "that it? Where to now?"

"Back to the Sands?"

"Ain't we gonna do the town up?" Jackie asked.

"With a hitman maybe lookin' for me, or Marilyn, or both of us? Not a good idea, Jackie."

"We're in Vegas, Eddie, not Miami Beach."

"You came here, he could come here, too," I said.

"He's right, Jackie," Marilyn said. "Besides, I'm tired from the flight."

"Okay, baby, okay," Jackie said. "We'll go back."

We piled into the limo and rode back to the Sands in silence, which suited me. The driver left us right at the front door.

"You wanna come up for a drink, Eddie?" Jackie asked.

"Marilyn's tired—" I started, but he cut me off.

"It's a big suite," he said. "Besides, I ain't finished talkin' to you. Come on, whataya say?"

"Sure," I said, "we'll come up in a little while."

"We?" Jackie asked.

"I go where Mr. G. goes," Jerry said. "Until this is over, anyway."

"Yeah, okay, Jerry," Jackie said. "I'll see ya both later."

He put his arm around Marilyn, and they went into the lobby.

"Now what?" Jerry asked.

"You still have to hear back from some calls you made, right?"

"That's right."

"Let's check with hotel operator, see if anybody called."

"Am I done, Mr. Gianelli?" the driver asked.

"Oh, yeah, sorry Paul. Here . . ." I put my hand in my pocket.

"That's okay, sir," Paul said. "Mr. Sinatra takes good care of me."

"I'll bet he does," I said, as he got back in the car.

As we went into the lobby Jerry said, "Should we go to the desk?"

"No," I said, "let's go to the suite. You can check for messages from there."

"Right."

We went to the elevator without anyone approaching us and rode up to our floor. In the suite we saw the message light flashing on the phone.

"I'll check in," he said.

"Fine."

I went to the bathroom, and, when I came out, he was just hanging up.

"I got two messages, both leaving numbers for me to call back."

I looked at my watch. It was after nine, which meant 11 or midnight in Chicago or New York.

"Go ahead and make the calls, even though it might be too late."

"Right, Mr. G."

I sat on the sofa to consider my options while Jerry started dialing.

I could tell Frank and Jackie that this was out of my league, dealing with some pro who went to Miami Beach to make a hit, and may have disappeared. But, if he was watching Marilyn, then at least he wasn't coming after me.

On the other hand, what I'd said in the restaurant was true. If Jackie and Marilyn came to Vegas, the killer might have done the same. If that was true, he was in my back yard.

And as mad as I was at Frank, did I want Frank getting mad at me? Maybe before I made a decision, I should talk to somebody who knew him real well. Maybe I should get some advice from Dean. Jackie knew him, but he was too involved to give me unbiased advice.

I heard Jerry hang up and looked up as he came across the room at me.

"I got through to one call, it was from Chicago. My guy doesn't know anything about a hitter in Miami."

"And the other one?"

"It came from Brooklyn," he said. "It's after midnight there. I'll have to try tomorrow."

"Okay," I said, "let's go have that drink with Jackie." I stood up, headed for the door, then changed direction and went to the phone. "Let me check and see if he called room service, if he didn't, I'll have them send some dessert."

But Jackie had made the call already, for coffee, tea and some cakes.

"What kind of cake?" Jerry asked, as we went out the door.

Chapter Thirty

Jackie let us in and acted like he hadn't seen us in weeks.

"Good ta see ya, pals!" he exclaimed, slapping us on the back. "Come on in!"

He crossed the large expanse of the room and got behind the bar, where he looked for all the world like Joe the Bartender—only I wasn't Crazy Guggenheim.

"How about a drink?"

"Where's Marilyn?" I asked.

"She went to bed," Jackie said. "She was exhausted. Come on, whataya have?"

On the bar was a tray with the coffee and cake they'd ordered.

"I'll have a cup of coffee," I said.

"Jerry?" Jackie asked.

"Coffee," Jerry said, "no milk, no sugar—and one of those cheesecakes."

I looked at him.

"What? It's a special occasion."

Jackie poured two coffees, and then a straight bourbon for himself. He put out his cigarette in an ashtray, and his hand went right into his right side pocket and came out with another one, which he fired up.

"You guys are makin' me feel like a boozehound."

"I gotta keep sharp in order to protect Mr. G.," Jerry said.

"And I've got work tomorrow," I said.

Jackie took a look at the variety of cakes on the tray and, as Jerry had, picked a cheesecake.

"Jack Entratter keep you jumpin'?" he asked.

"All the time," I said, "but he's real understanding about . . . special cases."

"Oh, like me, you mean?"

"Like any friend of Frank's," I said.

Jackie frowned at me for a moment before speaking again.

"Do we have a problem, Eddie?"

"Not that I know of."

"Because I like you, kid," Jackie said, "but I get the feelin' you don't like me."

"It's not you, Jackie," I said, "I'm just kinda . . . pissed at Frank."

"Ah, because he sprung me and Marilyn on you?"

"Exactly."

Jackie waved the hand that was holding the cigarette.

"Don't blame Frank," he said. "I just don't like anybody else talkin' about my business. I asked him to tell you as little as possible."

The bar had some stools in front of it. I sat on one and put my coffee down in front of me.

"Okay, then," I said, "let's talk about it. Suppose this guy doesn't mean Marilyn any harm?"

"He's a killer," Jackie pointed out. "A hitman."

"And if he wanted her dead, she probably would be," I countered.

"That sounds right," Jerry agreed.

"Okay," Jackie said, "so he's followin' her because he's got a crush on her. So maybe he's not a pro. Maybe he killed the guy in the elevator because he was followin' Marilyn, an' this guy didn't like it."

"No," I said, "the way he approached me in the bar, he's a pro. The police are working on that assumption."

"Okay," Jackie said, cocking his head to one side, "so we stay with the assumption he's a hitman. How long before he decides to get me out of the way?"

"That's a possibility," Jerry agreed.

"In that case," I said to Jackie, "you're better off with the police."

He pointed at me with the cigarette hand. "You're the guy."

"I wish you'd stop sayin' that," I said. "We're dealing with a pro, and I'm not a pro."

"As good as," Jerry said.

"There, see?" Jackie said.

I gave Jerry a look and he stuck a piece of cheesecake into his pie hole.

"All right," I said, thinking of Danny, "I do have a pro at my disposal. I'll make use of him."

"Whatever you gotta do," Jackie said. "I want this guy off of Marilyn's tail."

"How long are you gonna stay in Vegas?" I asked.

"Well, we came to see you," Jackie said, "but I guess we could stay a couple of days. We'll just have to get back to Miami to do the next show."

"Then I better get with it." I slid off the stool. "Come on, Jerry." To Jackie I said, "I'll be in touch."

"Come by and see us tomorrow night," Jackie said.

"I'll have Jerry keep an eye on you, so you can take in some of the sights, if you want."

"Sights," Jackie said, "right, like the Flamingo and the Desert Inn."

He walked us to the door, slapped us on the back again, and then closed the door as soon as we were out in the hall.

"Mr. G.," Jerry said, "I'm supposed to be keepin' an eye on you."

"I'm gonna see Danny," I said. "Meanwhile, we need to find out if Marilyn's really being watched, or if they're imagining it."

"I don't like it."

I Only Have Lies for You

"They won't be here long," I said, as we walked to the elevator. "Maybe we can wrap this up quick."

Chapter Thirty-One

In the morning I met with Danny in the Garden Café. I didn't tell that to Jerry, because he would have wanted to come rather than keep an eye on Jackie and Marilyn.

"When do I get to meet The Great One?" Danny asked, sliding into the booth across from me.

"Maybe later today," I said.

"What's this about, then?"

"I need a pro to catch a pro."

"I thought you wanted me to keep an eye on Gleason and his girl?"

"Well, I'm playin' this by ear," I said. "Now I've got Jerry watching them."

"And who's watchin' you?"

"We don't know that the guy is in Vegas," I said. "If he is—and this is according to Gleason—then he's following Marilyn."

"So now we think he's more interested in her than you?" Danny asked.

"Looks like it. At least, for now."

"So we need to know if a professional hitman has come into Vegas in the past . . . what? Day?"

"If he's followin' them, then he came in last night."

"Depends on how he's followin' them."

"What do you mean?"

"Sometimes the best way to tail somebody is in front of them."

"So you're sayin' if he knew they were coming here, he may have come in ahead of them."

"Right."

"So then we need to look and see if he came in within the past two days."

"It makes sense. I've got some contact at McCarron I'll check with them, but I'll need a description of the guy."

"We don't have that," I said. "I never saw him."

"What about Jackie and Marilyn?"

"Glimpses, maybe."

"Then I don't know who I'm lookin' for."

"Somebody antsy . . . nervous?"

"No, a pro is calm, smooth as ice"

"Okay, so look for somebody like that."

"All right," he said, with a sigh, "buy me breakfast and then I'll have a crack at it. At least we only have to deal with flights coming in from Miami."

***

After breakfast we walked out into the hotel lobby.

153

"Wait a minute," he said. "If I leave you here, you've got no backup."

"Like we said," I reminded him, "the guy's probably followin' Jackie and Marilyn."

"If anything happens to you," Danny said, "I'm gonna have a lot of explainin' to do to Jerry."

"I should be okay today," I said. "Let's risk it."

"I'll be back quick," he promised.

As he went out the door, a bell boy came running up to me.

"Mr. Entratter's lookin' for you, Mr. G.," he said.

"Thanks, Billy."

I took the elevator and entered Entratter's outer office.

"He's looking for you, Eddie," Wendy said.

I waved and said, "That's why I'm here."

"Go on in, then."

"Eddie!" he snapped, as I entered. "Have a seat, boy!"

He was in a good mood, almost ebullient. This couldn't be good.

"What's goin' on, Jack?" I asked, seating myself.

"I been talkin' with Frank, Eddie. He's gonna record a live album here at the Sands for his label."

"That sounds great."

"It is great!" he said, waving his arms. "Why aren't you more excited?"

"What good is it gonna do me, Jack?" I asked. "I'm happy for you and Meyer and whoever else is gonna benefit from it."

"He says he's gonna get the Count and his band to accompany him, and have Quincy Jones arrange it."

I knew "the Count" was Count Basie. I wasn't all that sure at the time who Quincy Jones was.

"When is this supposed to happen?" I asked, because he wanted me to.

"Oh, it'll take a while to get everybody's schedule in sync," he said, "so probably not til the end of the year."

"That's a long way off."

"Yeah, it is," he admitted, "but the important thing is it's gonna happen."

"If you say so, Jack."

Entratter frowned at me.

"You still ticked off at Frank for the Gleason thing?"

"What makes these guys think I can do anything about a professional hitman bein' on the loose."

"Maybe because you have a reputation for gettin' things done, no matter how hard they are?" he said. "Maybe because somebody's always talkin' you up."

"You mean Frank and Dino?"

"I mean me, asshole!" Entratter said. "Eddie, you're the guy—"

"Oh Jesus," I said. "there's that word again. Jackie keeps tellin' me that."

"That's because it's true," Jack said. "And when you use Big Jerry and your P.I. pal, Bardini, nothin's too hard for you to get done. It doesn't matter who you're goin' up against—Mo-Mo, the Kennedys, or a hitman."

I hadn't really gone up against "Mo-Mo" Giancana and the Kennedys, but I did manage to get my way with them a time or two.

"Where do we stand with Gleason, anyway?" he asked.

"He's in a suite, takin' a look at the town—the Flamingo, the Dunes—with Marilyn—"

"Then why are you here?"

"Jerry's watching them," I said, "trying to determine whether or not they're really being followed."

"So who's watchin' you? Bardini?"

"He's checkin' with a contact at the airport to see if maybe a pro was seen comin' in on a flight."

"So nobody's watchin' your back?'

"Not at the moment, but Jackie's worried that the guy's following Marilyn. If that's the case, then he's not worried about me."

"Yet."

"Yeah, yet."

"You know, I made a few calls, but didn't come up with a name for a guy operatin' in Miami."

"Maybe he's not connected," I said. "Might be completely freelance."

"He'd have to be good to go unnoticed."

"If only I'd turned my head for a second in Miami and gotten a glimpse of him."

"If you did, you'd probably be dead."

"Guess you're right."

"Well, okay then," he said, "I just wanted to tell somebody the news, somebody who knew Frank, and what this would mean to the Sands."

"It's exciting news, Jack," I said, "it really is. And as far as bein' pissed at Frank, I'll get over it."

"You'd better," Entratter said "He don't take kindly to his friends bein' pissed off at him. It tends to piss him off. And you know what can happen then. Just ask Lawford."

"Yeah, yeah, I get it," I said. "Is he still in Tahoe?"

"Been there all week," Jack said. "All right, go back to work. I just wanted to share the news with somebody who'd appreciate it."

I stood up. "I do appreciate it. I just have a lot of other, more immediate business on my mind."

"Then what are you doin' here?" he asked. "Go take care of it!"

Chapter Thirty-Two

I went back down to the casino floor, wondering what Jackie and Marilyn were up to, hoping Jerry was staying close, and waiting for Danny to come back with some information.

Meanwhile, the safest place for me, without Jerry or Danny to watch my back, was the Sands, my home turf. At least, I thought I was safe. When I got off the elevator, before I could get from the hotel lobby to the casino floor, I saw two men enter through the front doors. I knew them both, disliked one of them, intensely.

It was clear they were headed for the casino, so I moved to cut them off. When they saw me coming, they stopped.

"Look who we ran into," Detective Hargrove said. "Saves us the trouble of hunting you up, Gianelli."

I ignored him and looked at Detective Eisman, of the Miami Beach police. "You're keeping bad company, Detective."

"He's goin' by the book, Eddie," Hargrove said, not letting Eisman answer. "Came to town on business and contacted us. And when I heard that his business involved you, well, I just volunteered to be helpful."

"'Helpful,'" I repeated. "Not one of the words I would've used to describe you, Hargrove."

"So I guess you two know each other pretty well," Eisman said.

"Well enough to dislike each other," I said.

"'Dislike,'" Hargrove repeated. "Not the word I would've used to describe how I feel about you, Eddie." He looked at Eisman. "I delivered him to you. Let me know if you need anything else."

"I will," Eisman said. "Thanks."

"Just doin' my job," Hargrove said, and left the two of us standing there.

"There has to be a very interesting history between you two," Detective Eisman said.

"I'll tell you about it, some time."

"Meanwhile, can we talk, somewhere?" Eisman asked me.

"Come on," I said, "I'll buy you a drink."

He followed me across the casino floor and into the lounge. As we took two stools at the bar, he stared at the mural on the wall behind it.

"Las Vegas," he said, shaking his head.

"You don't like our town?"

"On the contrary," Eisman said, "I've been here a few times on vacation. I find the excesses almost welcoming. Except for the gambling, it's almost like Miami Beach."

"But no beach, just desert.

"Yeah," Eisman said, "that, too."

"Beer?"

"Sure."

I held two fingers up to the bartender, pointed to the beer taps. He nodded, drew two and brought them over.

"So, what gives?" I asked him. "What brings you to Vegas looking for me?"

"Our investigation into the murder in the elevator floundered," he said. "I tried everything to give it a kick, but this was the only thing I could think of."

"What was? Coming here and talking to me?"

"I figure you've had time to think it over," Eisman said. "There must be something you either saw or heard that can help."

"I have been thinking about it," I said. "And I've been waiting for him to show up here. I even have a bodyguard, and a detective looking for him. On top of that, Gleason is here and with Marilyn Taylor. They arrived a day before you."

"What are they doing here?"

"They seem to think the hitman is following her."

"Why would he do that?"

"Jackie thinks he may have a thing for Marilyn."

"You mean he fulfilled his contract, but fell in love?" Eisman asked.

"That's his idea."

"Jesus." Eisman shook his head. "I guess it's possible. A hitman in love. Who woulda thunk it."

"Not me," I said. "That wasn't the feeling I got about him from our brief exchange."

"So then they think he's going to follow them here," Eisman said. "What does Gleason want you to do. Go up against a pro?"

"That's exactly what he wants me to do."

"And you're going to do it?"

"I told you," I said. "I've got help, and they're both pros in their own right."

"This should be interesting, then," Eisman said. "Maybe I should stick around and watch."

"Don't you have to go back to work?"

"I actually had to take some time off in order to come here," Eisman said. "My bosses wanted me to move on to other cases. So, I took the time I had coming to me. Technically, I'm on vacation."

"Well, hanging around is up to you, then," I said, "but did you tell Hargrove you were on leave?"

"No," Eisman said, "I neglected to mention that part. But rest assured, I still have my badge."

"But no authority," I added.

Eisman finished his beer, set the empty mug down and asked, "How much authority do I need to observe?" he got down off his stool. "I'll be around,"

He left the lounge, and I finished my beer.

Chapter Thirty-Three

Truth be told, I didn't really give much credence to the possibility that the hitman had fallen for Marilyn Taylor. She was a good-looking woman, there was no doubt about that, but to think that she had caught the fancy of a professional killer while he was on a job was ludicrous. If he was on her trail, then there was some other reason—no matter what Jackie Gleason thought.

But whatever the reason was, we had to find out if the hitman was in Vegas. Only I was out of the action for the moment, so I turned my attention to my real job.

During the course of the day, I approved new credit limits for half a dozen regulars—including the singer, Julius LaRosa—sent show tickets to three couples who were staying with us, supplied girls for two high rollers, ordered flowers for the wife of another, and arranged dinner for still two other couples, one of which was Steve and Eydie.

I was back in the bar, this time having a bourbon rather than a beer, when Jerry came walking in.

"Where's Jackie?" I asked.

"They're back in their suite," he said.

"You want a beer?"

He hesitated, then said, "A small one."

The bartender brought it and Jerry took a stool next to me.

"How did the day go?"

"Fine, I guess," Jerry said. "Mr. Gleason did some gambling, and Miss Taylor stood by his side the whole time. Then she wanted to look at some shops, and he went with her."

"So they stayed together the whole time?"

"Yep," he said, "the whole time."

"And did you see anybody taking an interest in them?" I asked.

"Nobody," Jerry said, "except, of course, lots of people recognized Mr. Gleason. Some of them went up to him for autographs. I almost stopped a couple of them, but there was no trouble. What about here?"

"I asked Danny to check with the airport, see if anybody noticed someone squirley comin' in."

"A pro ain't gonna fly and look squirley," Jerry said, "unless he's afraid of flyin'."

"No harm in checking. Oh, and I had a surprise visitor."

"Who?"

"The detective from Miami Beach who's working on the murder."

"What did he want?"

"He's having trouble with his case, thought he might up start it by coming here and talking to me."

"Did it help?"

"I don't think so, but he's on vacation, so he's gonna stick around a while."

"Did he come alone?"

"Came from Miami alone," I said, "but Hargrove brought him here."

"That sonofabitch?"

"He didn't stay long," I said, "just made some snide remarks and left."

"When's that department gonna catch on and let him go?" Jerry asked.

"Who knows?" I said.

"Well, it ain't gonna happen today," Jerry said.

"What makes you say that?" I asked, looking into my glass.

"Because here he comes," Jerry said, "and he don't look happy."

I looked up and saw Hargrove coming toward me with another man in plain clothes, and two uniformed cops.

"Another new partner, Hargrove?" I asked. "They're starting to get fed up real quick."

"Not a time for jokes, Eddie," he said. "You're comin' with me."

"What for?"

"Questioning."

"About what?"

"Murder."

"What murder?"

"Your buddy."

My stomach dropped, and I went cold all over.

"Danny?" I asked.

"No," he said, "not your dick buddy, your Miami cop buddy, Eisman."

"Eisman's dead?"

"Killed," Hargrove said, "and, my guess is, you're the last one who saw him alive."

Chapter Thirty-Four

Hargrove wouldn't let Jerry come with me, so the big guy followed in my Caddy.

As usual, they stuck me in an interrogation room and left me alone for a while. Finally, Hargrove came in with his new partner, a fortyish guy who looked like a department lifer. His name was Everett.

"No coffee?" I asked, as they entered empty handed.

"This ain't a diner," Hargrove said. He sat across from me while Everett held up a wall with his arms folded.

"Tell me about Eisman," Hargrove said.

"Not much to tell. I found a body in Miami, and Eisman caught the case."

"And he let you leave town?"

"I wasn't a suspect," I said. "I was a witness. I told him what I knew." I didn't tell Hargrove about my meeting with the hitman. Fuck 'im.

"So what did he come here for?"

"Didn't he tell you?"

"He just came here, identified himself, and said he was lookin' for you. I figured he wanted to throw your ass in jail."

"Not the case."

"Too bad," Hargrove said. "Maybe he'd still be alive."

"How did he die?" I asked. "And where?"

"He was staying at a hotel off the strip. He was found there, stabbed to death."

"In his room?"

"No," Hargrove said, "A guest went for ice, and found Eisman in the ice machine."

"Jesus. When was he killed?"

"The body was cold, so he must've been in the machine for hours, but since you saw him this morning, he was killed between then and now."

"Brilliant."

"The M.E. will pinpoint it when he can, but we're only dealin' with hours."

"He was stabbed, you say?"

"That's right."

"That's how the guy in Miami was killed."

Hargrove sat back. Either he never thought I did it, or he was starting to think I didn't.

"Can you tell me anything else about the Miami case?"

"They figured the guy was killed by a hitman."

"A pro?"

I nodded.

"A pro who uses a blade," Everett said. "That's unusual. I'll see what I can find out."

"Fine," Hargrove said, and his partner left the room.

"What else can you tell me?"

I kept my mouth shut about Gleason and Marilyn Taylor. That was part of my job, to see that guests of the Sands didn't get hassled by the police.

"Not much."

"What did Eisman say?"

I shrugged. "He said the trail went cold in Miami. He thought there might be something else I remembered that might help him. I told him there was nothing. He said he thought maybe the hitman might come here for me, so he was gonna stick around for a while."

"He didn't have to get back?"

"Apparently," I said, "he took some vacation days to come here."

"So he wasn't official."

"I guess not."

"I'll have to call Miami P.D.," Hargrove said. He pushed his chair back and stood up.

"Hey," I said, "what about me?"

"Sit tight," he said. "I'll be back after I've talked to Miami. Depending on what they say, I'll let you leave."

"Hargrove—" I snapped, but he went out and locked the door behind him.

169

Another hour with no coffee or water. I knew Hargrove was being a dick—a real dick—on purpose.

I felt sorry for Eisman. He came all this way to work his case on his own time, only to die, probably at the hands of the very killer he was pursuing. I wondered if he saw it coming?

When the door opened again, it wasn't Hargrove, but Everett, the new partner.

"You find out what a shitheel your partner is, yet?"

"I went into this already knowin' that," he told me. "But they don't let us pick our partners." He stood aside and left the door open. "You can go."

"What'd Miami say?"

"They're sendin' somebody, probably to talk with Hargrove, and to take Eisman home."

"Maybe his partner, a guy named Winter."

"That's him," Everett said. "I talked to him a bit on the phone. He was shocked, didn't even know Eisman had left Miami Beach."

I stood up.

"Any problem with me talking to him when he gets here?"

"He said he wanted to," Everett said, "and I don't see why not. You can go."

"Yeah, thanks."

As I passed him, he said, "Sorry for the shitty treatment. I wanted to bring you some water, but Hargrove wouldn't let me."

"That's no surprise," I said. "Don't worry about it."

"Your friend's waitin' out front."

"My friend?"

"Big guy," he said, "in a Caddy."

"Ah, Jerry," I said. "Good to know I've got a ride. I'll be seein' you, detective."

I made my way to the front of the building without running into Hargrove, which suited me fine. Took the elevator down and found Jerry waiting out front, like Everett said. I'd been inside for hours, but it still wasn't completely dark.

"Hey, Mr. G." he called.

I waved, went down the stairs and got into the passenger seat of my car.

"Everythin' okay?" he asked.

"Oh, Hargrove was a shit, as usual, but yeah, everything's fine. He called Miami, and they must've given him the word that I'm not a suspect."

"So where to?" Jerry asked.

"We've got to find Danny," I said. "He's probably wondering where we are. And then I've got to talk with Jackie."

"So, back to the Sands?"

I nodded. "Back to the Sands."

Chapter Thirty-Five

We didn't have to look for Danny. He was waiting for us in the lounge, at the bar. It was dark when we pulled into the parking lot, and I could hear Jerry's stomach making hunger noises.

"I got the word that you got pinched," Danny said, as we approached. "But nobody knew why."

"Not pinched," I said, "just taken in for questioning." I waved to the bartender for two beers. I was dry as the desert around Las Vegas. "The Miami Beach detective who showed up here, Eisman, was found dead in his hotel."

"Jesus!" he said.

Jerry and I took stools on either side of Danny, who was working on a bourbon.

"But they let you go," he said.

"Yeah," I said, after a healthy swig from my beer, "they talked to Eisman's partner in Miami. I guess he gave me the all clear, but he's on his way here."

"He's gonna want to talk to you," Danny said.

"That's not a problem," I said. "What did you find out?"

"Not a thing," he said. "Came up dry. But what did you expect? Nobody was gonna tell me they spotted a guy getting off a plane who looked like a hitman."

"I guess not."

He smiled. "Although one guy did tell me about Jerry."

"What?" Jerry said.

"Yup," Danny said. "A ticket taker said the only guy he saw who looked like a gangster was this big guy who was wearing a houndstooth jacket."

"I don't look like no gangster!" Jerry snapped. "Do I?"

"Maybe," Danny said, "it's just the jacket."

Jerry looked down and touched his lapel.

"Never mind," I said. "The airport was a longshot."

"What's next on your agenda?" Danny asked.

"Me and Jerry are gonna eat here. You're welcome to join us," I said. "After that I'll wanna talk to Jackie, again."

"Thanks for the invite, but Penny's waitin' for me to take her to dinner, and I'm already late." He got off his stool. "Just so you know, I'm gonna blame you."

"No problem," I said. "Your girl will know better, anyway."

"Tell 'er I said hello," Jerry said, although his attention was still on his lapel.

"Will do, big guy." Danny looked at me. "I'll be around tomorrow."

"See you then."

As Danny left, Jerry moved over one stool and we finished our beers before going into the Garden Room for dinner.

"What makes this a gangster jacket?" he asked.

***

Jerry had some chicken and a salad, and picked on some fries from my plate, where they surrounded my steak.

"Well, your killer's definitely in town," he said. "It's too much of a coincidence that somebody else killed that Miami cop."

"I agree," I said. "He's either here for Marilyn, or for me."

"You don't believe that guff about him bein' sweet on the broad, do ya?" Jerry asked.

"No, I don't."

"Then you definitely think he's here for you."

"It makes the most sense," I said. "Why kill the investigating detective, and not the only witness?" Then something occurred to me. "Oh, shit!"

"What?"

"I wasn't the only witness."

Jerry got it. "The driver!"

"Right."

"Do you know his name?"

"Just his first name," I said. "Paul."

"Well, who would know his full name?"

I made a face. "Maybe Frank, since he hired him."

"And you don't wanna talk to Mr. S.," Jerry said.

"Not really."

"What about the cops?"

"Eisman's partner is on his way here."

"Well, I can call Mr. S.," he offered.

"No, no," I said, "it's my responsibility. I'll call him."
I signaled the bartender to bring me a phone, dialed the
Cal-Neva number in Tahoe from a small book I kept in
my pocket since I started working as a host.

"Frank Sinatra, please," I said when the phone was
answered.

"He don't talk to just anybody," a wise guy on the
other end said. "Who's callin'?"

"This is Eddie G. from the Sands? You wanna keep
your job, bub? Put me through!"

"Uh . . . oh . . .yeah, sure, right away. Sorry."

Other people referred to me as Eddie G., but I never
did. I felt bad for using my name to make the guy into a
stammering, apologizing fool. Kinda.

"Jesus, Eddie," Frank said, coming on the phone, "what'd you do to that guy? He's afraid he's gettin' fired."

"Yeah, sorry about that, Frank. He rubbed me the wrong way."

"Seems like that's happenin' a lot, lately."

I ignored the comment.

"Look, that detective who was investigating the murder in Miami came here to see me, and he ended up dead in his hotel."

"Crap, the hitman?"

"Looks like it."

"So he's in town. Lookin' for you?"

"That's what I was thinkin'," I said, "but then I remembered I wasn't the only witness."

"You weren't—oh, wait, Paul."

"That's right. I don't know his last name. Do you?"

"Jeez, no, I never did, I just . . . wait, I got a card in my wallet. Here's the number I call to get him." He read me a phone number.

"Okay, Frank," I said, "I'll see if I can get ahold of him. If he's okay, I'll warn him."

"But you guys didn't see nothin', right? Just the dead body in the elevator?"

"Right," I said, "but the hitman might have his own ideas about what we saw."

177

"Hey," Frank said, "let me know what happens, huh? And Eddie . . . I'm real sorry I got you into this. If you want, just tell Jackie you're out. I'll make him understand."

Somewhat mollified by the apology I said, "Naw, naw, it's okay, Frank. I already told him I'd help. I don't wanna go back on my word."

"Okay, Eddie," Frank said. "Keep in touch so I know you're all right."

"I will." I hung up.

"What happened?"

"He apologized."

"That's good, right?"

"Yeah, that's good." I tapped the phone a few times, then dialed the phone number Frank had given me for the driver in Miami Beach.

"Hello," a woman's voice said.

"Hello," I said, "I'm calling for Paul . . . Is he there?"

"Oh . . ." she said, and it sounded as if she dropped the phone.

"Hello? Hello?" I said.

The phone was picked up and a man said harshly, "Who is this?" I had a bad feeling.

"My name is Eddie Gianelli," I said. "I'm calling from Las Vegas. Frank Sinatra and I used Paul as a driver when we're in Miami Beach. I was wondering if I could talk to him.

"Oh," he said, "oh, I'm sorry Mr. Gianelli, I didn't know . . . that was Paul's wife who answered the phone. I'm her father. I have some bad news. Paul went out a few nights ago for a driving job, and never came home. They . . . they just found him today. He's . . . he was dead in his car."

"Oh, I'm so sorry," I said. "Do—did the police say how he died?"

"He was stabbed. It's . . . it's horrible. My daughter is very distraught."

"Understandably so," I said. "I won't bother your family any longer, sir. Please accept my condolences. Paul was a fine man."

"Yes," he said, "thank you."

The line went quiet.

"He's dead?" Jerry asked.

"Oh yeah," I said, "He's dead. Stabbed and left in his car."

"So what do we do now?"

"Now," I said, "we wait for Detective Eisman's partner to get here. Meanwhile, we'll talk to Jackie, again."

Chapter Thirty-Six

I called Jackie's suite and told him what had happened to Eisman. He said he didn't want to talk in his room. There was no reason to bother Marilyn with that news just yet.

"Where can we talk?" Jackie asked.

"Wherever you want," I said. "The bar, the Garden Room, Jack Entratter's office."

"Let's not involve him."

"He won't be there at this hour."

"Hell with it," Jackie said. "I'll meet you in the Garden Room in ten minutes."

"We'll be there."

"We? Oh, Jerry?"

"Yup."

"Good." He hung up. So did I.

"Garden Room?" Jerry asked.

"Right."

"That means I'll have to eat somethin'."

"Have to?"

"Well, just to be nice to Jackie," Jerry said. "We can't let him eat alone."

"What makes you think he's gonna eat?"

"Have you met Mr. Gleason?"

Well, I'd been in the police station for a long time. I *was* kind of hungry.

***

We were sitting at a table when Jackie walked into the Garden Room. I thought he'd prefer it to trying to slide into a booth.

"Hey, Jerry, ol' pal!" Jackie exclaimed.

"Hey, Mr. G."

"'Mr. G.'," Jackie said, looking at me. "I tol' the kid he can call me Jackie, but he calls me 'Mr. G.'"

"He calls me 'Mr. G.' and he's known me for years."

"Well, whataya know," Jackie said. "I guess it's a sign of respect, huh?"

"What's wrong with respect?" Jerry asked.

"Nothin', Jerry, ol' pal," Jackie said. "Nothin' at all." Jackie sat opposite me. Jerry was on my left. "You mind if I order somethin'?"

"No," I said, "I could use a snack. Being left hangin' in a police department interview room tends to make me hungry."

"They took you in, huh?"

"For questioning." I waved at the waitress. This one was a cute kid named Coco.

"Whataya have, Mr. G.?"

"A burger, Coco. No cheese, no fries."

"No fries?" Jerry asked.

"Order your own," I said.

"I can't," he said, glumly, and looked at pretty Coco. "A burger, with cheese."

"Comin' up." She looked at Jackie. "Hey, aren't you Ralph Kramden?"

"That's me, doll," Jackie said. "I'll have a cheeseburger and bring me the fries these guys aren't havin'."

"Yes, sir."

"Bring us three beers with the food, Coco."

"Right, Eddie."

"And baby," Jackie said, "make sure that burger is medium rare or, bang, zoom, to the moon!"

Coco hurried away, giggling.

Jackie took a cigarette out of his right pocket and lit it.

"Okay, Eddie," he said, "what's goin' on?"

Detective Eisman's not the only one dead, Jackie," I said. "Also the driver, Paul, who was with me when I found the body."

"Jesus," Jackie said, "so you're the last one left alive?"

"Me," I said, "and Marilyn."

"But she didn't see nothin'," he said.

"Well, neither did I, except for a dead guy in an elevator."

"So then why would he be after you?" Jackie asked.

"For the same reason he killed Paul, whatever that is," I reasoned.

"And he's not following Marilyn?"

"I don't know, Jackie," I said. "We can ask him that when we find him. But I doubt he's in love with her."

"So now we're actively lookin' for a professional hitman?"

"That seems to be a better idea than waitin' for him to find Mr. G.," Jerry said.

Coco came over and set all our plates down. Jackie's was covered with fries. He picked up his hamburger, bit into it, chewed, then looked at her and said, "Baby, you're the greatest."

Again, she scurried off, giggling.

"So if he's here," Jackie said, "maybe the best thing is for Marilyn and me to head back to Miami Beach."

"That may be," I said. "If he stays here, he's after me. If he goes back, then he's after her . . . or you."

"Me?" Jackie stopped chewing. "Why would he be after me?"

"We don't know why he'd be after any of us, Jackie," I said. "We don't even know why he killed that poor bastard in the elevator."

"Okay," Jackie said, "so Marilyn and me, we go home. Then we see what this hit guy does."

"When will you leave?" I asked.

"Well," Jackie said, "not til I finish these fries."

Chapter Thirty-Seven

Since Jackie and Marilyn had come in on Frank's plane, they could leave any time. All Jackie had to do was call Frank.

Jackie finished eating and stood up.

"Can I sign the check—" he started.

"Don't worry, I got it," I said, cutting him off. "Look, do me a favor."

"What's that?"

"Don't leave town until late tomorrow. I just need some time to make sure what's safe, and what isn't."

"Sure, pal," Jackie said, "but we do have to get back by the end of the week for the next show."

"Gotcha," I said.

"See ya later, Jerry," Jackie said, and left the Garden Room.

Coco came over and indicated the plates on the table.

"Okay to clear?" she asked.

"Sure," I answered.

She took Jerry's plate and mine, but as she reached for Jackie's, Jerry said, "Take that later!"

"Sure, big guy," she said, with a smile. "Hey, that Mr. Gleason's a riot, right?"

"He sure is," I said. "He's a regular riot."

As she walked away Jerry put Jackie's plate in front of him.

"Jerry."

"There's only a few fries left here," Jerry reasoned. "He ate most of 'em."

"You should see him chow down on Chinese food."

"Chinese food!" Jerry said. "Now that sounds good."

"You just had a burger," I said. "Relax and eat your fries."

He popped one fry into his mouth and asked, "What's on your mind?"

"Jackie."

"What about him?"

"I'm gettin' the feelin' he knows more than he's tellin'," I said.

"And that's why your Brooklyn is comin' out?"

"I don't like thinking he's holding out on us," I explained.

"You're not mad at Mr. S. anymore, but you're mad at Mr. Gleason?"

"I'm not mad," I said. "I'm . . . confused by the whole thing."

"So what do we do?"

"We wait for Eisman's partner to get here tomorrow and see what he has to say."

Jerry made a face.

"Is he gonna stop in and see Hargrove first, too?" he wondered.

"I don't know," I said. "Probably, if he follows protocol. But . . . maybe we can stop him."

"How do we do that?"

"He's coming in on a commercial flight," I said. "Let's find out when and meet him. That'll keep him away from Hargrove until after we talk to him."

"Great idea."

I waved at Coco and made motions for her to bring me a phone.

"What are you gonna do now?"

"Call Miami Beach P.D., see if I can get ahold of Detective Winter before he leaves or, at least, find out when he's leaving."

"If I knew you was gonna do that from here, I woulda ordered dessert."

Chapter Thirty-Eight

We didn't have dessert, but he did order coffee while I was on the line.

When I got off the phone, he pushed a coffee cup over to me.

"Thanks." I sipped. "They wouldn't give me any information, wouldn't give me his home number. Against the rules."

"So you came up empty?"

"Not exactly. When I said I wanted to leave a message for him to call me back immediately, the person on the other end said it wouldn't be that fast. She said he wasn't going to be in for a few days—starting tomorrow morning."

"So you figure he'll be in a plane in the mornin'."

"I figured that before the call," I said. "I mean, his partner was killed, he wasn't going to wait long. This call just confirms it."

"What if he flies in tonight, on a red eye. Or already did?" Jerry asked. "If we miss him, he'll get to Hargrove first—and you know he ain't gonna have nothin' good to say about you."

"That's true," I said. I didn't have Danny's contacts at the airport, but I did know one person—a man in security. "Let's see what I can find out tonight."

I picked up the phone receiver and Jerry turned and waved to Coco.

***

By the time I got off the phone, there were two pieces of pie on the table, both apple. The coffee cups had been refilled. Jerry had eaten half of his slice and pushed the rest away. I took a bite of mine.

It had taken some time, but my security contact at the airport confirmed that no red eye flights had come in from Miami Beach.

"Looks like he's gonna come in tomorrow," I said. "I've got two likely times for flights, so we'll drive out there in the morning and wait."

"You gonna recognize 'im?"

"I saw him once, but yeah, I think I will."

"If you don't, I will."

"You've never seen him."

"If he looks like a cop, I'll spot 'im."

We finished our pie—he slowly, reluctantly ate the rest of his—and then we went back into the casino. I intended to do my job for the rest of the evening, and he intended to do his and keep me alive.

***

In the morning we were at McCarron Airport when Detective Winter got off his plane. I looked around, but didn't see Hargrove anywhere, which suited me. I wanted a word with Winter before he got the lowdown on me from Hargrove.

He recognized me as we approached him, but gave Jerry a wary look.

"Detective Winter," I said, extending my hand, "we thought we'd give you a ride."

"We?" he asked, shaking my hand.

"This is my friend, Jerry."

"Friend," Jerry said, "and bodyguard."

"Ah," he said, "I get it." He shook hands with Jerry.

"We're sorry about your partner," I said. "I spoke to him the night before—"

"Didja? You can tell me about that in the car, then."

"Fine," I said, "it's this way. Is that your only bag?"

"This is it."

"I'll take it," Jerry said, and plucked it from the detective's hand.

"We can put you up at the Sands, if you like," I offered, as we walked.

"No, that's okay," he said. "I wanna stay where Eisman stayed—a hotel? Motel?"

"Sure," I said, "we'll take you over there."

Out in the parking lot Jerry tossed the suitcase into the back seat, and Winter insisted on riding with it. Jerry got behind the wheel and I got in the passenger seat in front.

That made it kind of hard to talk with Winter, but since I was doing most of the talking, I simply turned in my seat and gabbed. I told him about my conversation with Eisman the night before he died—or, actually, the night he died. He must have gotten killed as soon as he returned to his hotel.

The Decatur Court looked more like a motel, but they called it a hotel because it had three floors. All the rooms, however, were accessed from outside.

Jerry pulled up in front of the office and Winter got out with his bag.

"So what's the real reason you guys picked me up?" he asked.

"I was hoping to get to you before you talked to the local detective, Hargrove, who Eisman was in contact with. He's gonna bad mouth the hell out of me."

"He already did."

"What?"

"I spoke with him on the phone," Winter said. "He's a real jerk."

"You got that right," Jerry said.

"Don't worry," Winter said. "I value Eisman's opinion more than this guy Hargrove. Can we talk some more after I've seen him, and identified the body?"

"Sure," I said. "Come on over to the Sands anytime."

"I'll do that." He turned to go into the office.

"And don't get killed!" Jerry said.

He turned back and stared at Jerry. "I'll keep that in mind."

As he went into the office, I swatted Jerry on the arm. "What?"

"Don't get killed?"

"I don't even know why he's stayin' here, Mr. G. It's dangerous."

"He knows that," I said. "He probably wants the guy to try."

"Well," Jerry said, putting the Caddy in drive, "that ain't smart."

I stared straight out through the front windshield. My neck had a crick in it from the ride with my head turned.

"Let's head for the Sands," I said. "Danny's probably wondering where we are."

Chapter Thirty-Nine

As we entered the Sands lobby, I realized I was getting tired of it. I'd never felt that way before, but with a hitman in town, maybe looking for me, I was kind of trapped and I didn't like it.

"There you are!"

We turned, saw Danny coming toward us.

"I was tryin' to figure out where you were," Danny said. "I talked to Entratter, but he didn't know. Why do I annoy that guy so much?"

"Probably because you're a cop," Jerry said.

"I'm not a cop."

"Well," Jerry said, "close."

Danny looked at me. "Where you been?"

"Eisman's partner, Winter, came in this morning. We picked him up at the airport, took him to his partner's hotel."

"He's stayin' at the same place? Not smart."

"See?" Jerry said. "That's what I said."

"I can't control where the guy wants to stay," I said, "or who he wants to talk to."

"Like . . . Hargrove?"

"Exactly," I said.

"Did you warn him?"

"I didn't have to," I said. "He had already talked with Hargrove on the phone. He thinks he's an ass."

"Ah," Danny said, "a smart cop, for a change."

"Any word on our guy?" I asked.

"Nobody in town knows about an out-of-towner comin' in," Danny said. "What about you?" He looked at Jerry.

"I got nothin'," Jerry said. "I called Chicago, Boston, Philly. Nothin' but blanks."

"This guy must be a ghost," Danny said.

"Hey," I said, "he sat right next to me in a bar and I didn't see him."

"What about the bartender?" Danny asked.

"What?"

"The bartender on duty," Danny said. "He served him. didn't he see him?"

"I never asked." I felt like a dunce.

"Didn't the cops talk to 'im?" Jerry asked.

"I don't know," I admitted. "We'll have to ask Winter."

"You gonna see him again?" Danny asked.

"Yeah," I said, "after he talks to Hargrove, he's gonna come here."

"If the killer doesn't get him first."

"I warned him," Jerry said.

"If the killer's gonna come after anybody, it'll be me," I said.

"What about Gleason, and the Taylor girl?"

"He's takin' her back to Miami Beach on Frank's plane."

"When?"

"Probably tomorrow. He gave me another day."

"To do what?"

"I don't know," I admitted. "I never knew why he came here to see me. I keep thinking there's something Jackie's not telling me."

"Do you think he's told anyone?" Danny asked. "Maybe Sinatra?"

"Maybe," I said. "I can ask Frank, but if Gleason has sworn him to secrecy, I think I know which way Frank will lean."

"He's known Gleason a lot longer," Danny said.

I nodded. "There's only thing I can think of to do."

"What's that?" Jerry asked.

"Get help."

"From who?" Danny asked.

"I'm thinking if Frank won't tell me what Gleason's up to," I said, "maybe he'll tell somebody else."

"Come on, Eddie," Danny said. "Who are you talkin' about?"

"Dino."

"Why would he tell Dean Martin what he won't tell you?" Danny asked.

"I think Dean's the only one Frank thinks more of than Jackie."

"And why would Martin even ask him?"

"Because I'll ask him to."

"And you think you and Dino are close enough friends for him to do this for you? Sinatra is *Dean's* best friend."

"I know," I said. "I told you, it's the only thing I can think of. So maybe all I have to do is convince Dean that it's in everyone's best interest for me to hear the truth, whatever it is."

"So where's Dean now?"

"He should be in Burbank, shooting the first season of his new show."

"That means you can call him at home."

"Right."

"Well, all right, then," Danny said. "Is Jerry stayin' with you?"

"He is."

"Okay," Danny said, "I've got a few more ideas I want to chase down. Let me know what happens with Martin."

Chapter Forty

That entire conversation took place in the hotel lobby, and we separated right there.

"What do we do now?" Jerry said. "We're all comin' up empty on this guy."

"All I know is, I'm feeling kind of smothered in here. I'd like to get out and do something."

"Like what?"

"We drove Winter to that hotel, but we never went in and took a look. Or talked to the desk clerk."

"Don't you think Hargrove musta done that?"

"Maybe he didn't ask the questions we'll ask," I said. "Let's take a ride."

"Suits me."

It might've been an odd choice of what to do next, since we had just come from there, but we went back out to the Caddy and drove back to the Decatur Court.

Whether it was a hotel or motel was moot. They even called themselves a "court," which wasn't quite right, either. It had three floors, outside access, and a pool. We parked outside the main office and went in.

"Help ya?" a middle-aged clerk asked. He was balding, thin, had wire-framed glasses and a slight lilt to his voice which indicated he might've been from somewhere in the South.

"Yes," I said, "we're here about the police detective who was killed."

"More of you?" he asked. "First the locals came in, and then that cop's partner wanted the same room and asked a lot of questions. Now you?"

"We're just doing a follow-up," I said.

"Yeah," Jerry said, looking mean.

"Okay," the clerk said, leaning on the desk, "whataya want?"

"Other than the local cops, and the two Miami cops," I asked, "who else did you see in the past few days?"

"What kinda question is that?" the clerk asked. "Lots of people come in and out of here—locals and tourists."

"We're not talking about tourists," I said, "we're talking about . . . suspicious characters."

"Shit," he said, "half of them look suspicious. You look suspicious."

"Okay," I said, "when the first detective from Miami came here and checked in, did anyone come in asking about him?"

"Now that's something your local buddy didn't ask," the clerk said, "but the second Miami cop did."

"And what did you tell him?"

"There was one man who came in askin' about him," the clerk said. "He wanted to know what room he was in."

"Did you tell him?"

"Well . . ."

"How much did he pay you?" Jerry asked.

"Fifty bucks."

"And you want the same from us?" I asked.

He shrugged. "Fair's fair."

"Yes, fair is fair," I said. "How would you like it if my big partner here tore your head off?"

"And shit down your neck?" Jerry asked.

The clerk looked worried. "Y-you can't do that. You're cops."

"Who said we were cops?" I looked at Jerry. "Did we say we were cops?"

"No, we didn't," Jerry said.

"B-but I assumed—"

"You assumed wrong," I said.

"In fact," Jerry said, moving his coat aside so the clerk could see the cannon in his belt, "we're just the opposite of cops."

Now the man brightened, thinking he'd gotten it.

"Oh, well, why didn't you just say you were connected?" he asked. "I'll tell ya whatever ya wanna know."

"Start with a description of the man who asked about the dead cop's room," I suggested.

The description didn't help.

"Average," the clerk had told us. The man looked average. Height, weight, facial features. "He looked like, well anybody."

Had he seen him since the murder?

No.

And did anyone else besides cops come around asking any questions?

No.

The guy was no help, at all.

We turned to leave when I thought of another question.

"What about since this morning, when the other cop registered? Anybody been around?"

"Just you two."

"Has the other cop come back down since he checked in?" I asked.

"Y-yessir," the clerk stammered, "h-he came down a little while ago and took a cab."

Jerry had been halfway out the door. He came back in and approached the desk again. The clerk shrank back.

"And nobody should hear about us bein' here, Got it?"

"Y-yessir, I got it."

We went outside.

"Now what?" Jerry asked.

I Only Have Lies for You

"I'm not ready to go back to the Sands, yet," I said, "and I don't think Winter will be done with Hargrove, yet."

"So where do we go?"

"Can you eat hot dogs on this new diet of yours?"

Chapter Forty-One

Jerry knew the way to the hot dog stand at the end of Industrial Drive. We'd been there many times before. This time we ordered two dogs each, but our concession to his diabetes was no French fries.

"I could probably have a few fries if I only had one dog," he reasoned. "Or, ya know, if you ordered 'em I could, ya know, take a few."

"That's okay," I said. "I'm not that hungry. I was just looking for something to do rather than go back to the Sands. A hot dog is always something good to do."

"You got that right."

We carried our dogs and sodas to the wooden picnic tables and benches nearby. We'd already dressed our dog. Mustard and sauerkraut for Jerry, ketchup and relish for me. Yes, ketchup on my hot dog. I learned that from having Nathan's hot dogs while I lived in Brooklyn. So sue me. Jerry and I'd had many discussions about it, but he finally gave up on me.

We sat across from each other and ate.

"This killer," Jerry said. "He sounds too perfect."

"I know," I said. "Nobody's seen him, and the one person who might've says he's average,"

"That's the perfect hitman," Jerry said. "The one nobody ever notices. And he's a blade man, so he needs to be able to get in close."

"Seems to me he'd either have a helluva reputation, or he's a ghost."

"Well, since we can't find anybody who knows anythin', I guess he's a ghost."

"And that doesn't help us, at all," I said, "not that we really want to find a hitman."

"Findin' him would be better than havin' him find you, Mr. G.," Jerry said.

"I suppose you're right."

Jerry was looking longingly at the hot dog stand and I knew he was thinking about going back for more, so I said, "Okay, we better get out of here."

"Uh, yeah, okay, right."

We got rid of our trash and walked to the Caddy. I stopped before getting in and looked at Jerry on the other side.

"What if we change our tactics?" I asked.

"Whataya mean?"

"Instead of not wanting the hitman to find me, what if we let him find me?"

"You mean use you as bait?"

"Seems to me he could've got to Marilyn Taylor, or Jackie, any time he wanted to. No cops around, no bodyguards."

"Mr. Gleason had no bodyguard? No security?"

"Oh, there's security at the theater," I said, then realized I as contradicting myself. "Yeah, okay, so he couldn't have gotten to them there. But once they headed home, they were ripe for the picking, weren't they?"

"She is," Jerry said. "Anybody can get into that underground parking lot you told me about, right?"

"Right," I said. "Her stalker got in there."

"So how do you figure to do this?" he asked, opening his door.

"I don't know," I said, opening mine. "The idea just occurred to me."

We got in the car.

"Well," Jerry said, "you'd have to get rid of me. Then maybe go home, sit in your house, and wait."

I looked around. There was a man and a woman at the hot dog stand, a few passing cars, nobody on foot. In the distance were houses, and factories, some of them with three and four story rooftops.

"Well, there's one good thing," I said.

"What's that?"

"Being a blade man, he's not gonna shoot me from a distance."

204

Jerry looked around, then started the car and said, "Nope."

Chapter Forty-Two

We finally had to head back to the Sands. There was simply no place else to go. Not until we came up with a plan.

Several pit bosses rushed me when I appeared on the casino floor, and for the next few hours I was busy putting out fires, with Jerry right at my elbow.

It was actually nice for that time to be doing casino work and not worrying about a hitman. I left that up to Jerry, who was keeping a wary eye out for anyone who looked "average."

Inside the Sands it never mattered what time it was. In fact, the time didn't matter much in Las Vegas, in general. Everybody did what they were going to do until they got tired.

"I need a break," I said to Jerry.

"The Garden Room or the lounge?"

"Let's go next door."

"The Flamingo?" he asked.

I nodded.

"Why not?" he said. "Ain't no hitman gonna look for you there."

Unless he follows us there, I thought, but I didn't say it out loud.

We left the Sands by the front door, made a left and walked to the Flamingo. It wasn't exactly next door, but it was close enough.

My face was known in the Flamingo, some of the dealers and girls nodded or waved as we went by on the way to the bar. To a lot of people, the place was known as "Bugsy's Place." Back when Bugsy Siegel opened it, though, it was more like Bugsy's Folly. But the boys got rid of Benny Siegel and got the Flamingo on the right track.

"Hey, Eddie," the bartender said. "Whataya have?"

I knew his face, but his name wasn't coming to me.

"A coupla beers, thanks."

"Comin' up."

"This is a nice place," Jerry said. "I always wonder when we come in here what Siegel did wrong?"

"He wasn't a businessman, Jerry," I said. "The Flamingo closed soon after he opened it, in December of forty-six. It reopened about three months later when the hotel was refinished. Three months later, Bugsy was gunned down in Virginia Hill's house."

"It's too bad," Jerry said. "He was a Brooklyn boy from Williamsburg. He made good for a while. Too bad it went wrong for him."

"He did it to himself, Jerry," I said. "He made enemies in the mob, and that's not healthy."

"You said it," Jerry said. "They ventilated him with a M-one. That's overkill. That's why you gotta like this hitman we're lookin' for."

"Like him?"

"I mean, ya know, respect him," he said, explaining himself. "I mean, he ain't messy. He gets in close and does the job."

"He left a pretty good mess on the elevator floor in Miami Beach," I pointed out. "There was a ton of blood. I'd call that a mess."

"Hey," Jerry said, changing the subject, "weren't you gonna call Mr. Martin?"

"Yeah," I said, "I've been getting it straight in my head what I'm gonna say to him."

"Why not call him now?"

"He's home with Jeannie and the kids," I said. "I'll try and get him in the morning before he goes to the studio. If he's even going to the studio. I know he hates to rehearse."

"You really think he'll help?" Jerry asked. "Talk to Mr. S. for you? Get Mr. S. to talk about Mr. Gleason?"

"I don't know," I said. "That friendship between him and Frank, it's an odd one. I mean, I really think Dino could take it or leave it. It's Frank who wants Dino to be his best buddy. Dino just figures, fine, let him have what he wants. It's no skin off his nose for everybody to think of Frank as the leader, the Chairman of the Board. Dean Martin's got no ego when it comes to all that."

"I always thought they were best buds."

"They are," I said. "Frank wants it that way, and Dino goes along for the ride."

"So that's why you think he'll help you?"

"He'll help me," I said, "because I've helped them many, many times over the years, and haven't asked for anything in return."

"Didn't Mr. Martin save your neck that time in the Sands parking lot—"

"I don't make a habit of asking for help!" I said, cutting him off. "From them, that is. I do make a habit of asking you, though."

"Now that's because we're best buds," Jerry said, then frowned and stared at me. "Ain't we?"

"Definitely, Jerry," I responded. "Nothing could be more true."

209

Chapter Forty-Three

When we returned to the Sands, we went right up to the suite. Jerry turned the T.V. on and started watching some old Western, but I decided to get some sleep. By morning I hoped to have a better idea of what I should do.

When I came out in the morning, Jerry was still sitting on the sofa, but this time he was drinking coffee.

"Did you get any sleep at all?" I asked.

"Enough," he said. "I had room service send up coffee. It's on the bar."

I walked over to the bar and poured myself a cup, then sat on a stool.

"What are we doin' today?" he asked.

"I'm gonna guess and say you're hungry," I said. Before he could follow his nod with a verbal agreement I went on. "I thought we'd go downstairs for breakfast."

"Sounds good to me. Now?"

We were both dressed so I nodded and said, "Now." He jumped up from the sofa, I gulped down half my coffee, and got off the stool. At that point the phone rang.

"Yeah?" Jerry said, answering it. "Oh, yeah. Hang on." He looked at me. "It's that Miami cop."

"I'll take it."

I walked to him and took the receiver from his hand.

"Winter?"

"Is this Garden Room any good?" the detective asked.

"It's very good," I said. "In fact, we were just on our way down for breakfast."

"Mind if I join you?"

"Not at all," I said. "How's five minutes?"

"See you in five," he said, and hung up.

"We got company for breakfast?" Jerry asked.

"We do."

We left the room and went down to the lobby. It was check-out time, so guests were leaving. In a few hours it would be check-in time, and the new ones would be lining up.

We crossed the casino floor to the Garden Room and found Detective Winter sitting in a booth.

"You must eat here a lot," he commented.

"Too much," I said, sliding in across from him, "but it's good, and convenient."

We all ordered breakfast from Coco, the waitress, and then Jerry said to Winter, "I'm glad to see you're still alive."

"We're talkin' about a blade man," Winter said. "If he wants me, he has to get in real close. I welcome that."

Winter did not look like a man in the greatest shape. He'd been on the job too long, eaten too many free meals and donuts.

"I assume you're armed?" I asked.

"Right here," he said, patting his armpit area. "Anybody who gets too close gets a bullet, and I'll explain later."

"You tell that to Hargrove?" I asked.

"Hey, I'm a cop, he's a cop, and my partner was killed. Hargrove knows the score, even if he is a dick."

"How did that conversation go?"

"He's got nothing," Winter said. "He thinks I'm making a mistake, and that I'm hanging myself out to dry."

Jerry nudged me, indicating he was thinking the same thing, but he didn't say a word.

"Look," Winter said, "I know the score in Vegas, and I know who owns this place. I'm thinking you've got connections."

"We've made calls," I said, "nobody knows anything about this blade man."

"New York, Chicago," Jerry said, "and Philly, and some other places, they use guys with heaters. Using a blade man, there's too much room for a fuck-up. Takin' a guy out from a distance is the easiest way to go."

Winter looked at Jerry and seemed to take his time studying him. Then, as if he'd committed the big guy to memory, he nodded to himself, thinking he had Jerry pegged.

Coco brought the plates and handed them out, refilled all our coffees.

"So what's your plan?" I asked. "Just hang out around that hotel and wait for the guy to come at you?"

"You got a better idea?"

"I've still got a friend of mine working some local angles," I said. "We'll have to see what he gets. But if he comes up empty, I've been thinking that maybe we should just wait for the guy to come after me."

"That's a bad idea," Winter said. "You're an amateur, you wouldn't have a chance."

"My local guy is not an amateur," I pointed out.

"And neither am I," Jerry chimed in.

"And neither are you," I added. "Maybe the four of us can bring this guy out of hiding and take him down."

"You think he's hiding?" Winter asked. "That's a word I wouldn't use for him. Somebody who likes to work in close has an ego. That's what I think is going to trip this guy up."

"Okay," I said, "let's play to that ego."

Winter chewed, swallowed, and put down his fork.

"Why would you want to do this?" he asked. "What do you stand to gain?"

"Piece of mind, for one thing," I said. "I won't have to be lookin' over my shoulder, anymore. Also, I don't like

213

that this guy killed Eisman. I didn't know him like you did, but I liked him."

"Yeah," Winter said, "he was a good guy." He picked his fork up again. "So, okay, what do you propose?"

"Gleason and Marilyn Taylor are probably flying home today," I said. "If the guy stays here, then he's likely after me, not them."

"And how will we know if he stays or goes?" Winter asked.

"Good question," I said. "This sonofabitch is like the wind."

"That's real poetic," Winter said, "but true. The only way we're going to get him is if he comes after you."

"I guess."

"And you're willing to be bait."

"I guess," I said, again, but with less feeling.

"What about this other pro you say you've got," Winter said. "Who's he?"

"Danny Bardini," I said. "A local private eye I grew up with in Brooklyn."

"He any good?"

"Plenty good," Jerry said.

Winter looked at Jerry. "Are you any good?"

Jerry smiled, and it wasn't pretty. "Better."

"Okay," Winter said, shifting his attention to me, "I'll take you up on your earlier offer of a room here at the Sands. Makes sense if we're going to work together."

"Good," I said. "I'll take you up—"

"I've got to go back to my hotel, get my things, and check out." He pushed his plate away. "I'll meet you here in an hour."

"Okay," I said. "Make it out in the lobby."

Winter nodded, slid out of the booth, stood and left the Garden Room.

"Think he's on the level?" Jerry asked.

"Why not?"

Jerry shrugged.

"He's a cop."

Chapter Forty-Four

After Winter left, I made the call to Dino. It was later than I planned, but I hoped to find him home.

"Oh, hello, Eddie," his wife, Jeannie, said.

"Hi, Jeannie. How are you?"

"Oh, you know, getting by."

I didn't think being married to Dean Martin was the definition of "getting by."

"Is he around, or is he at the studio?"

"Doing what? Rehearsing?" She laughed. "Hold on, I'll get him."

After a few moments, Dino came on the line.

"Hey, Eddie, how you doin', Pally?"

"Hope I'm not buggin' you, Dean."

"Nah," he said, "I was workin' with my kid on his new song, 'I'm a Fool' that he's recording with Dino, Desi & Billy."

I remembered that Dean's teenage son had formed a rock group with Desi Arnaz, Jr. (Lucy and Desi's son) and their friend, Billy Hinsche. Dino had gotten them an audition with Frank at his Reprise Records, and they'd been signed. I knew they'd had a song out in '64 that didn't chart so well, which was probably why Dean was helping them with this one.

"I hope it's a hit for them, Dino."

"These kids," Dean said, "they're not even fifteen, yet. I'm real proud of 'em. Anyway, what's on your mind?"

"Frank."

"What'd he do now?" he asked, with both affection and amusement in his tone.

I reminded Dean what had happened in Miami, and then brought him up to date on things.

"So you think Jackie knows something he's not tellin'," he said, when I was done, "and that Frank knows what it is."

"I'm hoping Frank knows what it is," I said, "and that he'll tell me . . . if you ask him to."

"Why don't you ask him?"

"I have," I said. "He's been friends with Jackie longer than with me, so that's where his loyalty lies."

"Hell, he's known Jackie longer than me, too," he pointed out. "What makes you think he'd tell me?"

"Because you're his best buddy, Dino," I said. "Look, we've got a dead cop here, and I may be next on the list. I need whatever information I can get."

Suddenly, Dean got serious.

"Okay, Pally," he said. "We can't have you bein' next on the list, can we? I'll talk to Frank and get back to you."

"Thanks," I said. "I appreciate this, Dean."

"I'll be in touch," he said, and hung up.

I hung up the phone, signaled to Wendy that she could take it, and looked across the table at Jerry.

"He's gonna do it?" he asked.

"He's gonna do what he can," I said.

"And whatta we do til then?"

"We hang out here and wait for Winter to come back."

***

Winter never came back.

"I knew he shouldn'ta gone," Jerry said.

I called him at the hotel, but there was no answer. I spoke to the desk clerk, who said the guest hadn't checked out.

"Whataya think?" Jerry asked, later in the day.

"I don't wanna say what I think," I answered. We were standing in the casino, watching the live poker tables.

"You think he's dead?"

"He was being careful," I said. "If he's dead, then this guy is real good."

"Do you wanna go out and look for him?" Jerry asked.

"Where? We better wait for Danny. He can use his local contact to do it."

"When is Danny supposed to get here?"

I looked at Jerry. "He should've been here by now. He's supposed to check in with us."

"So now we gotta worry about him, too?"

"At this point," I said, "we've gotta worry about everybody."

***

At midday, Jackie and Marilyn came down in the elevator. Jackie sent a bellboy into the casino for me. When I came out, they were standing in the lobby with their luggage.

"We gotta get goin'," he said, as I reached them. "You know any reason why we shouldn't go home?"

I grabbed his arm and said, "Lemme talk to you a sec. Excuse us." I steered him away from Marilyn. Jerry stood halfway between us.

"What's goin' on Jackie?" I asked.

"Whataya mean, pal?"

"I mean you're keepin' somethin' from me," I told him. With him heading out to the front door, I couldn't afford to wait for Dean to get Frank to talk to me.

But when Jackie's face went cold, I knew I was going to have to wait.

"Look, Eddie, you're a pal of Frank's. That's swell. But you and me, we just met. That means you ain't my confidante. I don't have to tell you nothin'."

"Hey," I said, "you came to me for help."

"And maybe that was a mistake," he said. "We're headin' home, now. If you're pissed off, have the hotel send me a bill. I can afford it."

He turned and walked away, grabbed Marilyn's arm and marched her out the front door.

I walked over and stood next to Jerry.

"Nothin'?" he asked.

"Nothin' but attitude."

"Well," Jerry said, "let's go siddown somewhere and I'll tell you what the lady just told me."

Chapter Forty-Five

Rather than go back to the Garden Room, or into the lounge, we took a short walk. I opened a door and we stepped into the empty Copa Room. Empty, that is except for the Copa Girls, who were on stage being put through their paces by Antonio Morelli, who directed the girls during the 50's and 60's. The Copa Room had been home to many of the biggest acts of that time, not the least of which was the Summit—Frank, Dean, Sammy, Joey and Peter Lawford, referred to by the newspapers as the "Rat Pack." Frank actually hated the name—probably because it brought back memories of a time when he was a member of the Rat Pack that used to meet at the home of Humphrey Bogart and Lauren Bacall. Since then, Frank and Bacall had almost gotten married, but the ceremony never came off, and Bacall now openly loathed him.

We took seats at a table all the way in the back where we wouldn't bother the rehearsal. Of course, if Antonio spotted us, he'd kick us out immediately, but at the moment he was too occupied.

"Okay, what's this about?" I asked Jerry.

"Well, while you and Mr. Gleason were talking, Miss Taylor leaned over and spoke to me."

"You gonna make me ask?"

"She said to tell you to check deeper into Philip Rossi."

"Rossi."

"She didn't say who he was," Jerry said. "You know him?"

"Yeah," I said, "he was the dead guy in the elevator."

"Oh, him," Jerry said. "Why would she want you to check him out? Didn't the Miami police do that?"

"Maybe," I said, "they didn't look deep enough."

"So then, how do we do that?" Jerry asked. "Go to Miami Beach?"

"Maybe," I said.

"Maybe the dick can go," Jerry suggested. "You should probably stay close to home."

"We'll talk about it," I said. "You, me and Danny. She say anything else?"

"Yeah," Jerry said, "she wanted me to tell you that she's sorry. And she said you should talk to her sister."

"June?"

"That her name? She didn't say."

"Yeah, she's the head of the June Taylor dancers."

"Those are the ones on Mr. Gleason's show, that they shoot from above, right? They make all them designs with their legs?"

"That's right."

Jerry shrugged. "I wouldn't mind meetin' some of them girls." He looked up at the stage. "Or them, for that matter."

"You're such a bullshitter, Jerry."

He jerked his head back to me. "Huh?"

"You're way too much of a shy gentleman to meet those girls," I said.

"Maybe," he said, almost indignantly, "I ain't as shy as I used ta be."

He'd been super shy with the likes of Marilyn Monroe, Ava Gardner and Judy Garland, but maybe he had changed since then. I remember he ended up being pretty friendly—and I mean big brother friendly—with all three of those ladies.

"I guess we'll find out, then," I said.

"In Miami Beach?" Jerry asked. "I ain't never been there. All I know about it is what I see on Surfside Six, on T.V."

"I don't know if Jack's gonna give me more time off to go there again so soon," I said.

"Who you kiddin'?" he asked. "If you tell him it's for Mr. S. and Mr. Gleason, he'd drive you to the airport himself."

Jerry was right. Jack Entratter bent over backwards for certain people, especially celebrities. And for Frank in particular.

223

"Yeah, okay," I said. "Let's talk to Danny and then we can make up our minds."

"Right," Jerry said, "but before we talk to the dick, we gotta find 'im, first."

Chapter Forty-Six

When Danny finally showed up hours later, he was surprised when Jerry jumped on him. So was I.

"Where the hell have you been? Why didn't you call?" Jerry demanded, as we let Danny into our suite.

Danny grinned at Jerry.

"Sorry, Dad, I didn't know I had a curfew."

"The other cop from Miami is missing," I said to Danny. "We were worried when we didn't hear from you."

"Is he dead?"

"We don't know," I said.

"So right now he's only missin'."

"Right."

"I need a drink."

"Help yourself," I said.

He went to the bar. "Anyone else?"

"Not me," I said, sitting on the sofa.

"Me, neither." Jerry sat in one of the armchairs.

Danny poured himself a bourbon on the rocks and carried it to the other armchair.

"This is what I'm startin' to think," Danny said. "Our guy may not even be a hitman."

"Why do you say that?" I asked.

"Because there's nothin', not a peep, out there any-where about a hitman who uses a blade like this guy. Hitmen are smart. They don't wanna get close to their prey. They wanna shoot to kill from a distance. It's safer." He looked at Jerry. "What do you think, big guy?"

"That makes sense," Jerry said. "I figured he hadda be a dope for working that close. Sooner or later, it'd back-fire on him."

"So," I said, "we have a killer, but not a hitman."

"Right."

"That changes things," I said.

"Why'd he kill the guy in the elevator if he wasn't paid to?" Danny said.

"And why'd he kill the Miami cop?" I asked.

"Well, that makes more sense," Danny said. "Maybe the cop was gettin' too close."

"But Winter came here to see what I remember," I said. "I don't think he had a thing."

"Well, the killer didn't agree with you," Danny said. "And now maybe he's killed the other cop."

"I think I'll have that drink now," I said, and went to the bar. "Jerry?"

"Nah. What're we gonna do now, Mr. G.?"

I poured my drink and then remained behind the bar.

"If we're gonna work on the premise that there's no hitman, Jerry," I explained, "then I think you and me are flyin' to Miami Beach."

"Why do that?" Danny asked.

"Jackie and Marilyn left this morning," I said. "Jackie pretty much told me to mind my own business. But Marilyn told Jerry to tell me we should be concentrating on the dead man in the elevator, Rossi."

"So what about me?" Danny asked, smiling hopefully. "Do I get a trip to Miami?"

"You better stay here, Danny," I said. "See if you can find that other cop."

"Don't you think the Vegas cops are lookin' for him?" Danny asked.

"Yeah," I said, "Hargrove."

"I get your point," Danny said. "But if the guy's already dead—"

"We'll stay in touch," I said. "If he turns up dead, there won't be any point to your stayin' here, and I'll buy you a plane ticket."

"You got a deal!"

Chapter Forty-Seven

I asked Jack Entratter for two plane tickets the next day to Miami Beach.

"Forget that," he said. "I'll have a plane waitin' for you at the airport. But do you really think this is the way to go? I mean, back to Miami?"

"The girl told Jerry that we need to check into Philip Rossi more," I said.

"The dead guy in the elevator."

"Right. Somethin's goin' on, Jack, something Jackie's not tellin' me. The only place to find anything out is back in Miami."

Entratter agreed and made a call to arrange for the plane. "It won't be like Frank's, but it'll do the trick."

That was okay with me. I didn't want to use Frank's plane because I didn't want him to know I was going back to Miami—mainly because I didn't want Jackie to know.

***

We got off the plane that afternoon in Miami and went out to the cab stand. We were both carrying one bag.

"So where to?" Jerry asked. "The Fontainebleau?"

"Wouldn't that be nice," I said, "but not on my dime. We'll have to stay in a motel."

"As long as it's got a pool," Jerry said. "With girls in bikinis."

"No matter where we stay," I said, "I think there'll be a beach."

We got into the back of a cab and as the driver asked, "Where to?" something occurred to me.

"Do you know a motel called the Pink Grotto, on Collins?"

"I know it," he said, "but that ain't the best part of Collins Avenue."

"Don't worry," I said. "For us it'll do."

Not being in any of the luxury hotels also made it less likely that somebody connected to Jackie Gleason would spot us.

"Wow," Jerry said, as we drove past some of the bigger hotels.

"One of these days, Jerry," I promised.

"Sure, Mr. G."

***

The cabbie pulled up in front of the Pink Grotto, which didn't look quite as bad as I remembered.

229

"You won't wanna go walkin' around here," the cabbie said, as I paid him. "Unless you take your big friend with ya."

"Thanks, I'll remember. This place any good?"

"Usta be," the cabbie said. "It's kinda fallen on hard times, like a lot of places at this end of Collins."

"Thanks."

I joined Jerry on the curb. He was looking at the two-story pink stucco motel.

"Want to go somewhere else?" I asked.

"I seen worse motels than this in Sheepshead Bay," he said. "And they didn't have a beach. Besides, we're not here on vacation."

"Let's check in," I said, "if they have rooms available."

Not only were they available, but we were able to each get our own. I looked out the back window and saw the beach, but there were no girls in bikinis there. Neither were there any at the pool we'd passed on the way to the office.

I'd left my door ajar, so Jerry knocked and came in.

"Where to first, Mr. G.?" he asked.

"How about we get something to eat," I suggested, "and go from there."

"I thought you'd never ask."

"And I know just the place," I said. "Beer and burgers."

"We need another cab?" he asked, as we went out the door.

"No, we can walk. It's a few blocks."

"That cabbie said we shouldn't walk."

"Unless I took you with me," I added. "Come on."

***

We did pass some homeless souls along the way, but nobody who was very threatening. As we took the circular walk down to the bar, Jerry asked. "How did you know about this place?"

"I had a meeting with Eisman here last time I was in Miami."

"Is the food any good?"

"I don't know, I didn't eat last time."

"Then why are we goin' back?"

"Because," I answered, "Eisman told me he owned a piece of it."

We went inside and it looked pretty much the same as last time I was there. It even looked as if the four people seated at the bar were the same ones.

I led Jerry to the same booth I'd sat in with Eisman. Before long, the bartender came over—the same bartender.

"Get ya somethin'?" he asked.

"Two beers, two burgers," I said, "and some answers."

"Beer and burgers I got," the man said. "Answers are harder to come by."

"Do you own this place?" I asked.

"I do," the man said, after a moment of hesitation. "What of it?"

"I was here a few weeks ago with Eisman."

The bartender nodded. "I thought you looked familiar. We don't get too much repeat business here, except for regulars. I couldn't place you."

"But now you can?"

"Yeah."

"What's your name?" I asked.

"I'm Nate Morgan."

"I'm Eddie Gianelli. This is Jerry Epstein. Now that you know I was here with Eisman, you know he'd want you to talk to us."

"Why don't you ask Eisman what you want to know?"

"Because . . . he's dead."

"What? When? Where?"

"A few days ago, in Las Vegas. He was working on the same case that he and I were talking about here. And now I need your help."

"What can I do?"

"Well," Jerry said, "you can start by gettin' us those beers and burgers."

"Right," the man said. "Comin' up."

He turned and went back around the bar, and then into a back room that was apparently the kitchen.

"What kind of help do you think he can be?" Jerry asked.

"I don't know," I said, "but he knew Eisman. Maybe he can tell us somethin' helpful that he doesn't even know is helpful."

"Hopefully," Jerry said, "we'll know it's helpful when we hear it."

Chapter Forty-Eight

Morgan returned with two plates. The burgers were thick and juicy, piled high with onions, pickles and tomatoes, on soft buns. Also, on the plates were home-made potato chips.

Jerry and I each took a bite and exchanged surprised glances.

"If you can cook like this," I asked, "why don't you have more people here?"

"The city said they were gonna renovate this whole end of Collins Avenue," he said. "That's why Eisman wanted to buy in."

"And it never happened," I said.

"The money went into some politician's pocket, instead," Morgan said.

"This is probably the best hamburger I've ever had," Jerry said.

"Thanks."

"Can you sit and talk while we eat?" I asked.

He didn't even look at the bar. There wasn't much going on there.

"Sure thing."

Jerry and I were sitting across from each other, so Morgan chose to slide in next to me.

"Whataya wanna know?"

"The case Eisman was working," I said. "Did he talk to you about it?"

"He didn't talk about any of his cases with me," Morgan said.

"Weren't you friends?"

"No," Morgan said, "business partners. We only ever talked about this place, and maybe sports."

I looked at Jerry, who bit into his burger and shrugged.

"Okay, then," I said, "did he ever bring others around here, like he met me here?"

"Well . . ." he rubbed his jaw. ". . . on occasion he'd meet somebody, sit right here like he did with you."

"Men?" I asked.

"Men, women."

"Was it always police business?"

"I wasn't privy to what it was about, but to me it seemed that way."

"Did he bring anyone else here after me?"

Morgan frowned before answering.

"He did bring a woman in here a few days after he brought you."

"A woman. What'd she look like?"

"Beautiful, classy, long dark hair, even longer legs."

"Like a dancer?" I asked.

"Yeah," Morgan said, nodding, "a dancer."

"A dancer," Jerry repeated.

This time it was me who nodded. "A dancer."

***

After we finished the delicious burger and the perfect homemade chips, I paid the bill and thanked Morgan for his help.

"Did I help?" he asked, from behind the bar. "I don't feel like I did anything."

"You did more than you know," I said.

"Well then," he replied, "I hope you find out who killed Eisman."

"We're gonna try our best."

Jerry and I left and walked back up to Collins Avenue. Once there we headed for our motel.

"We need a car," I said.

"Do you wanna rent one?"

"No," I said, "we don't know how to get around here. We need a car and a driver."

"A cab, then."

"No," I said, "better than that."

"What then?"

"I still have the phone number Frank gave me for his car and driver, here."

"But the driver's dead."

"Then they can send a car with another driver," I said. "Especially when they hear we're trying to find out who killed their driver, Paul."

"Then let's do it."

"As soon as we get back to the room, I'll make the call."

"And then what?"

"And then you and I are gonna go and see a dancer."

"You know which one was with Eisman back there?"

"I have a pretty good idea," I said. "The description can fit a lot of dancers, but it fit June Taylor to a tee."

"You mean, that other one's sister? The one with all the girls on Mr. Gleason's show?"

"That's the one," I said. "And she's the first one who came to me and got me involved in this. Maybe she knows more than she told me."

"Why are people keepin' things from you?" Jerry asked. "First Mr. Gleason, and now Miss Taylor?"

"That's what we're gonna find out."

"Wait—" Jerry said, grabbing my arm.

"What?" We stopped walking, but were within sight of our pink motel.

"Marilyn Taylor," he said, "when she told me you had to look into Rossi she also started to say something else,

237

but stopped when Mr. Gleason came over and grabbed her arm."

"Somethin' like 'talk to June—'" he said. "I thought she was talkin' about the month."

"Okay," I said, "so now we have two reasons to go and talk to June Taylor."

"Both of us?" he asked.

"Yeah, both of us."

Chapter Forty-Nine

We went to my hotel room, I fished the card out of my wallet and called the number of the car service. An operator answered and I asked for her boss.

"What's this about, sir?"

I said the first thing I thought of that might get me put through.

"Frank Sinatra."

"Just a minute."

After two minutes a man came on the line. "Mr. Sinatra. So nice to hear from you again so soon."

"This isn't Frank," I said, "it's a friend of his."

"What? Who?"

"My name's Eddie Gianelli, from Las Vegas. I was here with Frank last time he was in town. We were driven by Paul."

"Paul's dead."

"I know that. Frank said if I ever came back, I should call you for a car and driver."

"Would you mind if I checked with Mr. Sinatra about that?" the man asked.

"Not at all," I said, "but I'll be paying for this service, myself."

The man hesitated.

"Hello?"

"Yeah, I'm here."

"What's your name?"

"Phil," he said, "Phil Herman."

"Phil, can I get a car and a driver?"

"Yeah, sure," he said. "Where are you?"

"A place called the Pink Grotto,"

"Wow," he said, "what're you doin' there?"

"Keepin' a low profile."

"Then you don't want a limo, do you?"

"Ah, actually, no. Any kind of car would do."

"Okay," he said, "I've got a Chevy, a Ford—"

"Chevy's good."

"When do you want it?"

"As soon as possible."

"Where's your first stop gonna be?" he asked.

"The Miami Beach Municipal Auditorium."

"Where they shoot the Gleason show?" he asked.

"That's right."

"So you know Gleason, and Sinatra?"

"Yes."

"Well, that's okay, then," he said. "The car will be there in fifteen minutes. The driver's name is Esteban. He's, uh, Cuban. Is that a problem?"

"Does he speak English?"

"Perfectly."

"Then there's no problem."

***

While we waited, we talked about Philip Rossi.

"Well, he was Italian," Jerry said.

"That doesn't mean he's connected," I argued.

"We asked around about a hitman," Jerry said. "We didn't ask about him."

"Good point," I said. "After we talk with June, we should make some of those calls. Maybe something will come up. Somebody will know him. Although . . ."

"Although what?"

"The cops here must've checked him out."

"They're just cops," Jerry said. "On top of bein' dumb, there are people who just won't talk to them. But they'll talk to us."

"To you, maybe."

"That's just as good, then."

Jerry was right about that. His contact, if they knew who Rossi was, would tell him things they would never have told the cops, or me.

"Let's wait for the car outside."

***

241

A black, 4-door Chevy pulled up in front of the Pink Grotto 14 minutes later. From the driver's side stepped a young man in a dark suit, and chauffer's cap. He had dark skin and looked decidedly Cuban.

"Mr. Gianelli?" he asked.

"That's right. Are you Esteban?"

"Yes sir."

He looked about 25 years old, tall, slender and very spiffy in his dark clothes.

"This is Jerry."

Esteban nodded.

"Are you still going to the theater?' he asked.

"We are."

Esteban nodded again, turned, opened the back door, and waited. I got in first, so Jerry wouldn't have to slide his bulk over. Esteban then closed the door, ran around and got behind the wheel. He took his hat off, started the car and pulled away.

Chapter Fifty

Esteban stopped the car right in front of the main entrance to the theater. Donning his hat, he got out of the car, ran around and opened the door for us.

"Should I wait here, sir?"

"Yes," I said, "and don't call me 'sir.' It's Eddie."

"That wouldn't be right, uh, sir."

Jerry put his hand on the young man's shoulder. "Call him Mr. G. That's what I do."

Esteban smiled. "Okay, that's what I'll do . . . Mr. G."

"Fine," I said. "Wait here. We'll be out soon."

If we even got in.

The security man on the door stopped us cold. He didn't even open the door all the way.

"Rehearsals goin' on," he said. "Are you with the show?"

"No," I said. "We need to talk with June Taylor."

"I can't—" he started, but I cut him off.

"If you don't tell her I'm here, there'll be trouble," I said. "None of us want that."

He frowned, then said, "Wait here."

"What if Mr. Gleason's here?" Jerry said. "We don't want him to know we're in Miami, right?"

"He won't be here."

"How do you know?"

"You heard the guard," I said. "They're rehearsing. Gleason never rehearses. He only comes to do the show."

Security reappeared, opening the door fully for us.

"You can come in."

"Thanks."

I looked back at Esteban and we exchanged a nod. Jerry and I went in.

I remembered where the dressing rooms were, but that didn't matter. June Taylor was waiting for us outside the doors to the theater.

"Eddie," she said. "What brings you back?"

"June, this is my friend, Jerry. We need to talk somewhere private."

"My dressing room," she said. She was wearing a gaudy red-and-yellow outfit with her long legs encased in dark nylon. As we followed her, Jerry and I couldn't take our eyes off her twitching butt.

Inside the dressing room, she grabbed a robe from the back of the door and put it on, allowing us to concentrate on business.

"Sit," she said, seating herself in front of her dressing mirror. "What's going on?"

"Have you spoken with Jackie and your sister since they came back?" I asked.

"Well, yes," she said, "but mostly Jackie and I talked about the show."

"And Marilyn?"

"She was upset, Eddie," June said. "I don't think their trip to Vegas accomplished what they wanted it to."

"And what was that?" I asked. "Do you know?"

"I'm not sure," she said. "Marilyn wasn't even sure. She said Jackie told her they were going, so they went. He even flew, and he's terrified of flying."

"It must've been important, then," I said.

"It had to be."

"What's he been doing since they got back?"

"Working."

"And Marilyn?"

"She's been working," June said. "In fact, she's here right now."

"She is?" I said. "Can you get her in here?"

"Sure," she said, getting to her feet.

As June left the dressing room, I said to Jerry, "Let's see if Marilyn can shed any light on this."

"But she said we should talk to June."

"So now we're talking to them both," I said.

June came back with Marilyn, who was wearing the same gaudy outfit, and carrying a headdress.

"Hello, Marilyn," I said.

"What's up, Eddie?"

"You two know Jackie better than anybody," I said, deciding to go for the jugular. "What's he hiding?"

The sisters looked at each other.

"Come on," I said, "there's something he's not telling me. There's something *nobody* is telling me, which has some bearing on this whole mess."

Marilyn bit her lower lip. June looked at the ceiling.

"Marilyn," I said, "in Vegas you told Jerry to tell me to look deeper into the dead guy, Rossi. What am I gonna find?"

"If I tell you . . ." she started and trailed off.

"Look," I said, "June, you asked me for help, and then Marilyn came to Vegas with Jackie, and Jackie asked me. Everybody's asking for help, but nobody's helping me."

The two sisters looked at each other again, and then June finally spoke in a tone that made me think she had come to a decision.

"Why don't you go back to work," she said, putting her hand on Marilyn's shoulder, "that way you can say you didn't know what happened here."

"But what if—"

"Go ahead," June said, cutting her sister off. "I'll talk to Eddie." She rubbed her sister's arm. "I'll tell him what he needs to know."

Marilyn bit her lip again, then left the dressing room.

"Okay, boys," she said, "have a seat."

246

Chapter Fifty-One

"Jackie has a . . . belief that not many people know about."

"Okay," I said, "so how many people do know about it?"

"Well, there's me, Marilyn . . . Philip Rossi apparently knew."

"Oh shit," I said, "you're telling me Jackie knew Rossi?"

"Well . . . we all kind of knew Rossi."

"Wait, wait a minute," I said, looking at Jerry, who shrugged. "You're blowin' my mind, here."

"His Brooklyn comes out when you blow his mind," Jerry said, and I had heard it, too.

"Look," I said to June, who had once again sat down with her back to her dressing mirror. She looked up at me and I thought, in that moment, that she was really beautiful. For a moment, I got lost in those eyes.

"Yes?" she said.

"Sorry, sorry," I said, shaking my head. "What are we talking about, here?"

"Well . . ."

"What's this belief of Jackie's?" I prompted. "Does Frank know about it?"

"I actually can't answer that second one," she said. "Jackie doesn't tell me what he confides in Frank about."

"Isn't Frank his best male friend?"

"Maybe."

"Who else would there be? Who else would he confide in?"

She thought a moment, then said, "Art Carney."

"Norton?" Jerry said.

"Yes," she said, "Norton. They're very close."

Carney played Ed Norton on "The Honeymooners."

"Okay, well," I said, "clearly he's close to you and Marilyn. So go ahead, shock me."

"Shock you?"

"What's this belief that nobody wants to tell me about?"

She hesitated a moment, then said, "Occult . . . no wait . . . the supernatural . . . no, what did he call it? The paranormal."

"The what?" Jerry asked.

"You mean . . . like . . . witchcraft?" I asked.

"No, not witchcraft," she said, "exactly. More like . . . palm readers, tarot cards . . ."

"Fortune tellers!" I said.

"Yes! Psychics." she said, then, "Sort of . . . he also has some belief in . . . well . . . UFOs."

I hesitated, then said, "Well, okay, so he's got some wonky beliefs. What's that got to do with anything?"

"He doesn't want the word to get out, Eddie," she said. "He doesn't want anyone to know he believes in those things."

"Are you saying . . . Jackie was being blackmailed?"

"Yes," she said, "but no."

"June," I said, "you're confusing me."

"I know," she said, "it's confusing to me, too. Look, Jackie has gone to see this . . . fortune teller, for want of a better phrase . . . a few times. She was predicting things for him, and he was believing that they were coming true."

"Like what?"

"Like the ratings of the show going up," she said. "Like certain stars agreeing to appear."

"Why would anyone refuse?" I asked. "That's the kind of prediction anyone could make."

"True, but Jackie was believing it."

"So?"

"One day a man showed up at Jackie's house."

"Rossi?"

She nodded.

"He told Jackie he knew about his beliefs, but that a certain amount of money would keep them from being revealed."

"That's blackmail."

"Rossi said it was an investment."

"And Jackie paid him?"

"No," June said, "he kicked him out."

"And what happened?

"Rossi started following Marilyn. He never did anything, he just followed her, but it scared Marilyn."

"So did Jackie pay then?"

"No," she said, "he went to his fortune teller and asked about Rossi, but she claimed not to know anyone by that name."

"And he believed her?"

"She convinced him," June said. "But I didn't. That was why I came to you."

"But why didn't you tell me everything?"

"I couldn't," she said "Jackie would've been . . . furious. But even though I didn't tell you everything, you agreed to help, and you followed Marilyn. When you found Rossi dead, we thought it was over."

"But . . . we didn't find out who killed him."

"It didn't really matter," June said. "Jackie said as long as he was dead, that was all he cared about."

"And then what?"

"Some time passed, and then . . . somebody called Jackie, and made the demand again for money."

"Who called?"

"Another man."

"Did he go back to the fortune teller again?"

"Yes," June said, "but she was gone."

"At that point why didn't Jackie tell me the truth?"

"Jackie wants everyone to think he's always in control," she said. "But . . . I think he decided to tell you, that was why he and Marilyn went to Vegas."

"But he didn't tell me."

"I think, at the last minute, he decided to just pay. Now, he's waiting for the next call."

"Then we have time," I said.

"Do you know who it is?"

"No," I said. "We thought that a hit man killed Rossi, but now we've decided it wasn't a professional. That means it has to be someone connected to the fortune teller."

"Why would she have Rossi killed if she was involved?" June asked.

"Maybe they had a falling out," I said. "Rossi was going to make Jackie pay, and not cut the woman in. So she found herself another man to take care of him."

"What about the Miami policeman who was killed in Vegas?" she asked. "Jackie told me about him."

"He might've been getting too close. And now his partner's missing, too."

"Oh, no!"

"June," I said, "what's the woman's name?"

"If I tell you that, Jackie will have my head."

"Do you think Jackie will tell me?"

"Never."

"Then you have to," I said. "You or Marilyn."

"Marilyn never would."

"Okay, then," I said, "it's up to you."

June bit her lip, reminding me of her sister.

"It's the only way we're gonna find out anythin'," Jerry told her.

"Her name," she said, slowly, "was Madame Merlina."

"Really?" I said. "Is that her real name?"

"That's the name Jackie knows her by," June said.

I looked at Jerry. He'd been quiet for most of the conversation, and now he just shrugged.

"Okay," I said, "Madame Merlina. Where was she located?"

"A place called Cassadaga."

"Where's that?"

"Somewhere between Daytona Beach and Orlando."

"Do we have to fly there?"

"If you fly to either place, you'll still have to drive. Jackie had his driver take him there from here. But remember, he hates flying."

"Wait a minute," I said. "I remember reading in the paper that Rossi lived in Orlando."

"So we can kill two birds with one stick," Jerry said.

"Stone," I said. "Two birds with one stone, but I know what you mean. Check out Madame Merlina, and Rossi in one trip."

"Why Rossi?" June asked. "I mean, he obviously worked for Merlina."

"Then who killed him?" I asked. "And why? We need to find that out." I looked at Jerry. "We're going to Orlando, and Cassadaga."

Chapter Fifty-Two

Jerry and I agreed not to tell Jackie Gleason or Marilyn Taylor what we were doing. And June went along with it.

"When will you tell Jackie what you've done?" she asked.

"When we find the killer," I said, "and everybody is safe."

"Will you tell him that I told you about the psychic?"

"Not if you don't want me to."

"Then who would you say told you about her?" she asked.

"I don't know. I'll figure out something."

"No," she said, then, "I should tell him, and let the chips fall where they may."

"That'll be up to you."

She brightened slightly. "Where are you staying?"

"A place called The Pink Grotto."

"I know that place," she said. "It's a hot sheet hotel, where hookers take their johns."

"We haven't spent a night there, yet," I said. "I guess we would have found that out tonight."

"You can't sleep there," she said. "Come home with me."

"Home?" Jerry asked.

"I have a house, and plenty of room. It's too late for you to drive to Orlando today. You can get an early start in the morning. Do you have a car?"

"A car and driver," I said.

"Stick around here for about another hour," she said. "You can take me home, and I'll show you to your rooms."

I looked at Jerry. "Sounds better than the Pink Grotto," he said.

"Okay, then," I said. "We'll go to the hotel and get our things, then pick you up."

"Good." She put her hand on my arm. "I'm glad you're here, Eddie."

We left her dressing room. She went back to work, and we went back to the car.

***

Esteban pulled up in front of the Pink Grotto.

"Wait here," I told him. "We just have to get our things and check out."

"Right."

As we started for our room, we saw a girl walking ahead of us with her arm through a man's arm. He was a

255

portly man who couldn't have scored a girl like that unless she was a pro.

After we grabbed our luggage, we went to the lobby to check out. As we did, another girl came in with a thin, homely man, got a key from the clerk, and then took the man out. The two girls I'd seen would never make it in Vegas. They were too cheap.

"Checkin' out?" the clerk asked. "Already."

"Who you kiddin'?" Jerry said. "You were shocked when we checked in. You shoulda told us what kind of place this was."

The clerk, a middle-aged, grey haired man, said, "No skin off my nose where ya wanna stay."

"I can make it skin off your nose," Jerry offered.

The clerk drew back.

"Forget it, Jerry," I said. "What do we owe you?"

"You didn't even stay a night," the man said, eyeing Jerry. "Forget it."

"Yeah," Jerry said, "let's forget it."

"Suits me," I said.

We carried our bags out to the car, where Esteban put them in the trunk.

"Where to, Mr. G.?" he asked.

"Back to the theater," I said. "We're picking up a lady."

"Yes sir."

As we drove Jerry said, "I feel like a dope."

"Why?"

"Shoulda known what kinda place that was."

"We didn't see any girls when we checked in," I said. "We knew it was cheap, though."

"And dirty."

"In more ways than one."

Jerry laughed.

"I can take you someplace better," Esteban said. "Not the Fontainebleau, but cleaner rooms and a nicer beach."

"That's okay," I said. "We already got a better offer."

"The Lady?"

"Yes," I said, "and she is a lady, so don't get the wrong idea."

"Sorry, sir. I wasn't thinking anything."

"No, I'm sorry," I said. "We're just feeling a little frustrated, lately."

When we pulled up in front of the theater doors, June was waiting outside alone. Jerry opened the window and waved, and she came down the stairs. He got out to hold the door for her and let her get in the back with me, and then he got in front with Esteban. She looked beautiful and smelled great.

"Just give Esteban your address, and we'll be on our way," I said.

She smiled, gave him the address, and then sat back and sighed.

"Tough day?" I asked.

"No," she said, "Long, but I always enjoy working with my girls. It's just . . . having this other stuff on my mind that's draining."

"Well," I said, "maybe we can solve this thing and give your mind a rest."

"I know you can, Eddie," she said. "It's like Frank and Jackie keep saying. You're 'the guy.'"

That, again!

Chapter Fifty-Three

Esteban drove us to June's North Beach house. He popped out of the driver's seat and got our bags from the trunk.

"Thank you for the ride, Esteban," June said.

"You're very welcome, Ma'am."

"Esteban," I said, "tomorrow we want to drive to Orlando. Any idea how long that will take?"

"For most people, three-and-a-half to four hours, Mr. G. It'll take me three."

"Okay," I said, "and then we're gonna want to drive to a town called Cassadaga. Do you know where that is?"

"Yes, sir," he said. "Between Orlando and Daytona Beach. In fact, it's closer to Sanford than Orlando. It'll probably take half an hour."

"Can we do all that and drive back in one day?" I asked.

"It depends on what you'll be doing in both places," he said. "You'll probably have to stay over somewhere between here and there."

"Can you okay that with your boss?"

"Tomorrow I start two days off, Mr. G.," he said, "but I can still be here."

"So we can make our own deal for the two days?"

"Yes, sir!"

"Okay, then. Pick us up in the morning around . . . nine?" I said.

"I'll be here at nine on the dot, Mr. G."

"See you then, Esteban. And thanks."

"My pleasure, si—Mr. G."

He got back in the car and drove away.

"Let's go inside," June said. "I'll show you to your rooms and then we can have dinner."

"Dinner, too?" I asked.

She smiled. "June's B&B. Come on."

We grabbed our bags and followed her up the walk to the front door.

Her home was a beautiful one-story glass-and-stucco beach house. As soon as we entered, we could see through to the glass French doors that led out to a patio, and the beach beyond it.

The furniture was both expensive and comfortable looking.

"Wow," Jerry said, looking at the sectional sofa set, "I could sleep on that."

"You won't have to," June said. "I have four bed-rooms, so you can each have your own. Just go on and pick one out. I'm going to my room, get changed, and start dinner. Is lamb okay?"

"Lamb sounds great," I said.

Jerry and I walked down a hall and each picked out a room that looked identical to each other; king-sized bed, large dresser and a chest of drawers, sliding doors out to the patio, and each room had its own bathroom. The floors had deep-piled carpet, except in front of the sliding doors, where there were tiles for you to walk on when you were wet.

"I can't believe she's gonna cook for us," Jerry said, coming into my room. "I mean, that's a T.V. star, right?"

"She sure is," I said. "She's won awards."

"Emmy awards," he said.

"I'm gonna wash up," I said. "I'll see you in a few minutes."

"Yeah," he said, "I will, too."

He went to his room, and I went into the bathroom, scrubbed my face and hands, mostly to get the Pink Grotto dirt off. This place was so pretty I just had to be clean.

When I came out into the living room Jerry was there, looking around him.

"What are you looking for?" I asked him.

"Someplace to sit," he said. "This is all so . . . nice."

"Sit anywhere, Jerry," June said, coming back to join us. She had changed into slacks and a short sleeved-blouse and was barefoot. "You're my guests."

Jerry looked at me, then turned and sat down gently on the sofa. There was a matching chair, which I took. That was when I saw a man's pipe on the table next to it.

"Do you live here alone?" I asked.

"No," she answered, "I live here with my husband, Sol. He's a lawyer."

"Is he home? Or coming home?"

"He's away on business," she said. "He's often away. I spend a lot of time here alone, but I like it." She pointed to the open kitchen. "I'm going to make dinner."

"Won't that take a lot of work?" I asked.

"I prepared the lamb last night," she said. "All I have to do is cook it."

"You were gonna cook it for yourself?"

"I like cooking," she said, with a shrug. "And leftovers. But I'll happily share it with the two of you. Would you both like a beer while you wait?"

"Yes," I said, "we would."

She went to the kitchen, came back with two cans of Piels.

"Why don't you enjoy them out on the patio, or down by the beach," she suggested. "I'll come out and join you when the lamb's in the oven."

Jerry and I went outside, decided to stay on the patio. There were chaise lounges there, and we each took one. A cool breeze wafted in from over the water. For that moment, maybe even for the evening, we could relax.

About ten minutes later June came out, carrying a glass of red wine. Now that she didn't have all the show biz make-up on, I could see she was a very lovely 45 or so.

"The lamb's in the oven," she said. "It won't be long." She also sat on a chaise lounge. "I love sitting out here."

"I can see why," I said. "It's beautiful."

"Especially at this time of the winter," she said, "when there's a cool breeze."

"Why does Marilyn live in that apartment building?" I asked.

"Jackie wanted to buy her a house, but she wouldn't let him," June said. "There are certain aspects of her relationship with him that she's still not comfortable with."

"Because he's married?" I asked.

She nodded. "He's been separated from Genevieve for over ten years, but she's a devout Catholic and won't give him a divorce."

"That's crazy," Jerry said. June looked at him. "I mean, for somebody to hang on that long to somebody they don't wanna be with."

263

"Jackie's asked over the years. He says if he keeps asking that, eventually, she'll cave in and give him the divorce."

"Can Marilyn wait that long?" I asked.

June bit her lip. "It's something she's having doubts about, lately. She's starting to feel foolish for waiting around."

"But she's on the show," I said. "And she's one of your dancers."

"Which is part of the problem."

"So if the show went off the air, would she leave, then?" I asked.

"Maybe. But every time the ratings start to lag, Jackie reinvents the format. Right now, he's really playing up the whole Honeymooners revival."

I hadn't seen the new Honeymooners stuff. I never told anybody that I wasn't a real Gleason fan. I liked the old Honeymooners, but his Life of Riley had left me cold, and I hadn't watched any of his variety shows. I didn't even watch the episode Dino had done when I was down there with Frank.

"The lamb should be ready," she said, getting to her feet. "Come inside in five minutes."

"Okay."

She walked into the house.

"She's real classy," Jerry said.

"Yes, she is."

"Her husband shouldn't leave her alone so much. She might meet somebody better."

We finished our Piels and carried the empty cans back into the house with us when we went in for dinner.

Chapter Fifty-Four

June Taylor was almost as good a cook as she was a choreographer. The lamb was cooked perfectly, covered with breadcrumbs, accompanied by carrots and potatoes.

"This is great!" Jerry said, working his way through everything she had put on his plate. He felt he had to eat everything, so as not to insult her.

"He's right," I said. "It's delicious."

"I'm sure you've eaten in a lot of fine restaurants, especially in Vegas," June said.

"I'm not kidding," I said. "This is better than what I've had in those restaurants."

"I'm so glad to hear that," she said. "Thank you. More?"

"Hell, yeah!" Jerry said, holding out his plate. "Jeez, I'm sorry, Miss—"

"Don't be silly," she said. "Don't apologize for being anxious for more of my food."

She loaded his plate down and he started working his way through his second helping.

"Eddie?"

"Not a full helping," I said, wanting her to feel good, but getting pretty full from my first plate.

She gave me a lot less than she had given Jerry, then took even less for her own plate.

"More wine?" she asked.

"Thank you," I said.

She poured some in my glass, then looked at Jerry's empty glass.

"I'll stay with beer," Jerry said.

She nodded and set the wine bottle down.

"Have you cooked for Jackie?" I asked.

"Oh, no," she said, "I work for him. We don't eat together."

"Aren't you friends?"

"I've been working for him since 'Cavalcade of Stars,'" she said. "That's nineteen-fifty. We're close, mind you, but no, we don't eat together."

"Is that when you met him?" Jerry asked. "Nineteen-fifty?"

"I met him in forty-six," she said. "We were both in a Baltimore nightclub and had a terrible case of stage fright. I helped him overcome it, and the rest—as they say—is history."

"Well," I said, "he's missing out on a helluva cook."

"Marilyn comes here once in a while," June went on, "but without Jackie. He's not a beach person. He likes to be near it, likes looking at the girls, but he doesn't go on the beach, himself. He only ever wears a bathing suit on stage."

"I never wear a bathing suit," Jerry said.

June and I looked at him.

"I'm too big," he said. "It ain't a pretty sight."

"But . . . you've got muscles," June said.

"Nah," he said, "I'm just big. Oh, I'm strong, but I ain't got none of them weight lifter muscles."

It occurred to me, then, that even though we'd roomed together in the past, I couldn't remember ever seeing Jerry without a shirt—or, for that matter, a jacket.

"Huh," I muttered.

"What?" Jerry asked.

"Nothin'," I said. "Just thinking."

When dinner was over, June once again shooed us out onto the patio with beers, while she got dessert ready. It was getting dark, the breeze was mild, and we could see some lights out in the water.

"Ships," Jerry said. "I wonder where they're goin'?"

"Or coming back from," I said.

"Ever been on a ship, Mr. G.?"

"You know, Jerry," I said, "I never have been. But then, I've never wanted to be."

"Me, neither," he said. "Some fishin' boats in Sheeps-head Bay, but not on a big ship."

"Never had the urge to take a cruise?"

"Nope."

"Me, neither."

June came out with three cups of coffee and some pastries on a tray.

"Sfogliatelle!" Jerry said, in surprise. "Here?"

"There's a wonderful Italian bakery here," June said.

"I haven't seen those since I left Brooklyn," I said, as she set them down on a table that matched the chaise lounges. When I was a kid, they were a staple in my house of Sunday mornings, along with eclairs, creme puffs and Napoleons.

Sfogliatelle were shell shaped pastries filled with different things, but the most traditional were . . .

"What are they filled with?" Jerry asked, taking one.

"What else?" June asked. "Ricotta."

We enjoyed our coffee and Italian pastries, and then Jerry excused himself and went to bed.

"I'm gettin' old," he complained, as he went off.

That left me alone with June.

"What do you think you'll be able to do, Eddie?" she asked.

"Well, we'll check out where Rossi lived in Orlando, then go and look for this psychic in Cassadaga, see what she has to say for herself."

"We heard she left there," June said.

"Did anyone go and check?'

"Well, I don't know. Maybe those two detectives."

"Is that who told you she was gone?"

"Yes," June said, "I think they told Jackie that."

"And," I said, "that's probably not even her real name. Jerry and I'll look around and see what we can find out."

"But . . . you'll be careful, won't you?"

"Of course," I said.

We both stood up. With June's beauty, the moon on the water, and the breeze, it was a very romantic moment. We stood close to each other and looked into one another's eyes.

And then it passed.

"I have a husband," she said, taking my hand. "Or it might be different."

"I understand," I said. "Good-night."

"Good-night."

She went inside. I turned and looked out at the water. If I had gone with her to her room, it would only have been for the one time. I didn't love her, and she didn't love me. She had a man she loved.

And someday, I'd have a woman I loved . . . maybe . . . but not that night.

Chapter Fifty-Five

Esteban picked us up the next morning, and we headed north to Orlando.

Esteban took us on the Tamiami Trail to Tampa, and then U.S. 41 to Orlando. As promised, he made the drive in just over three hours.

When we got to Orlando, we found that Rossi didn't live in the city. He lived a few exits after it. When we got off, the exit sign said we were in Altamonte Springs, Florida.

June had given us Rossi's address. She said Jackie had gotten it from the police. I wondered how and why, but assumed that Jackie Gleason had some connections in Miami Beach.

We found our way to a neighborhood of old, adobe homes that looked as if they had been there for a long time.

"This is the address," Esteban said, stopping.

There was a fence around a bare front yard, with the gate hanging from one hinge. The adobe walls of the house had cracks on them. I had no way of knowing if they were surface, or if they went all the way through.

"Why would Rossi be living here?" I said, aloud.

"We don't know what he really did, do we?" Jerry asked.

"No," I said. "Just that he worked for a . . . a psychic."

"Maybe he was her muscle," Jerry said. "Was he a big guy?"

"The only time I ever saw him, he was dead on the floor of an elevator," I said. "He looked kind of . . . shrunken."

"We might as well take a look."

"You can wait in the car, Esteban."

"Sure, Mr. G."

It had been hot in Miami Beach, but for some reason it felt even hotter in Orlando.

The house was very like the one on the right and left of it. In fact, like most of them on the block. It was a bit past noon, kids were in school, people at their jobs. Nobody was in the yard or on the street. On the other hand, we didn't see any cars, either. The neighborhood seemed to be deserted.

We walked through the gate without knocking it off its remaining hinge, and up the cracked, slate walk to the front door. There was no porch, just concrete steps going up.

In the absence of a doorbell, we knocked on the flimsy front door. Nobody answered.

Jerry moved along the front of the house, looking in the windows.

"Looks deserted, Mr. G.," Jerry said. "I think we been had."

"Us?" I said. "Or the Miami Beach police?"

"All of us," Jerry said. "Wait, I'll look around back."

I waited by the front door and Jerry came back in what seemed like seconds.

"Nothin' in the back windows, either, Mr. G."

I looked both ways, and across the street.

"You think all the houses are like this?"

"I saw a tricycle and wagon in the back yard of the house on the right. A barbecue in the yard on the left."

"There doesn't seem to be anyone around now, though, does there?"

"Nope," he said. "Do we wanna go in?"

"Can you open the door?"

He put his hand on the front door and pressed. It popped open.

"I think so," he said.

Chapter Fifty-Six

We stepped inside.

It looked even more deserted standing in it than it had looking through the windows.

"Nobody lives here," Jerry said.

"Check the bedroom."

Jerry went through a doorway, came back after a few minutes. I was in the kitchen.

"Only one bedroom, and nothin' there, Mr. G. The dresser drawers are empty. There are hangers in the closet, but nothin' on 'em."

"If the house is deserted, why would there be hangers?" I asked.

Jerry shrugged. "Whoever used to live here left 'em there."

"Are they old hangers?"

"How do I know—wait, some are plastic, some are wire."

"The kitchen's empty, too, but there's a canister set on the countertop. One of them has tea bags in it. And they're not very old."

"So what are you sayin'?"

"Maybe after Rossi was killed, somebody came in here and cleaned it out."

Jerry bent down and ran his finger along the top of a cheap Formica coffee table.

"Dust," he said.

"Yeah, somebody cleaned it out, and nobody's been here since."

"We could talk to the neighbors," Jerry said, "if there are any."

"We don't have time," I said. "Let's try the house on either side, and then get going to Cassadaga."

We each took a house.

I went to the one with the tricycle and wagon in the back. A woman who had been sexy a few years ago, before she had kids, answered the door. She was a dishwater blonde wearing a tube top to accentuate bulging breasts and insistent nipples. Maybe she was hoping the big boobs would keep men from looking at the spare tire around her waist. In the background I could hear two kids, one talking, one crying.

"Well," she said, leaning against the doorjamb. "what're you sellin' handsome? I'll take two if you'll come inside and let me sample it, first." Then she turned her head. "Shaddup in there!"

"Ma'am," I said, "I was just lookin' for your neighbor, a man named Rossi?"

"Him?" she said. "Whataya want with him? Jeez, what a borin' guy. I stopped in one day to borrow a cup of sugar or somethin', and he wasn't interested at all. Can you believe that?"

"Uh, no, I can't," I said.

"Naw," she said, "I can see by the way yer lookin' at my tits, yer interested."

"I am," I lied, "but I'm also in a hurry. Besides, what if your husband gets home."

She cocked her hips even more and said, "He'll just hafta wait outside until we're through. Of course, it'll cost ya twenty."

So that was it. She was turning tricks from home while hubby was off at work. Or doing whatever it was he did for money.

"I'll have to take a rain check," I said. "Have you seen your neighbor?"

"Not since the paper said he was dead."

"And before that?"

"Sure, I saw him before that. Jeez, he lived next door."

"I mean, when did you see him last?" I asked.

"Jeez, I dunno," she said, "but I did see somebody after he got hisself killed."

"Oh? Who?"

"Fella and a broad, came by, went into Rossi's house and cleaned it out."

"Did you call the police?"

"Hell, no," she said, "why would I want the cops around here?" She turned her head. "Shut the hell up, will ya?"

"You say they cleaned the place out. Of what? They didn't take any furniture."

"They came out carrying suitcases, and some plastic bags. Tossed them all in the trunk and then drove off."

"What kind of car?"

"Green."

"Do you know the model?"

"All I know is, it wasn't a convertible. What do I know from cars?"

"Would you recognize them again if you saw them?"

Suddenly, a crafty look came into her eyes. She folded her arms over her breasts and straightened up. "Seems to me this info might be worth somethin' to ya."

Since she offered me sex for $20.00, I took a $20 out and gave it to her.

"I wouldn't know them again if I saw them," she said, "but the woman was in her forties, lotsa black hair all over the place, with some grey in it. She wore a bandana kinda thing on her head, and big hoop earrings. You know, like a gypsy."

Or, I thought, a fortune teller.

She looked past me. I sneaked a glance, saw Jerry waiting on the sidewalk.

"Think your friend would be interested?" she asked, fanning herself with the $20 bill I gave her. "He's a big one. I'd do you both for twenty-five."

"I'm sure he would," I said, "but like I said, we're in a hurry."

"Well, come on back," she said, "both of ya. I'll do a two-for-one deal, if ya know what I mean."

I knew. It wasn't a pretty picture.

I turned and went down the walk to Jerry.

"Anythin?" He asked.

"Some info," I said, "and a two-for-one offer."

"For what?"

I looked back at the woman, who was still posing in the doorway. Shorts and legs that used to be shapely but were now kind of fleshy topped off the picture.

"Take a guess."

We got back in the car. Esteban started the engine and was pulling away from the curb when Jerry suddenly got it, and said, "Ohhhh."

Chapter Fifty-Seven

There was an older woman on Jerry's side who offered him cookies rather than sex. But that was it. No info.

"You mean she wasn't the kind of old lady who spends her day looking out the window?"

"She's too busy makin' cookies, I guess."

"Any good?"

He made a face, took a cookie from his pocket. It had one small bite in it.

"No flavor," he said, putting it back.

"Where to, Mr. G.?" Esteban asked.

"Cassadaga," I said, leaning forward. "You know where it is?"

"I got an idea. We can take the new I-four."

"Whatever," I said. "How long?"

"Maybe half an hour."

I sat back.

"So," Jerry said, "now we're gonna look for this Madame Melinda?"

"Merlina."

"Right," Jerry said. "Either way, not her real name."

"Right. But we might have a description." I told him what the mama/whore had told me about the woman with all the hair and hoop earrings. "Oh, and a bandana."

"Sounds like a gypsy."

"I know."

"So where are we gonna start?"

"I don't know," I said. "Why don't we wait til we get there and see what we've got."

"And when are we gonna eat?"

"Same answer."

***

Cassadaga was a collection of private homes, most of them with signs in front advertising psychics, palm readers, tarot card readers and such inside.

"I don't see a restaurant," Jerry said, as we drove the streets.

"We passed a couple on the way in," Esteban reminded him. "Might have to go back."

"We can stop on the way back," I said. I reached over the seat and gave Esteban a slip of paper. "Let's find this address."

"Right!"

We drove around, saw people walking the streets, coming in and out of the houses. Some looked happy at what they'd been told, others looked sad. But what they all had in common was spending money.

We had gotten Madame Merlina's address from June Taylor, who had gotten it from Marilyn, who copied it from Jackie Gleason's phone book.

"I think this is it."

I looked out the window at a large, two story building with a wraparound front porch.

"It's a hotel," I said.

"Yep," Esteban said, "sure is."

"A hotel," Jerry repeated. "Maybe they'll have a forwarding address."

"Sure they will," I said.

Jerry and I got out of the car. Esteban started to get out.

"Just stay there and wait," I told him.

"Yes, sir."

When we entered the lobby, we realized they not only rented rooms, but also had rooms with psychics in them.

"Merlina probably had a room here to do business," I said. "Jackie must have come here."

"So if she left, and we find the manager, maybe he'll know where she went."

"It's worth a shot," I said. "That's why we're here."

We entered the lobby.

"Gentlemen, nice of you to join us," a man said, approaching us. "Are you here for the seminar?"

"Seminar?" I asked.

He smiled and pointed to a sign that announced a psychic seminar taking place in the hotel today.

"Are you the manager?" I asked.

"I am," he said. "My name is Simeon Westfield."

"Simeon," I repeated. "You wouldn't happen to be a psychic, would you?"

The man laughed. "As a matter of fact, I am, but I am not hosting the seminar. Today I'm simply the manager of the hotel."

"Well," I said, "today we're here to talk to someone about a lady named Madame Merlina."

"Merlina." The smile faded from the man's face. "I'm afraid Madame no longer has a room here."

"She lived here?" I asked.

"No," Westfield said, "she had a room where she conducted her, uh, business."

People were walking through the lobby, apparently there to attend the seminar.

"Look, Mr. Westfield, can we go somewhere and talk?"

"Well, I am rather busy today, what with the seminar and all, but . . . very well. This way to my office."

Jerry and I followed him across the lobby and down a hall to a small but well-appointed office. After we entered, Jerry closed the door and Westfield sat behind his desk.

"Please, gentlemen, have a seat. Then tell me what I can do for you."

Chapter Fifty-Eight

"My name is Eddie Gianelli," I said, "this is Jerry Epstein. We're here from Miami Beach, by way of Vegas."

"Las Vegas," Westfield said. "I've never been there." He was tall, fair-haired, pale-skinned, probably in his late thirties. He also had pale blue eyes, which probably helped him with his psychic thing.

"What's your interest in Madame Merlina?"

"Well," I said, "a man named Rossi was killed in Miami Beach. Apparently, he knew or worked for Madame Merlina."

"Who told you that?"

"Someone who came here to see her, professionally."

"Professionally!" he almost spat.

"What's that mean?"

"Merlina's real name is Rachel Foster. She's a phony."

"*She's* a phony?" Jerry said.

Westfield looked at him.

"I think what Jerry means is, aren't all psychics phonies?" I said.

He turned his head and looked at me with those creepy, pale blue eyes.

"If that's what you think, why are you here?" he demanded.

"Hey," I said, "we didn't mean any offense—"

"What if I said everybody who worked in Vegas was a gangster? Or a thief?"

"Okay," I said, putting my hands out, "I get it, I'm sorry."

He looked at Jerry, but the big guy didn't apologize. He just stared. Then he said, "Actually, I am a gangster."

"Well," Westfield said, not intimidated. "I'm a psychic. Most of the people who live here are connected to the supernatural in some way or another. Others, like Merlina, come here to rip people off."

"And you let them stay?"

"As long as they pay their rent."

"That seems very . . . understanding."

"We don't judge how people live their lives, here," Westfield said. "People come to Cassadaga looking for answers. Sometimes they find the answers they want in the wrong place. If it helps them, who's to judge?"

"Okay," I said, "we're not here to judge anyone, either. Is Merlina—Rachel Foster—still living in town?"

"No."

"But she did live here."

"Yes."

"Can you tell me where?"

Westfield looked at his watch. "I can do better than that. I can take you there."

***

When we stepped outside I said to Jerry, "You feel that?"

"What, Mr. G.?"

"It's cooler here, for some reason," I said. It was not only cool, but overcast. I found it odd that the sun seemed to be shining everywhere but on that little town.

Rachel Foster's house was walking distance from the hotel. Like most of the houses in town it was small, and well-cared for.

"People here are not allowed to let their homes get run down," Westfield explained. "When visitors come and walk around, they have to feel at home."

"I get it," I said. Jerry rolled his eyes behind Westfield's back.

"When did she leave?" I asked.

"I'm not sure," he said. "It was some time after the murder in Miami Beach made the news. And it happened overnight."

"So she just . . . disappeared?"

"That's right."

"What about Phil Rossi?" I asked. "Did you know him?"

"Probably."

"What does that mean?"

"She had more than one man around her," Westfield said. "I don't know who worked for her, or who was fucking her. To tell you the truth, I don't know which one was Rossi. But somebody in town might."

"Am I understanding this right? You were the landlord here?"

"Yes," he said. "I collected her rent, but I didn't associate with her."

We walked up to the front door.

"Can we get inside?"

"Go ahead," Westfield said. "I have to get back."

"Wait," I said, "is there police, or a sheriff in town that we could get into trouble with?"

"We don't have a police department," he said. "When we need to, we call the state police. I think you're pretty safe. That's actually part of the reason the phonies come here."

"And because they don't get judged," Jerry added.

Westfield looked at him and said, "You have such negative energy."

He didn't wait for Jerry to answer him, he just turned and headed back to the hotel.

"Jesus, Mr. G.," Jerry said, "we're surrounded by crack pots."

"Maybe so," I said, "but we're not here to make friends. Let's go inside and see what we can find."

I turned the doorknob and the door opened.

It was a small, one-bedroom set-up. The main room was both a sitting room and a dining room.

"You take the kitchen, I'll take the bedroom," I suggested. "Those are probably the only places we might find something personal."

Chapter Fifty-Nine

The bedroom had the usual furniture in it—a dresser, a chest, what looked like a double bed. It didn't have a bathroom. That was down the hall.

I opened all the drawers, looked under the bed, then walked down the hall to the kitchen. What I was looking for I didn't know. I just hoped I'd know it when I found it.

I heard Jerry in the kitchen, cabinets opening and closing, pots and pans, he even ran the water in the sink for some reason.

When we met up in the living room, we both said the same word.

"Nothing."

"If she had more than one man coming around," I said, "And a man helped her clean out Rossi's house in Altamonte Springs, then the other man has to be the killer."

"Makes sense."

"So we need to find somebody who knows who he is," I said.

"Somebody in the neighborhood?"

"Somebody in town," I said. "I think we're gonna need to get a room."

His eyes went wide.

"At that hotel?"

***

We walked back to the hotel, where the seminar had started up. There were people in a large room, sitting in rows of chairs, listening to several people sitting at a table in front of them.

Westfield was standing in the doorway at the back of the room; he saw us when we were crossing the lobby and came over.

"Finished already?"

"No," I said. "We're going to have to be in town a little longer, talking to some people. So . . . can you tell us where the closest motel is?"

"You'd have to get back on I-four and go a few exits," he said. "Or . . . you can stay here."

"So you do rent rooms?"

"Of course, we're a hotel, after all. Do you need one or two?"

"Three, actually," I said. "We have a driver outside."

"Three rooms," he said. "Excellent. And, of course, you'll pay?"

"Of course."

"Come with me to the front desk."

At the desk he instructed the clerk to check us into three rooms, and then excused himself to go back to the seminar. While I got us signed in, Jerry went out to get Esteban.

By the time they came back, I was holding three keys. Jerry and Esteban were carrying not only our bags, but an overnight bag Esteban must have had in the trunk.

"How about the car?" I asked.

"I parked it down the street," Esteban said. "I think it's legal. I didn't see any signs."

"It's probably fine," I said. "I didn't see any tow trucks in town."

A young man, presumably a bell boy, although he was wearing a simple suit, carried two of our bags and led us to rooms on the second floor.

"Must be busy," I commented, "what with the seminar and all."

"Oh, most of the people attending aren't staying here," he said. He didn't explain any further.

He showed us to three identical rooms, two in a row on one side of the hall, and one across the way. The two on the same side had connecting doors, so Jerry and I took those. We put Esteban across the hall.

"Thank you," Esteban said, and closed his door. He'd been carrying his own bag.

The bell boy put our bags in our rooms, and I tipped him. That done, and the doors closed, I went to the connecting door and knocked. Jerry opened it.

"Now what?" he asked.

"We need to talk to as many people in town who might have known Rachel Foster or seen her with one or two of her male friends. We need a description, or more."

"What's that?" Jerry asked. He walked to the window and looked out. "It's rainin'." He turned and looked at me. "I thought it didn't rain in Florida."

"It rains everywhere, sometime," I said.

"And there's somethin' out there. See it?"

I walked over, stood next to him and looked out. For a moment I thought I saw a dark shape, but it could have been someone running from the rain.

"I don't see anything," I said, only half lying.

"Maybe this whole town is haunted."

"Ghosts, Jerry?"

"Ain't that what psychics do?" he asked. "Talk to ghosts?"

"You mean, real psychics?"

"If you believe that hotel manager, then some of these people are real."

"I thought you didn't believe in this stuff?"

"Yeah but . . . it's rainin'. Somethin's up."

I couldn't believe the big boy was getting spooked, so to distract him I said, "I'm hungry. Let's go downstairs and see what we can rustle up."

We considered knocking on Esteban's door, but after all, he was our driver, not our buddy. And we might have to do it later, if we needed him to drive someplace for food. We left it at that.

Downstairs it was oddly deserted in the lobby, and in the room where the seminar was being held.

"Where'd everybody go?" I asked the desk clerk.'

"Home," the young man said. "The weather."

"The rain? Is that unusual?"

"It's the rain, and the cold."

Jerry nudged me. "See?"

"It's a little cool," I said, "but not exactly cold."

"Folks around here don't like this kind of weather," the clerk said. "They say it brings bad . . . things around."

"Things?"

"You know," the clerk said, poking at the air, "things."

Jerry nudged me again.

"Cut it out!" I hissed, then went back to the clerk. "Look, is there any place we can get some food?"

"There are some restaurants along I-four," he said, "but you don't want to go out in this weather."

"Nothing closer?"

"We have a kitchen," he said. "I can have them make you some sandwiches, if you like, and the bell boy can bring them to your room."

"Do you have a dining room, here?"

"That would be the room where they were holding the seminar," the clerk said, "so it's closed tonight."

"I see. Well, I guess sandwiches are okay."

"I can't promise anything fancy," the clerk said.

"Just send anything up," I said. "Enough for three. And some cans of beer, if you have 'em."

"Yes sir," the clerk said. Jerry had wandered over to take a peek out the front door. "Is he one of the three?"

"Yeah, he is."

"Okay," he said, "I'll have them make plenty."

"Thanks."

I walked over to where Jerry was standing.

"What do you see?"

"It's rainin'," he said, "and cool, and it's dark. It ain't supposed to be dark this early."

"So it's overcast."

"No," he said, "it's dark."

"Come on," I said, "they're gonna send up some sandwiches and beer."

We headed for the stairs.

"What kind of sandwiches?" he asked.

Chapter Sixty

It took about twenty minutes for the young bell boy to knock on my door. Jerry was there with me, and we had the T.V. on. Jerry had managed to find a rerun of an old Mike Hammer with Darren McGavin.

"Here you go, sir," the boy said. "The cook did the best he could. And we had this in the kitchen." He handed me a six-pack of Piels.

"Thanks," I said. "Here you go." I tipped him a few bucks.

"Thank you, sir!"

"Tell me something," I said. "Are you afraid that this weather might bring out some . . . things."

"Things, sir?"

"That's what the desk clerk told me," I said, pointing at the air. "Things."

"Oh, sir," he said, with a smile, "that's just a bunch of hooey."

"Yeah, okay," I said. "Thanks."

As he walked down the hall, I stepped out and knocked on Esteban's door. I figured it would only be fair to share the sandwiches with him. But there was no answer. Just in case he had gone to sleep—after all, he had been driving all day—I didn't pound any louder on it and went back in my room.

Jerry had already unwrapped a sandwich and popped the top off a beer.

"This ain't bad, Mr. G.," he said. "Ham and cheese on this one. And some good mustard."

I wasn't crazy about mustard, so I looked through the sandwiches and found one without it. It was roast beef, which suited me. It had mayo, which didn't suit me, but beggars couldn't be choosers at that moment.

I popped a beer and sat on my bed. Jerry was sitting at the small table by the window.

"So where do we start tomorrow?" he asked, starting on his second sandwich—pastrami.

"The neighborhood of the house she lived in," I said. "Somebody must have known her or seen something."

"Like in Altamonte Springs?" he asked.

"You know," I said, "I can't figure out what Rossi was doing living there."

"He must not have had enough money to live anywhere else."

"Why didn't he live here?" I asked. "If he was working with this Rachel Foster—Merlina—why didn't he live with her?"

"Maybe she already had a man livin' with her," Jerry said. "The killer."

"Why would a psychic have a killer working for her?"

"Psychics—most of them, anyway—are flim-flam artists. Criminals. Why not have a killer work for them?"

"But why kill their marks? They can't get money from them if they do."

"Maybe they kill relatives of the marks," Jerry said, "so they'll inherit more money."

"That's crafty thinking," I said.

He waved that away. "It's an old story, done all the time so the con artist can get to the family money."

"Then why was the killer in Miami Beach, following Marilyn Taylor? Or Rossi?"

"And why was Rossi there?"

"These are the questions we need answers to," I said. "Along with who killed Detective Eisman, and why?"

"And what about Mr. Gleason?" Jerry asked. "He's at the center of this, ain't he?"

"Definitely," I said, "only I can't believe it's only his belief in psychics he was trying to hide. There's something else, something he may not have even told Frank."

"What about Mr. Martin?" Jerry asked. "He was gonna try to find out something from Mr. S. for you."

"Good point," I said, finishing my last bite of my sandwich. "I'll call Dino."

But Dean had nothing for me. He said he called Frank, trying to make him believe that it was important for him to tell me what he knew.

"I tried to make him see the light," Dino said, "but he wouldn't even tell me. He *did* say he'd think about telling you."

"Well, I hope he does," I said, "before somebody else dies."

"Good luck, Pally."

I hung up and looked at Jerry. He was on his third sandwich.

"Aren't you supposed to be watching what you eat?" I asked him.

"Hey," he said, with his mouth full, "we been busy, and I'm hungry."

I looked at the table. There were two sandwiches left, which meant they'd given us six. I decided to have another and leave the last one for Esteban—if he ever woke up, of course.

I ate and told Jerry what Dean had said.

"You know, Mr. G.," he said, "if somebody had just told the truth from the very beginnin', this all might have ended much sooner."

"Believe me," I said, "when this is over, I'm gonna make that point very clear."

The rain continued to come down and, in fact, began to fall harder. So hard, in fact, that we lost our television reception.

We stayed in my room, talking about everything from sports, family, show business and the case. We finished the six pack of beer, and Jerry kept eyeing that final sandwich sitting on the table.

"Go ahead and eat it," I said. "He's probably gonna sleep all night."

He reached for it immediately and started eating.

"When you're done, I guess we better get some sleep," I said. "Tomorrow's gonna be a long day, and I only want to spend one more night here, if that."

He finished the sandwich, said goodnight and went back to his own room.

And then somebody tried to kill me.

Chapter Sixty-One

I wasn't sleeping soundly, which saved my life. Somebody entered my room and was moving through the darkness. For a moment I thought it might be Jerry, but I saw a dark figure and it wasn't that big.

I think because it was my room and I'd been staring at the ceiling, my vision in the dark was better than his. When he raised his hand, I knew he was pointing something at the bed. I reacted immediately, rolling off the mattress and to the floor just as there was a *phhht* sound and something took a chunk out of the headboard above where my head had been.

I reached out for something, anything to defend myself with. I ended up grabbing the lamp off the night table and throwing it at him. He ducked away and fired again. This time the bullet buried itself in the mattress just in front of me. I grabbed something again from the table, a clock, but this time I threw it at the door, which was open. It sailed out and bounced soundly off of Jerry's door across the room.

"Jerry! Jerry!" I shouted."

My assailant must have known Jerry would be trouble. As soon as I yelled, he turned and ran out the door. I got up and chased after him like a fool, running after a man with a gun. The connecting door opened, and Jerry came out, .45 in his hand.

"Mr. G. wha—"

"Down the hall!" I shouted and pointed. "He took two shots at me."

Jerry took off past me, down the hall, and I followed. I noticed that he was still wearing his pants, but his torso and feet were bare. I still had my shirt and pants on, but my feet were bare, as well.

We went bounding down the stairs to the lobby, stopping there to look around. The front desk looked deserted, but suddenly the clerk stood up from behind it and saw us.

"He went out the front door!" he shouted.

We took off out the door, into the rain. The shooter must have stumbled, because he was just getting up from the grass in front of the hotel, preparing to run again. Jerry raised his .45 and fired. The man kept running into the darkness, and we took off after him. However, we didn't get very far. Once we got to the sidewalk, he made better time than we did, since he had shoes on and we didn't. We ran for what seemed like blocks, but finally had to give up. We'd lost sight of him.

"Damnit!" Jerry shouted. Then he turned and looked at me. "Are you okay?"

"I'm fine" I said. "Scared, but fine."

The rain was pouring down and we were drenched.

"Let's get inside!" I said.

He nodded.

As we reentered the hotel, Lonny the clerk, was still crouched behind the desk, but the manager, Mr. Westfield, was there in front of the desk.

"Get up, damn it!" he was snapping at the clerk.

Lonny stood, then yelled, "There they are. They have a gun!"

Westfield turned and looked at us.

"Why am I not surprised? Why are you running through my lobby with a gun?"

"Somebody broke into my room and took two shots at me," I said. "We were chasing him."

"Did you catch him?"

We stared at him.

"No, of course not. That was a stupid question."

"You!" Jerry said, pointing at the clerk.

"Me?" he squeaked.

"You saw him run out."

"Yessir."

"Did you see him come in?"

"Nossir!"

"Were you here the whole time?"

"Yessir, the whole time."

"Then how did he get into the hotel?" Jerry asked.

"And how did he get into my room?" I demanded.

"Did he damage the door?" the manager asked. "Let's go up and have a look."

Jerry and I went up the stairs with the manager while the clerk remained hidden behind the desk. The door to my room was wide open.

"Well," Westfield said, "it doesn't look damaged."

"It doesn't even look jimmied, Mr. G.," Jerry said, bending over the lock.

"So somebody had a key," I said. "I must've heard it in the lock. If I wasn't lying half-awake, I'd probably be dead by now."

"Look at the headboard!" Westfield snapped.

"Fuck the headboard, that could've been my head!" I snapped back at him.

'Yes, of course." He stared mournfully at the scorched mattress and sheet.

"Is there another way into the hotel other than through the lobby?" I asked.

"There's a back door from the kitchen where there are trash dumpsters, but anyone coming in that way would still have to go up the stairs in the lobby."

"So the desk clerk must've seen them," I said, "or been away from the desk."

"Or," Jerry said, and we both looked at him, "the shooter was already in the hotel."

"One of my staff?" Westfield asked, aghast.

"Or," Jerry said, "a guest."

"Speaking of guests," I said, "where's Esteban? All this ruckus must've woken him up."

We went out the door and across the hall. Esteban's door was still closed.

"Nobody's that heavy a sleeper," I said, and pounded on the door.

There was no answer.

"Do you have a master key?" I asked the manager.

"Of course, but—"

"Open it!" I told Westfield.

"A guest's privacy is—"

"If you have a dead guest, how are you gonna explain it to the cops?"

He hurriedly produced his master key and unlocked the door.

"Let me, Mr. G.," Jerry said. Leading the way with his gun, he went inside. I followed. It was dark, but Jerry found the lamp on the night table and turned it on.'

"Oh my God!" Westfield said.

There seemed to be blood everywhere. Esteban was half on, half off the bed, dressed, soaking wet, with a hole in his side. He had obviously tried to staunch the flow of blood with pillow cases, but to no avail. The window was open, indicating somebody had come in that way.

Jerry checked his carotid artery.

"He's dead, Mr. G."

"So the killer got him first, and then me?" I said. "But why him?"

Jerry examined the body, then pointed out, "He's all wet, Mr. G. He was outside and came in the window."

"Are you saying—"

Jerry nodded.

"Esteban's the one who tried to kill you."

Chapter Sixty-Two

Jerry was convinced that the wound in Esteban's side was made by his .45.

"I got him as he was runnin' from us," he said. "I don't even know how he managed to climb back up here."

"You killed him?" Westfield asked.

"After he tried to kill me," I pointed out, "but if I was you, I'd call the police. We're gonna have a lot of explainin' to do."

Somebody else was going to have a lot of explaining to do—the agency who sent us the car and driver. But that would have to wait until morning.

Westfield left the room to reluctantly call the police.

"Mr. G.," Jerry said, "before the cops get here, let's see if we can locate his gun."

"Yeah, without that we're gonna be in some trouble."

"Well," he said, "I am, since I'm the one who killed him."

"We're in this together, Jerry," I pointed out. "Now let's take a quick look around."

***

When the police started to arrive, it was a mess.

As it turned out, Cassadaga did not have its own police department. The first car that arrived was from a
place called Lake Helen. It was a small city just to the
North of Cassadaga, but they didn't know what to do.
They called for a car from Orange City, which was to the
south, but they didn't know what to do, either. As the
night wore on, we got police presence from Sanford and
DeLand, but we didn't get detectives until they called the
Orlando Police Department.

They, in turn, called the detectives in Miami Beach
when we explained the situation to them. They actually
spoke to the Chief-of-Detectives there, because he got
involved when Eisman was killed in Vegas, and then his
partner, Winter, disappeared.

Detective Lemon hung up the phone on the manager's
desk and looked up at his partner, Detective Lowell, who
was across the room. We were seated between them, Jerry
and I. Westfield, had been interviewed, and was not in the
room.

"Well," Lemon said, to his partner, "Chief Gentry
from Miami Beach says these two are not suspects in
what happened down there, and what happened to his
detectives."

Jerry, who had been getting more and more annoyed
as the night went on, said, "We told you that."

Lemon, a man in his forties, raised his eyebrows, but still looked at his younger partner rather than us.

"And we should've taken their word for that," he said.

His partner, who hadn't said a word yet, just shrugged.

Then Lemon looked at us.

"First," he said, pointing at Jerry, "I could lock your ass up for that gun." He indicated the .45, which was on the desk in front of him.

"If he didn't have that gun," I said, "I might be dead."

I was stretching the point, since the shooter had been on the run by the time Jerry came out of his room with *his* gun. But I had to defend him.

"That might be the only reason he's not in a cell right now," Lemon said. "Apparently, the guy you put down is a killer. It remains to be seen if he's the guy they're looking for in Miami Beach."

"So we're free to go?" I asked.

"Go where?" Lemon asked. "Where are you going from here?"

"Back to Miami Beach, and then on to Las Vegas."

"Does that mean you found out what you came here to find out?" he asked.

"We're not sure," I said. "We have some people to talk to in Miami Beach."

"Yeah, you do," Lemon said, "and one of them is the Chief-of-Detectives there, Arthur Gentry. Understand? That's the only reason we're letting you go."

"We understand," I said. "We want to talk to the Chief."

"You report to police headquarters there as soon as you get back to town," Lemon said. "If you don't, a warrant will be issued for both of your arrests."

"Got it," I said. "We'll be leaving in the morning."

"Good."

We waited for more, and when it didn't come, I asked, "Is that it?"

"That's it," Lemon said. "Go!"

We stood up and Jerry started to reach for his gun. Lemon put his hand over it.

"Nuh-uh," he said. "We'll be sending this to the Miami Beach Police Department. If they decide you can have it back, they'll give it to you."

"And what are we supposed to do in the meantime if somebody tries again?"

"Why would they?" Lemon asked. "You got the guy, right?"

"Come on, Jerry." I nudged his arm. As he turned away, I asked Lemon, "We still have rooms here, right?"

"That's up to the manager."

"Yeah, right."

309

As we left the office, we found Westfield waiting right outside.

"Do we still have rooms?" I asked.

"If you don't mind sleeping in a bed with a hole in it," he said.

"I'll make do," I said. "We'll be checking out in the morning."

"Thank God!"

Chapter Sixty-Three

The next morning Jerry insisted on driving. We found the keys to the car in Esteban's room.

"Do you know the way?" I asked.

"Mr. G.," he said, "we just have to retrace our steps."

He got us back on the I-4 and we stopped for breakfast at the first Waffle House we saw.

While eating breakfast we went over the events, step-by-step.

"Let's try to put this all in order," I suggested. "Gleason comes here to see a psychic. Merlina—Rachel Foster—gets her hooks into him."

"So she threatens to tell the world that he believes in psychics," Jerry said, picking up the thread. "And he don't want that."

"No, he doesn't," I said. "Maybe she asks for money, and he says no. So she sends somebody to Miami beach to threaten his girl."

"And he follows her around," Jerry said. "But then why does somebody kill him?"

"That's the first question," I said. "Maybe Merlina sent two men to bird dog Marilyn, and they had a falling out."

"Okay, so one kills the other," Jerry said. "He wasn't a hit man. But he had the balls to brace you at the bar in the hotel."

"Figurin' he'd scare me."

"Which he did."

"Well . . ."

"You called me," Jerry said.

"Okay, yeah, I decided to be careful," I grumbled, then picked our thread up again. "So Gleason either doesn't want to tell me about the men working for Merlina, or he doesn't connect them to her."

"Seems to me if she sent a man to follow his girl, she'd let him know."

"Yeah, I think so, too," I said, "but he still doesn't tell me about it."

"So why did he ask you for help?"

"He didn't. Remember, it was June Taylor who came to me for help."

"Ah, that's right. So why'd he come to Vegas?"

"I think maybe June told him she asked me for help. I think he came to Vegas to see what I knew about his— let's call it, a hobby."

"And he brings his girl with him."

"Because the second man is still following her."

"Why?"

"Second question."

"I thought the second question was, why didn't Mr. Gleason tell you everythin'?"

"Yeah, okay," I said, "so this is the third question. Then Eisman comes to Vegas to see me."

"Why?"

"He's still working the case and he's stumped," I said. "He wanted to know if I remembered anything."

"He coulda called ya and ask that."

"Right, so question . . . four? . . ." Jerry nodded. "Why did he come to Vegas?"

Jerry counted on his fingers, then nodded to himself.

"So Eisman gets killed the same way Rossi did," I said, "which means by the same killer."

"Or," Jerry said, "by someone who wants everybody to think it's the same killer."

"Okay," I said, "so question five has an aye and a bee. Aye, who killed Eisman and bee, why?"

"Right." Jerry ate the last of his waffle, still had a couple of crisp pieces of bacon to gnaw on.

"Okay, so Jackie gets pissed at something and goes back to Miami. Only Marilyn decided to tell us about Rossi, and to talk to June again."

"No question there," Jerry said. "I figure she wanted to be helpful."

"Meanwhile, Eisman's partner, Winter, comes to town and promptly disappears."

"No question there. He came to town to find out what happened to his partner."

"But question six is, why'd he disappear?"

"Right."

"You know," I said, "one of us should've been writin' all this down."

"We ain't cops," Jerry said, "and we ain't a dick, like Bardini."

"Just two dumb jamokes tryin' to figure this thing out."

"Right."

We both ate our last pieces of bacon.

"And now," I said, "question number seven. Who the hell was Esteban?" We hadn't had a chance to call the car service to ask that question. "I'll have to call the service when we get back. Also, by then the Miami Beach cops can probably tell us who Esteban really was."

"Maybe he really was the killer," Jerry said, "and we got him."

"Except for one thing."

"What's that?"

"He didn't try to kill me with a knife."

Chapter Sixty-Four

We were exhausted when we got back to Miami Beach. Jerry made the drive from Cassadaga in just four hours. He had successfully retraced our steps, and not made any wrong turns along the way.

Thankfully, June had told us to come back to her house when we returned and had given me a key. I let us in and we both dropped our bags to the floor and sat.

"Why did I even get involved in this?" I asked.

"You know why, Mr. G."

"Yeah, yeah," I said, "I'm 'the guy.' Well, maybe I'm tired of bein' 'the guy.'"

"Nah," Jerry said, "you're just tired from last night." He looked at his watch. "We got plenty of time for a nap, a shower, and then goin' over and talkin' to this Chief-of-Detectives."

We had left Cassadaga very early, so it was only afternoon, and he was right. We did have time.

"How about we forget the nap, and just take the shower?" I suggested.

"Suits me, Mr. G."

"And then I'll call the car service before we go to police headquarters."

"You're the—"

"Don't say guy!"
"—boss, Mr. G."

***

After we showered, I put in a call to the car service. I asked for the man I had spoken to last time, Phil Herman. I assumed he was in authority, if he wasn't the owner.

"Mr. Gianelli?" he came on.

"Yes, Mr. Herman. I'm sorry to be callin' with bad news, but your driver, Esteban—"

"Who? We don't have a driver by that name, sir."

"Well, when he picked us up, he said he was from your service."

"Mr. Gianelli, did you not call back that same day and cancel your car?"

"I did not."

"Oh, my, I-I'm sorry, but someone called, used your name and canceled."

"I see. Well, Mr. Herman, you're probably going to be hearing from the police, either today or tomorrow."

"Good," he said. "I'm going to want that phony driver arrested."

"I'm afraid that won't be possible, Mr. Herman."

"Oh? And why not? He's besmirched our good name!"

"That may be," I said, "but he's also dead."

***

Since the car we had didn't belong to Phil Herman's car service, we decided to keep using it until the police told us to stop.

The Police Department was located at 1100 Washington Avenue. We found some maps in the glove compartment of the car, one of which was of Miami Beach, and used it to find our way. Apparently, if Jerry was a genius at anything, it was reading maps.

On the way we kept spitballing, trying to come up with answers to our questions, but we just seemed to be finding new questions.

"I'm getting real frustrated," I admitted, "so let's try something."

"Like what?"

"Like thinking outside the box."

"What box?"

"I mean something off the wall."

"Oh . . . like what?"

"You tell me," I said. "You know cops."

"What I know about cops you don't wanna know."

"Try me."

"They're dirty."

317

"All of them?"

"Lots of 'em," he said. "Most of the ones I've met. Look at Hargrove."

"He's dumb," I said, "but dirty?"

"A cop in Vegas?" Jerry said. "How can he not be dirty?"

"What about Miami Beach cops?"

"Sure, why not."

"Well, Eisman did own a bar."

"He wasn't dirty," Jerry said.

"What makes you say that?"

"If he was," Jerry said, "He woulda owned a better place than that."

"Okay, good point," I said. "Also, he came to Vegas lookin' for answers."

"And so did his partner."

"Well, Winter came to Vegas lookin' for Eisman," I said, "or who killed him."

"And he disappeared and ain't shown up dead."

"Okay," Jerry said, "you said you want off the wall, right?"

"That's right."

"What if Winter came to Vegas to see you," he said.

"What for?"

"Maybe he wanted to know what you told Eisman."

"That wouldn't make him dirty," I said, "That's just him workin' the case."

"Okay," Jerry said, "so that ain't so off the wall."

"But what if," I went on, "he didn't want to know what I told Eisman. What if he wanted to know what Eisman told me?"

"About him?"

I shrugged. "I'm just spittballin'."

"So Winter's dirty, and Eisman ain't, and he's afraid Eisman told you about it."

"What if . . . no, that can't be."

"What?"

"What if Winter killed Eisman?"

"He came to Vegas after Eisman was dead."

"That's what he told us."

"A cop kills a cop?"

"And he makes it look like the same killer did it."

"That's off the wall, all right."

"And you know what we've overlooked?"

"What?"

"Danny."

"If the dick had anything, he woulda called you."

But we haven't been anyplace that he could call us," I said. "He didn't know we were at June's, and he couldn't get us when we went to Orlando."

"You want I should pull over and find a phone?" he asked.

"No," I said, "let's go and talk to this Chief Gentry. When we get back to June's I'll call him. Maybe he's got something that'll help clear this whole mess up."

Chapter Sixty-Five

We parked and went inside the building at 1100 Washington, asked for the Chief-of-Detectives.

"Who shall I say is calling?" the cop on the desk asked sarcastically, as if he knew we'd never get in to see the big man.

"Gianelli and Epstein," I said. "We just got in from Cassadaga."

"Cadda what?"

"The Orlando area," I said. "The Detectives there called him about us."

"Wait over there." He pointed to a bench against a wall. We walked over and sat down.

"You gonna ask him about Eisman or Winter bein' dirty?" Jerry asked.

"Let's just see how the conversation goes," I suggested.

A uniformed officer came striding up to us and said, "Follow me. The Chief will see you."

We stood and followed.

Chief Gentry was a big, white-haired man in his 60's. He was sitting behind his desk and didn't bother to rise as we entered his office.

"That's all, Officer," he said.

"Yes, sir."

"Have a seat," he said to us."

We both sat across from him, side-by-side.

"I've had quite a few conversations about you with the detectives from Orlando. I know what went on there. I also have this." He put his hand on a folder.

"And what's that?"

"It's Detective Eisman's case file on the murder that occurred while you were in Miami Beach. The dead man in the elevator."

"Then you know everything," I said. "We went to Orlando and Cassadaga to try and find out something about the murders, not only the one here, but also of Eisman in Vegas."

"And did you?"

"No," I said, "all I did was almost get murdered myself."

"By your driver."

"Only he wasn't the driver," I said. "Somebody canceled the car and driver I ordered, and substituted Esteban."

"Esteban, as you call him," Gentry said, opening another file on his desk, "was actually a man named Samuel Foster. He lived in Orlando."

"Foster?"

"That's right. Mean something to you?"

"The psychic we went looking for, Merlina, her real name is Rachel Foster."

He picked up a pen and wrote the name down in the folder."

"What does she have to do with all of this?" he asked.

"We believe that whoever killed Rossi, and was following Marilyn Taylor, was sent by Merlina."

"Why?"

"That's what we went to Cassadaga to try to find out."

"They must be related," Gentry said. "Husband and wife, brother and sister."

"Or cousins," Jerry said.

Gentry looked at him, but didn't comment.

"How much do you know about Eisman and Winter?" I asked.

"They're my men," he said. "I know everything about them."

"Do you know why Eisman came to see me in Vegas?"

"I assumed it was to work the case."

"And Winter?"

"I figured he was going to try and find out who killed his partner."

"Have you heard from him since he left?"

"No."

"Do you know when he left?"

"Four or five days ago."

"That's days before he came to see me. Where did he go first?"

Gentry hesitated, then said, "I don't know."

I looked at his desk. There were other folders there, one of them very thick.

"You've got other cases," I said, jerking my chin. "And you've been workin' them for a long time. What's goin' on, Chief?"

He hesitated again, then seemed to come to some kind of decision.

"Close that door," he said.

Jerry got up and closed the office door.

"What we talk about now goes no further than this room. Got it?"

"Got it," I said.

Jerry had remained standing after closing the door, but now he sat down again.

"I got it," he said to Gentry.

Reluctantly, Chief Gentry opened the thickest of folders on his desk.

"This is a case that has been being worked for months, well before you came here, before Philip Rossi was murdered." He hesitated, as if second guessing himself. "The only reason I'm telling you about this is because you are not part of this department."

I Only Have Lies for You

"We're not gonna say a word," I promised.

Chapter Sixty-Six

"There has been an Internal Affairs investigation going on for several months concerning Detectives Eisman and Winter."

Bingo. I didn't know how I had pulled that one out of a hat only an hour before. It could only have been a result of having thought outside the box.

"I didn't know Eisman that well," I said, "but I had a couple of meetings with him after the initial interview regarding the murder. We met once at this bar he owns off of Collins, and then again when he came to Vegas. I gotta say, he didn't strike me as being dirty."

"No," Chief Gentry said, "after the first few weeks the I.A. detectives cleared him, but they were still looking into Winter."

"Did Eisman know Winter was dirty?" I asked. "I mean, they were partners. He would've had to know, right?"

"Eisman resisted for a long time, but he finally agreed to work with us."

"And what did he tell you?"

"The I.A. guys thought he was about to talk. In fact, they had a meeting set with him for when he got back from Vegas."

"Only he never came back."

"Right."

"And Winter came to Vegas, only he went someplace else first, didn't he?"

Gentry fell silent, got that second-guessing look again.

"Either you, or your I.A. guys, think Winter came to Vegas and killed Eisman, don't you? Because he knew about the meeting with I.A. when he returned."

"That's what they think, yes. Only he left days before you say he got there."

I looked at Jerry, who had been silent this whole time. "What do you think?"

"I think maybe Winter came to Vegas, killed his partner, then left and came back on the day he met with us at the airport, to make it look like he just got there."

"That's what I think." I looked at Gentry. "I've got a P.I. buddy in Vegas who can probably check this out even quicker than you can. But Winter could've flown into L.A. and driven to Vegas, killed his partner, driven back to L.A., and then flown into Vegas."

"Didn't you check on incoming flights that day?" Gentry asked. "You would've seen if he had come in on a flight from L.A."

I looked at Jerry. "I don't remember if we checked on incoming flights," he said. "I think we just stood there and waited to see him."

327

"In any case," I said, "he could also have flown from here to L.A., and then flown right out to Vegas."

"Well," Gentry said, "your guy can check on that from your end, and mine can check this end."

"I'm gonna call my guy as soon as we're done, here. But the question still remains, what does all of this have to do with the murder of Phil Rossi, and the attempt on me."

"Gentry put his beefy hands together, and then spread them apart.

"They could be two separate things. It might just be a coincidence that Eisman and Winter caught your case of the dead guy in the elevator."

"So Winter killed Eisman, but somebody else killed Rossi and tried to kill me."

"Could be."

"Or it could all be malarkey," Jerry said.

"That's possible, too," Gentry said. "Maybe we're all just reaching."

I had to admit I thought I had been reaching when I started to think about dirty cops. Now I wasn't so sure.

As far as the murder of Philip Rossi went, Gentry didn't know anything about Rachel Foster, aka Merlina.

"There's nothing about her in Eisman and Winter's case file," Gentry said. "I'll assign a new pair of detectives. Is there anything else they should know?"

"It looks like Merlina left Cassadaga," I said, "so they won't find her there."

"We figure either the killer is with her, or the killer was Esteban, the man I shot," Jerry said.

"Still," I said, "he didn't come for me with a blade. I don't think he killed Rossi."

"Oh," Gentry said.

"What?"

"I just realized if Winter killed his partner with a blade, he was trying to make it look like the same killer did Rossi. That's . . . cold."

Chapter Sixty-Seven

Before we left, the Chief took Jerry's gun out of his desk.

"I'm going to give this back to you," he said. "As far as I'm concerned, you saved Mr. Gianelli's life in Cassadaga."

"Thank you," Jerry said, reaching for it.

"Just please," the Chief said, "don't make me regret it. Try not to shoot anybody in Miami Beach."

"I'll do that," Jerry said, picking up the gun. "For a cop, you ain't a bad guy."

"I'll take that as a compliment," Gentry said. "Are you guys headed back to Vegas?"

"Probably tomorrow."

"Will you keep me informed, if you see or hear anything from Winter?"

"You got it, Chief," Jerry said.

We agreed to let the Chief and his men work on the murders of Phil Rossi and Detective Eisman. We were going to try to solve Jackie Gleason's problem, if we could properly identify it. Of course, we didn't tell the Chief what we thought Gleason's problem was, that his psychic was blackmailing him.

We went out the front door and got into the appropriated car, which we had forgotten to tell the Chief about. While Jerry reloaded his gun, I looked in the glove compartment and found some papers on the car that we could show to a cop if we got stopped.

From Police Headquarters, we drove back to June Taylor's house, stopping first at a deli Jerry spotted. We bought enough food for the three of us, so June wouldn't have to come home and cook.

When we reached June's house at the beach, Jerry took charge of the kitchen, while I used the phone to call Danny. As soon as he realized it was me, he reamed my ass.

"Where the fuck have you guys been? I've been calling the Sands lookin' for you. I thought you went missin' like that cop, or maybe you were dead."

"I'm sorry," I said. "We've been movin' around, and haven't really had time to check in."

"What the fuck," he said, again. "Busy doin' what?"

I filled him in on moving to June's house, driving to Orlando and Cassadaga, the attempted murder, the drive back to Miami Beach and the meeting with the Chief-of-Detectives.

"Jesus Christ," Danny said. "Jerry killed a guy and the cops gave him his gun back?"

"The Chief here is very understanding," I said.

331

"Well, I'll tell you who ain't understandin'," Danny said. "Jackie Gleason."

"What about him?"

"When I called the Sands lookin' for you guys, they told me that Gleason has been callin' too. He wants to talk to you in a big way."

"Okay, well, do you have anything to tell us?"

"Yeah, your guy, Winter?" Danny said. "From what I can see, he was here twice. Looks like he drove in from L.A. while his partner was here. Then he drove back, turned in his rental car, and disappeared. I'm betting he flew back to L.A. under an assumed name, and then flew back to Vegas under his own name to see you."

"And then disappeared after he found out that I didn't know anything."

"If I'm puttin' money on anythin', it's that he killed his partner."

I told Danny how the Miami Beach P.D. had been investigating Eisman and Winter, but had cleared Eisman.

"And was Eisman cooperating, then?"

"He was."

"So they think Winter killed him?"

"They don't want to think about a man killing his own partner, but they are."

"So if they're workin' on that premise, what's left for us to do? They still workin' the first murder, the guy in the elevator?"

"They are."

"What are you and Jerry gonna be doin'?"

"Well, we were going to talk to Jackie, and find out what he's hot and bothered about."

"Blackmail will do that to a person."

"Let's see if he admits that's what's been goin' on."

"But I gotta tell you," Danny said, "seems to me there's more at stake than havin' his public find out he believes in psychics and ghosts, or whatever."

"I agree," I said. "Somethin' else is goin' on."

"And it's bringin' out your Brooklyn," Danny said. "I can hear it."

"Yeah, me, too. With any luck, we'll see you tomorrow."

"Just don't forget I'm out here worryin', okay?"

"Deal."

"And tell the big guy."

"I will."

As I hung up, there was a key in the lock and June came walking in.

"I saw the car outside," she said. "Are you guys okay?" She dropped her carryall bag, with her dance gear in it, to the floor.

"We're fine," Jerry said. "We got some food for you."

"Great! I'm starved!"

"Before we eat," I said to her, "I've just been told Jackie's been trying to call me in Vegas."

"Yes," she said, "he's been desperate to get ahold of you."

"And you didn't tell him I'm not in Vegas?"

"You didn't want me to."

"No, I didn't."

"Then I didn't."

"Can you get ahold of him and set us up to meet to-morrow?" I asked. "We want to talk to him, and I guess it's obvious he wants to talk to us."

"I'll call him tonight."

"You know where he's going to be?"

"Of course," she said. "With Marilyn."

"Okay, then."

"Can we eat now?"

"We can eat."

She looked at Jerry.

"What do we have, big fella?"

"Pastrami . . ." Jerry started.

Chapter Sixty-Eight

June was exhausted from the day's rehearsals and went to bed early. Jerry and I were also worn out from our trip to Orlando and Cassadaga and back, so we also hit the sack early.

By morning June had arranged a meeting between us and Jackie.

"He doesn't want to wait, and he doesn't want to do it in a restaurant," she said. "So, he suggested you both come with me to the theater this morning, so you can talk there."

"He's gonna be at the theater for rehearsal?" I asked. "He must really be worried about something."

June didn't respond. We were eating bagels, which Jerry had also bought at the deli the night before. She paid special attention to smearing cream cheese on hers.

"Come on, June," I said. "It's got to be more than just not wanting his fans to know he believes in psychics."

"I'm sorry, Eddie," she said, "but I've already told you all I can about this situation. The rest is up to Jackie, himself."

Jackie was her friend, her employer, and I was just a guy she'd met a short time ago. I got it.

"Okay," I said, biting into my bagel.

June looked at me.

"Is it really okay?"

"It's fine," I said. "Let's just see what Jackie has to say."

***

"I'm gonna pay the blackmail."

That's what Jackie had to say.

"What blackmail?" I didn't want him to know that June had been filling us is.

"That don't matter, Eddie." We were in Jackie's dressing room: him, me, and Jerry. "I just want you to pay it."

"And that's why you've been trying to reach me?" I asked.

"Yes," he said. "And they want you to make the drop."

"Me?" Why were people constantly trying to give me jobs I wasn't trained for. "Why me?"

"Because," Jackie said, "they want the payoff to be made in Las Vegas."

Okay, wait a minute. That wasn't so bad. That was my home turf, and I'd have Jerry and Danny with me.

"When?"

"I told them I had to get ahold of you and then set it up," Jackie said. "They've been callin' me for the last three nights."

"It's obvious they ain't pros," Jerry said.

"Howzat?" Jackie asked.

"They're lettin' you call the shots," Jerry said. "Pros wouldn't do that. They wouldn't be waitin' for you to get ahold of Mr. G. They'd have you make the payment with somebody else."

"No," Jackie said, "you don't get it." He flicked the ash off the ever-present cigarette. "*They* want Eddie to make the payoff, and they want him to make it alone."

"Did they say why?"

"They said since I had chosen to involve you, and you lived in Vegas, you might as well be useful."

"But why Vegas?"

"I don't know. It doesn't matter. I just want to get this thing over with."

"What whole thing?"

"Huh? This," Jackie said, "the . . . blackmail."

"It could've been over sooner, if you'd leveled with us from the beginning," I said.

"I know, I know," Jackie said, "I was an idiot. Frank can tell you, I do that, sometimes. But I'm ready to actually let you help me, now."

"Help you pay the blackmail."

337

"Yes."

"But blackmail for what, Jackie?" I wanted to make him explain it all to me.

Jackie put his cigarette out, plucked a fresh one from his pocket and lit it before answering.

"I can't have my viewers knowing that I went to Cassadaga to see a psychic," he said, finally. "They'd think I was . . . crazy."

"You're a funnyman, Jackie," I said. "You don't think they already think you're crazy?"

"Ha! Crazy funny is different than crazy nutty, don't you think?"

"I think you're still holding something back."

"You do, huh?" Jackie asked. "And you think you're entitled to know what it is?"

"Hell, yes."

Jackie looked at Jerry.

"How much is the blackmail?" Jerry asked,

"Fifty grand," Jackie said. "You think I'm gonna pay fifty grand to keep somethin' quiet, and then tell you about it?"

"Do you think I'm gonna take my life in my hands to deliver your fifty grand, and not know why?" I asked, trying to keep my anger in check.

Jackie drew on his cigarette and blew the smoke out disgustedly.

"No, I suppose not." He looked down at the cigarette in his right hand, flicked the ash. "It's something that happened a long time ago, something I'm not proud of. Madame Merlina said she could help me."

"How?"

"How else?" he asked. "Putting me in touch with the dead."

"And did she?"

"No," Jackie said, "but I told her my secret. After I came back here, she waited months before contacting me, and threatening to tell if I didn't pay."

"You said no."

"Initially," he said. "I had no intention of giving that phony any more of my money. Then a man came to town, stopped me in the parking lot of the theater one day."

"Rossi."

He nodded.

"He renewed the threat, made some lewd comments about Marilyn. I still said no. So he began to follow her, frightening her."

"Why did June think I could do anything?"

"Frank talked about you, told me all the problems you've fixed in the past, the people you've helped. Ava, Judy . . . Bing. Even told me about Elvis. I told Marilyn. She must've told June."

"Why did June bring me in, not you?"

339

"June acted before I did," he said. "Rossi ended up dead, and I thought it was over."

"But it wasn't."

"No, I heard from Merlina again. Turns out Rossi wasn't acting for her. He was trying to go around her and hit me up for money, himself. He even brought the price down. Twenty grand. I still said no." He shrugged. "I'm stubborn."

"And the man who killed Rossi?"

"He was working for her," Jackie said. "She said now I knew how serious she was. That's when I took Marilyn and flew to Vegas to see you."

"But you still didn't tell me what was going on."

"Then you called my suite and told me about that cop gettin' killed," Jackie said. "That's when I knew things had gotten way out of hand. I couldn't risk anybody else gettin' killed, not Marilyn, not you. So we came home, and I started plannn' to pay."

"Fifty grand," I said.

He nodded.

"And you think she'll stop after that?"

"I told her it's a one-time payment," he said, "that if she came back at me, I'd go to the cops. I had no intention of lettin' her bleed me dry. I think she got the message."

"So you're sure you want to play it this way?"

"I'm sure, Eddie," Jackie said. "Do I have to tell you more about my little . . . secret?"

I studied him. He looked more vulnerable than I'd ever seen him.

"Not now," I said. "Maybe some other time."

"Sure," he said, "some other time."

Chapter Sixty-Nine

Jerry and I flew back to Vegas with a leather briefcase bearing Jackie Gleason's $50,000. I decided there was no hit man looking for me, so I'd go home. I also suggested that Jerry fly back to Brooklyn.

"Not til this is over, Mr. G.," he said. "You know me better than that."

"I just thought I'd make the suggestion."

Jerry insisted on driving me home in the Caddy and staying the night on the sofa. We took the $50G's with us.

When we got into my house, I called Danny.

"Come on over and bring some food," I said. "We have to talk."

"Chinks?" he asked.

"Chinks okay?" I asked Jerry.

"Sure," Jerry said, "but plenty of pork fried rice, huh?"

"I heard 'im," Danny said. "See you in half an hour."

I hung up.

"What're you gonna tell the dick?" Jerry asked,

"Everything."

"Mr. Gleason gonna like that?"

"Danny deserves to know what he's getting into."

"Why?" Jerry asked. "You know he'd help you, anyway. All you gotta do is ask."

"How do you know that?"

"Because that's what I'd do."

***

Danny showed up 35 minutes later, and 10 seconds after that the kitchen table was covered with Chinese food take out containers. He also brought two six packs of Ballantine beer.

"And a bottle of diet soda for you, big guy."

"Forget it," Jerry growled, "I ain't drinkin' that crap."

Danny laughed and put the soda in the frig. Then we sat down and started to divvy up the food. Danny brought paper plates and, for all three of us, plastic forks. We were all hopeless with chopsticks.

"If you're back home, you must be feelin' pretty safe," Danny said.

"They're not gonna kill me," I said, "when they need me to deliver some blackmail money."

"What? Gleason's gonna pay?"

"Fifty grand," I said.

"You got it here?"

I nodded with a mouth full of lo mein.

"Jesus. So you're gonna make the delivery?"

343

I sat back and looked at him.

"I thought maybe between you, me and Jerry, we could catch this guy."

"Guy?"

"Well, it's a woman who's actually blackmailing him, but it'll be a man collecting the money."

"Would this man happen to be the blade killer?"

"That's what we think," I said, looking at Jerry.

"This gypsy woman has had one guy she can count on," Jerry said. "He killed the guy in the elevator and had the nerve to approach Mr. G. in the hotel bar."

"And she had two men she couldn't count on," Danny went on. "One got himself killed because he went out on his own, and the other got himself killed by going up against you."

"Right."

"Do we think they're both here in Vegas? Merlina and the blade guy?"

"We do," I said. "Two blackmailers lookin' for a place to lay low until they pick up the money."

"You want me to see if I can find them," Danny said.

"Yes," I said, "and failing that, maybe we can catch him at the drop and make him take us to her."

"And then hand them over to Hargrove?"

I made a face.

"What, the Highway Patrol?" he asked.

Now Danny made a face. "They're part of the De-partment of Motor Vehicles. That's not real police."

"Okay, then what about Ralph Lamb?" Danny sug-gested.

Lamb was the sheriff of Clark County, had been for several years, and was respected.

"All we have to do is tell him he has to hand them over to the Miami Beach Police," I added.

"You've met Lamb," Danny said.

"No."

"I have," Danny said. "He doesn't like me much."

"Okay, then," I said, "I promised the Chief-of-Detective in Miami Beach I'd keep him informed. What if we call him, and have him send a couple of men to pick them up?"

"And what do we do with them until they get here?" Danny asked.

"Sit on 'em," Jerry said.

"We're gonna have to make sure Hargrove never finds out about this," Danny warned us. "You know what a glory hound he is."

"Only the three of us are gonna know," I pointed out, "and none of us are gonna tell him. Right?"

They both nodded their heads.

"Pass the pepper steak," Jerry said.

Chapter Seventy

Of course, I had to fill Jack Entratter in on what was going on, but not what we intended to do when we caught the blackmailers.

"Jesus, Gleason almost got you killed gettin' you involved in this."

"And Frank."

"Well, now—"

"I'm pretty convinced that this wasn't a coincidence," I said. "He invited me to go to Miami Beach with him so Gleason could check me out."

"But it was the Taylor dame who asked you for help."

"Right, she jumped the gun without knowing it, but that worked in Jackie's favor."

"Okay, so they all almost got you killed."

"Right."

"But now all you're gonna do is make this payoff."

"Right, again," I lied.

"Do you know what Gleason is getting blackmailed about?" Jack asked.

I hated to lie to him again, but I said, "No idea. He won't say."

"Then why are you makin' the payment?"

"Come on, Jack," I said. "He's Frank's friend, and in the end we've gotta make Frank happy."

"You got that right."

I stood up.

"You still in that suite?"

"I'm keepin' it for Jerry while he's here," I said, "but there's no reason I can't go home and sleep."

"So you can get a call—I mean, I can call you at home or in the suite?"

I knew what he was asking. "Yeah, tell Frank to call me at either number."

"I think he wants to apologize."

"Yeah, sure."

I went out, gave his girl a wave and hit the elevator.

***

Jerry was waiting down in the lobby.

"What'd your boss have to say?"

"That Frank is gonna be calling me to apologize."

"Whataya think of that?"

"I think it's the least he can do, since somebody took two shots at me."

"You still pissed at him?"

"Maybe now more than ever."

"You gonna tell 'im?"

"What do you think?"

***

The call came in to Jerry's suite while we were up there trying to strategize. How would we make the drop, and then hang around to catch the guy, without being seen?

"You're the local guy," Jerry said. "They should let you pick the place."

"Is that what blackmailers do?" I asked. "Leave the location in somebody else's hands?"

"Not pros," Jerry said, "but we ain't dealin' with pros, here. We're dealin' with a crazy gypsy broad and her boyfriend who likes to work with a knife."

"How do we know they didn't recruit another guy with a gun?"

"We don't," Jerry said, "but they lost two other guys, already. I'm thinkin' they're just gonna trust each other."

"That's good thinking," I said.

The phone rang at that point. I picked it up, thinking it would be the blackmailers. I wasn't. It was Frank.

Well, it was the hotel operator telling me Frank was looking for me.

"Put him through," I said.

"Yes, Mr. Gianelli," she said.

"Eddie?"

"Hello, Frank."

"Jeez, kid, I'm sorry," he said, quickly. "I heard what happened. I sure didn't mean for you to almost get killed. Neither did Jackie."

"I know that, Frank," I said. "Nobody wanted me to get killed. But I was kept in the dark about a lot of things."

"I know, kid, Frank said, "so was I. Believe me, I tore Jackie a new one when I heard what happened. I told him to come clean. Did he?"

"Almost," I said.

"Whataya mean?"

"He told me he's being blackmailed," I said, "as a result of going to see a psychic. But he didn't tell me for what, exactly."

"Are you still gonna help him?"

"I'm in this pretty deep, Frank," I said, "and the blackmailers asked specifically for me to deliver the money, so yes, I'm still gonna help him."

Chapter Seventy-One

The blackmailers were supposed to call Jackie, and then Jackie would call me. Still, when the phone rang and it was Frank, I couldn't help wondering if it was the blackmailers. Were they going to stick to the plan?

"These are amateurs, Mr. G.," Jerry told me over breakfast the next morning, "not pros. In some ways that makes them even more dangerous."

"How so?"

We had ordered room service, and were sitting across from each other at the table they had wheeled in. Once again, I had spent the night in the suite.

"We can't predict what they're gonna do," Jerry said.

"And they don't know what we're gonna do."

"That's right."

I put my knife and fork down and sat back with my coffee cup in hand.

"Jerry, I need you more than ever for this. I'm in the dark, here."

"I've dealt with blackmailers before," Jerry said, "but they were pros. But I'll do the best I can, Mr. G."

"That's all I ask."

"You better be ready with a time and place," Jerry said. "That is, if they let you pick either."

"I'll make them a fifty-fifty proposition," I said. "One of us picks the time, the other picks the place."

"That's a start," he said, taking some more bacon and toast.

"What happened to your diet?" I asked.

He chewed and said, "After. I'm gonna need all my strength for this."

I took two more pieces of toast, added bacon and held the sandwich in my hand.

"Me, too." I took a bite.

***

We had no way of knowing when the blackmailers would call Jackie, or me. So I simply went back to work, with Jerry dogging my heels the whole time.

It was two days later that the call came in from Jackie. I had given him my home number, and that's where Jerry and I were when he rang.

"Eddie? I just got off the phone with them."

"What'd they say? Where do they want the drop? Is it a drop or a meet?"

"I don't know any of that," he said, frustrated. "They asked me if you had the money and I said yes. Then they said they're gonna call you."

"When?"

351

"That they didn't say."

"Did you talk to a man or a woman?"

"A man."

"How did he sound?"

"I don't know . . . confident. Well spoken."

That fit the guy who had talked to me in the Fontainebleau bar in Miami Beach. But it also fit a lot of people.

"Jackie, have you ever heard the voice before?"

There was a pause, and then he said, "Now that you mention it, he did sound familiar."

"Do me a favor," I said. "If it comes to you where you heard it before, give me a call and let me know."

"All right," he said. "And you call me when you hear from them. I wanna know when this is gonna end."

"You got a deal."

"They call?" Jerry asked as I hung up. He was sitting on the sofa with a can of beer.

"They did, but they didn't say much." I relayed Jackie's side of the conversation to him.

"So now we gotta wait for them to call you," Jerry said. "Great. How bad do they want this money?"

"I don't know. Guess we'll know more when they call."

I sat at the other end of the sofa and picked up a beer bottle.

"The dick comin' over tonight?" he asked.

"Yeah, he said he might have somethin'."

We both sucked on our bottles and looked at the blank T.V. screen

"Where do you think you wanna set up the meet?" he asked.

"I've been giving that a lot of thought," I admitted. "The middle of nowhere at night, or during the day with people all around?"

"If it's a drop," Jerry said, "at night. If it's a meet and a payoff, then during the day."

"Okay, then," I said. "The middle of nowhere, out in the desert, where we can see in all directions."

"And they can see us."

"Good point. Somewhere on a deserted road, then. In a parking lot. We can see from a window, or a roof."

"And during the day?"

I thought a moment, "The Sands, by the pool."

"They'd never agree to that."

"We'll see what they agree to," I said. "They may not even give us any choices."

The doorbell rang.

"That must be Danny," I said.

"I hope he brought food."

I opened the door and let Danny in. As Jerry had hoped, he had take-out bags.

"Don't cook tonight call Chicken Delight," he said, holding up the two bags.

"There aren't any Chicken Delights in Vegas," I pointed out.

"They got 'em in New York," Jerry said.

"So it's just chicken," Danny said. "And fries, and beans, and biscuits. Okay?"

"Sounds good," Jerry said, coming off the couch. He grabbed the bags from Danny and took them to the kitchen.

"I hope you've got more than chicken," I said.

"I thought I did."

"Thought?"

"I heard somethin' about a man and a woman squattin' in a motel, plannin' somethin'. Turned out to be a couple of Bonnie and Clyde wannabes. Not the two we're lookin' for. Sorry."

"Don't worry about it," I said. "We'll eat and keep waiting for a call."

Chapter Seventy-Two

But they didn't call that night.

Or the next.

On the third day Jerry and I were in the Horseshoe Coffee Shop, waiting for Danny to arrive when a familiar figure walked in.

"Holy shit!" I said.

Jerry turned to see what I had seen.

Detective Winter of the Miami Beach Police Department was walking toward us.

"Eddie G.," he said, with a grin. "Good to see you again. Mind if I join you?"

Before I could object, he slid in the booth next to me.

"You want me to wring his neck, Mr. G.?" Jerry asked.

"I'm armed," Winter said, moving his coat aside to show us his shoulder holster.

"So is Jerry," I said, and Jerry showed Winter the butt of the .45 in his belt.

"So we're even. But that wouldn't be good for any of us," Winter pointed out.

"And why not?" I asked.

"Because then I wouldn't be able to tell you where to deliver the blackmail payment."

"You?" I said. "You're working with the blackmailers?"

"Not originally," he admitted, "but then there came a point where our interests sort of . . . aligned."

"Why would you throw in with amateurs?" Jerry asked.

Winter looked at Jerry. "It just seemed to be the thing to do."

"Where have you been?" I asked,

"Around."

"And how did you know we were here?"

"I followed you." He looked around. "How's the food here?"

"Great—" Jerry said, annoyed that he'd answered before he could cut himself off.

"Are we waiting for your P.I. friend, or can we order?" Winter asked.

"It's just us," I lied.

"Then what should I order? Ah, I think the burger platter," he said, looking at the menu.

"Why don't we just get down to it?" I asked.

"Because I'm hungry," Winter said. "Come on, now, fellas, let's have lunch together, and then we'll talk."

"I wanna talk during lunch," I said.

"Fine with me," he said, "about anything but blackmail. That will come after."

Jerry and I both ordered the burger platter . . .

"So did you kill your partner?" I asked, as we ate.

Winter laughed. "If I did, would I tell you?"

"He must've had the goods on you," Jerry said.

"What goods?"

"To prove you were on the take."

"He couldn't prove that," Winter said.

"Why not?"

"Because then he would have had to admit that he was on the take, too."

The Miami Beach P.D. Internal Affairs Detectives must have known that Winter was guilty of something much more serious than his partner, otherwise why recruit Eisman?

"Come on," Jerry said, "he probably took a buck or two, but you must've been gettin' more—or doin' more for it."

"What makes you think so?"

"Because you're alive," Jerry said, "and he ain't."

Winter looked sideways at me.

"Does this guy do all your talking for you, Eddie?"

"People don't generally know this," I said, "but he's the smart one."

Winter laughed uproariously at that.

"What's so funny?" Jerry demanded.

"Hey," Winter said, "no offense. I just thought he was making a joke."

Our platters arrived and we started to eat. I was hungry enough that eating next to a man with a gun didn't ruin my appetite.

"Why don't you tell us what the plan is?" I said to Winter, "and I'll tell you where we can make the drop."

"You've got that part wrong already," Winter said. "We'll tell you where the drop is being made."

"That's not smart," I said. "This is my town."

"That's exactly why you're not picking the place," Winter said. "I'm surrounded by amateurs, and you're one of them, Eddie. I've taken over the planning of this little gambit, so I'll be making the rules."

"Your partners don't object to that?"

"My partners, as you call then, have done everything wrong up to now. They know if they want a payday, they've got to play by my rules."

I looked at Jerry, who had bristled at the word "amateur" but said nothing. If Winter was going to think of Jerry as an amateur, maybe that would work to our benefit.

"Okay, then, Winter," I said, "go ahead and make your rules."

Chapter Seventy-Three

Winter laid it out. Jerry just glared at the man while I listened intently.

"The reason I've been here so many days was to scope the area out," Winter said. "Now that I've got the lay of the land, I picked out the best place for the pass."

"Pass?" I asked. "Not a drop?"

"No drop," Winter said. "You're gonna pass the money right to me."

"Your partners are goin' along with that?" Jerry asked.

"They don't have a choice," Winter said, pushing his plate away. "Neither do you."

Jerry and I had cleaned our plates. Winter had left a few bites of his burger, and about half his fries. As evidence of just how much Jerry disliked the cop, he wasn't even looking at the food.

"Okay, when?" I asked.

"Tonight."

"That's quick," Jerry said.

Winter grinned. It was only then I realized how much the man looked like a wolf.

"I'm not giving you time to come up with a plan." He pointed at Jerry. "And you won't be anywhere nearby. Eddie makes this pass alone."

"And then you put a bullet in me," I said.

"I don't have any reason to," he said, "but I'd advise you not to give me one." He slid out of the booth, dropped a piece of paper onto the table. "There's the time, place, and instructions, laid out nice and neat. Don't deviate from that, Eddie. Understand?"

He didn't wait for me to answer, just walked away, out of the restaurant.

"So," Jerry asked, "what do we do now?"

"Have dessert," I said, "and figure out how we're gonna deviate."

***

The note said the pass would be made at midnight. That gave us about four hours.

"What place did he pick?" Jerry asked.

I read it, and grinned.

"What's funny?"

"I'll show you," I said. "Let's take a ride."

***

We got in the Caddy and I had Jerry drive South on Industrial Road until we reached Blue Diamond Road, that intersection was deserted except for a few abandoned buildings, and a vacant parking lot.

We pulled to a stop alongside the lot.

"He picked this place," I said,

"There's nothing for miles around," Jerry said. "How am I gonna protect you?" He looked at me. "And why are you grinnin'?"

Of the three abandoned buildings, two of them had collapsed walls, so no one would be able to hide inside.

"That building there?" I said, pointing to the third one. "You have to live in Las Vegas, and be in the know, to know that it's not abandoned."

"It's not?"

"Come on," I said, getting out of the car.

Jerry got out and followed me across the parking lot to the building in question. It was like a cement block, with a wrought iron front door that was chained.

"How you gonna get that chain off to go inside?" Jerry asked.

"I'll show you."

I stepped up to the door and pounded on it. A small eye-slit opened and I said, "Hey."

There was the sound of a couple of locks being thrown, and then the door opened. The chain remained where it was, allowing the door to swing out. It wasn't locking anything, it was just for show.

"Eddie G.!" a man shouted. "How ya doin', man?"

"Hey, A.J.," I said. "This is Jerry. He's with me. He's all right."

"If you say so. Come on in."

I entered, followed by Jerry, and then A.J. closed the door and locked it.

"What brings you here, Eddie?" A.J. asked. He was in his late thirties, with shoulder length blonde hair and clear blue eyes. I had heard more than one woman describe him as looking like "a fallen angel."

"Just provin' a point to my friend here, that everything isn't always what it seems."

"Well," A.J. said, "whatever you want . . ."

"Thanks."

He went down one hall, and I took Jerry down another until we came to a room with a bar. A few people were sitting at it. There were also some tables, a few of which were occupied by one or two people—a man alone, two men drinking together, and a young couple with eyes only for each other.

"Why ain't there no cars parked outside?" Jerry asked.

"Folks get dropped off," I said. "Friends, cabs, whatever."

"So what is this place?" Jerry asked.

"Kind of a club," I said, "for people who don't like the glitz and glamour of the strip. This place has whatever they want."

"Anything?"

"You can get what you want to drink, snort or shoot," I said. "They have to know you to let you in. There's even a small horse-and-sports book in the back, plus the occasional poker game."

"What, no slot machines?"

"That's part of the noise these people are gettin' away from," I said.

"What's it called?"

"Folks just say they're goin' to 'The Place.'"

"So, since Winter ain't from Vegas, he doesn't know nothin' about it."

"Right. He picked this parking lot because he thinks it's completely off the grid. The presence of The Place is only known to those of us who are well informed."

Jerry got it. "So I can watch you from here."

"Right."

"But all that means is, if he kills you, I can kill him."

"Right."

"After."

"Right again."

"I still don't like it," Jerry said. "I need to be closer."

"Well, you can't be."

"Yeah, I can," Jerry said.

"How?"

"Just make sure the pass takes place close to this building, and not out in the middle of the parking lot. I need to not only see, but hear."

"Well," I said, "I'll do my best."

"Mr. G.," Jerry said, "you gotta do better than that."

Chapter Seventy-Four

We went to my house to pick up the money.

"You know," I said, as we sat in my living room and had a beer first, "I don't see that Gleason's fifty grand is a big enough prize for Winter to want part of."

"So you're thinkin' he's gonna take it for himself?"

"Like he said," I answered, "he's dealin' with amateurs."

"Except for me."

"He's gonna be sorry he overlooked you, Jerry."

"You got that right."

There was a knock at the door at that point.

"That'll be Danny," I said. We had called him when we got to the house. He had to drive out to Blue Diamond Road with Jerry, because I needed to drive my Caddy out alone. I didn't want either of them to hide in my back seat, because I thought that was the first place anybody would look. As for the trunk, they might not even look in there, but just pump a few slugs through the door.

"Catch!" Jerry said, and tossed a can of beer Danny's way. The dick caught it with one hand.

"Thanks."

We all sat and I filled Danny in on the plan.

"So Jerry and I will be in the place, and you'll be out in the parking lot alone?"

"That's right."

"With this Detective Winter. And he'll have a gun and you won't."

"That was part of the instructions he wrote down," I said. "I'm to come alone, and unarmed, with the money."

"Fifty grand?"

"Right here," I said, slapping the briefcase that sat on the coffee table.

"And Winter's gonna take that and share it?" Danny asked.

"Jerry and me, we were just talkin' about that before you came," I said. "It doesn't seem like enough, does it?"

"No," Danny said. "The way I figure it, he's out for his own payday. He ain't gonna share it."

"Which means," I said, "he'll have to kill this Madame Merlina, and whoever she's got with her."

"The blade guy," Danny said.

"Against a Miami cop with a gun," Jerry said.

"My money's on the cop," I said.

"But first he's gotta get the money from you," Danny pointed out. "And then he's gotta kill you."

"Well," Jerry said to Danny, "we're gonna do our best to make sure that don't happen, right?"

"Right," Danny said.

I Only Have Lies for You

***

Danny and Jerry left in Danny's car two hours before me. Danny knew how to drive to "The Place" without being seen from Industrial Road. They would walk a few blocks to get there and be in position. A.J. knew Danny, and would remember Jerry, so he'd let them in.

I was nervous. Even with my two friends nearby—not close by, but nearby—I was out there all alone with an armed dirty cop. As a rule, I'm not crazy about cops, and the only thing worse than a dirty cop like Winter was a dumb cop like Hargrove.

Hargrove. I wondered if I should call him, then decided that was dumb thinking on my part. If he thought I was hanging myself out to dry and might get killed, he'd stay away. I had a strong dislike for him, but he had an unreasonable hatred for me. He wouldn't lift a finger to help me unless he thought it would get him a medal, or a promotion.

So no Hargrove.

Danny had offered me a gun. I hadn't taken it. Guns are not my thing and besides, I was sure Winter would frisk me.

I sat on the sofa and had a glass of bourbon. What the hell was I doing? What kind of plan was this? Walk right

367

into the lion's den and hand him a briefcase filled with 50G's. Then what?

Well, what the hell did I think I was there to do? Jackie Gleason wanted the man paid, I should just pay him and be done with it. Wasn't that what Jackie was asking me to do? Why was it up to me to try and stop the guy? The Miami Beach police were working on the murders, so why not leave this to them, as well? But Gleason wasn't even going to file a complaint about being blackmailed, so if he didn't care, why did I?

And then why did I have to go and get my friends involved, as well? Jerry ended up killing a man, and who knew what Danny was gonna have to do to try and keep me from getting killed?

Yet, there I was, ready to go through with it. And I knew why. We all knew why, right?

Right.

I was the guy.

Chapter Seventy-Five

I drove the Caddy to the meet, my stomach fluttering. There were no other cars in the abandoned parking lot as I pulled in. I looked over at The Place, secure in the knowledge that Jerry and Danny were watching. I just hoped they wouldn't end up watching me get shot.

I got out of my car and waited. It occurred to me that either Jerry or Danny could have ridden in the trunk or hunkered down in the back seat. Either one probably would've made me feel a lot better.

I kept an eye out for headlights, but when I heard somebody's feet crunching on the gravel surface of the parking lot, I realized that Winter was walking toward me.

There were no lights in the lot, so the only illumination was coming from the moon, and one light pole over by The Place.

Finally, after hearing the crunching footsteps for what seemed like hours—they were echoing in my head—Winter came from out of the darkness with an amused grin on his face.

"Eddie," he said, "nice to see you. Is that my money?"

I gestured with the hand that held the briefcase and said, "Every cent."

He took out his gun and pointed it at me.

"What's that for?" I asked.

"Just want to check," he said, "make sure you're not armed or wired. Spread your arms, please."

I did as he asked and as I'd expected, he frisked me, doing a pretty good job.

"Very nice," he said, "now just stand still, I want to check your car."

"For what?"

"I doubt your bug buddy could hunker down far enough in the back seat . . ." He took a quick look. ". . . right, didn't think so, but maybe he's in the trunk, huh?"

"I think that'd be an even tighter fit," I said.

"All the same," he said, standing behind my car, "maybe I should pump a few slugs into it, just to be sure."

"All you're gonna do is make holes in a beautiful car," I said.

He stared at me. Underneath his fedora his eyes were shaded by the moonlight, so I really couldn't see much of an expression.

"Ah, you're probably right," he said, walking over to me. He put out his empty left hand. "Keys. We'll just take a look."

I took out the keys and handed them over. He opened the trunk, jumped back, ready to shoot whoever was in there, but it was empty.

"Jesus, Eddie," he said, "so far you've done everything I asked." He slammed the trunk shut. I had an idea that if he wasn't going to kill me, he'd hand the keys back. If he was, he'd either just toss them away, or put them in his pocket.

I wasn't encouraged when he dropped them onto the back seat.

I wanted to get him over near The Place, but I didn't want to suggest it. Still, that was the only place there was a light . . .

"You wanna take a look at your money now?" I asked, starting to unbuckle the briefcase.

"In this light?" he asked. "Which is to say, no light at all. You'd like to slip some funny money past me in the dark, wouldn't you?"

"What are you talkin' about?"

"You know why I picked this spot for a pass, Eddie?" he asked. "Because of that light." He pointed to the lamp post. "The only light. Let's go. I want to see my money right under that light."

I wondered where his car was? Was there somebody out in the dark who had driven him? If so, they'd certainly be able to see us standing under that light. But then, so would Jerry and Danny.

I started walking.

371

Chapter Seventy-Six

Again, the gravel crunching beneath our feet sounded incredibly loud to me. I know they say when you're about to die your life flashes before your eyes, but I wondered if your hearing also got very acute?

We entered the circle thrown by the light and Winter said, "That's far enough."

I could see the front door of The Place. I couldn't tell if the eye slit was open or closed.

"Open it!" he commanded.

I opened the briefcase and held it out to him. He reached in with his free hand, came out with a packet of ten thousand dollars. With the other hand, he kept his gun pointed at me. I wondered if his plan was to just shoot me and leave me lying there?

He studied the top bill, then riffled the pack one-handed as well as he could.

"Looks good," he said.

"It is," I said. "Why would Gleason pay with funny money? Where would he even get it?"

He stuck the packet back into the briefcase, took out another one. Satisfied, he put it back.

"Close it up!"

I redid the buckle on the front of the briefcase.

"Give it to me."

I handed it over, stood there empty-handed, waiting. I wondered if I should try to jump him, hang onto his gun arm until Jerry and Danny came out to help me? Or would I just get shot? And what was the difference? Wasn't I going to get shot, anyway?

Holding the briefcase in his left hand, and the gun in his right, he opened his mouth to say something, but was interrupted when suddenly, there were headlights. We hadn't heard an engine start, but there it was, something with headlights, barreling toward us.

The tires crunched over the gravel, and as it got closer, I could see it was a car, a dark sedan.

"Damn it!" Winter swore. He turned to face the car, held the gun out. But even as he fired, it came at us, and I couldn't wait to see what he accomplished. It meant to hit both of us.

I jumped out of the way as he fired a couple of shots, and then it was roaring past. I didn't know if it had struck him, but it missed me.

The driver hit the brakes and the car skidded on the gravel, then stopped. The doors opened on both sides and two people got out, a man from the driver's side, and a woman. The woman had a gun, I could see it in the light from the pole. I could also see wild black hair and hoop earrings.

Madame Merlina.

She pointed the gun, but not at me. That was when I saw Winter on the ground, where he'd jumped out of the way of the car, as I had.

"You bitch!" he shouted. "You tried to kill me."

"I'm not done trying!" she shouted back and pulled the trigger.

Winter had dropped both the briefcase of money and the gun when he leaped. Now he scrambled around, searching for his gun.

At the same time, the man who got out of the car came toward me. The light from the pole gleamed off the blade he held in his hand.

"Too bad you didn't listen to what I told you in the bar in Miami, Eddie," he said.

I tried to scramble away from him and get to my feet, but I slipped on the gravel.

There was more gunfire, and then I realized there were more people. Jerry had come charging out The Place's front door, and into the fray. He slammed into the blade man, knocking him completely off his feet.

"I got this!" he shouted to Danny, who was behind him.

There was another shot and Danny turned that way, his gun in hand. He found himself facing Madame Merlina, who had picked up the briefcase, and still had her gun in her hand. Winter was down, bleeding from a gunshot wound.

"Take it easy, Lady," Danny said.

"Who the hell are you?" she demanded.

"He's with me," I said, getting to my feet.

Off to the side her blade man got to his feet and said to Jerry, "I'm gonna cut you good."

Jerry produced his .45 and pointed it at the man.

"You're done stickin' people," he said.

We were now all encircled by the light from the single pole. Jerry faced the blade man, Danny and I were facing the armed Madame Merlina, and Winter was on the ground, moaning and holding his chest.

Merlina pointed her gun at Danny and me.

"Madame Merlina," I said, "this is over. Your plan to blackmail Jackie Gleason, your plan to double-cross your partner, Detective Winter over there? All over."

"He's not my partner," she said. "He tried to horn in on us after he killed his partner and needed money to disappear. Well, he wasn't gonna get our money."

"You mean Jackie Gleason's money, don't you?"

"It's ours now!" she screamed. "We worked hard for it. Tell that big idiot to stop pointing his gun at Leonard."

"Leonard?" Jerry asked.

"I'm Lenny the blade," the man with the knife said, as much to Madame Merlina as to us.

"Jesus," Jerry laughed, "you shoulda stuck with Leonard."

"Merlina," I said, "he's not going to put his gun down, and neither is Danny, here. So you want to start pulling that trigger, go ahead."

And then we all heard it in the distance: police sirens.

"Leonard, get in the car!" Merlina shouted. "Let's go!"

"Don't move a muscle, Mr. Blade," Jerry told him, laughing again.

"If you didn't have that gun, I'd cut you up," Leonard told Jerry. He was tall and slender, I recognized his voice from the Fontainebleau in Miami. Even if Jerry put his gun down, Leonard wouldn't have had a chance against him.

"Drop the gun, Merlina," I said. "And the briefcase."

Merlina looked at us, then at Jerry, assessed the situation, and dropped the gun to the gravel. She didn't drop the briefcase, though. She held that with both hands, tight to her chest, and was still holding it that way when the police cars arrived.

Chapter Seventy-Seven

After several squad cars arrived, an ambulance came for Winter, then an unmarked car with Hargrove and his partner, as well as a surprise guest.

Miami Beach Chief-of-Detectives Gentry.

The presence of Gentry—who outranked him, even if it was with another department—seemed to temper Hargrove's hatred of me.

"You should have called us instead of trying to handle this yourselves," Hargrove said.

"I think we handled things pretty well," I said.

"For a bunch of amateurs," Hargrove said.

"Funny how the only one to get hurt was a career cop gone bad," I observed.

"Chief Gentry told me he was under investigation," Hargrove said, "and that he believed Winter killed his partner."

"He did."

"Then he's trash," Hargrove said. "He should have died here."

"But he didn't," I said, "so I guess Gentry will be taking him back."

"You're lucky, Eddie," Hargrove said, "that your hood and your pet P.I. never discharged their weapons."

"They didn't have to. I told you, we handled it."

Hargrove looked around the parking lot, which was now filled with people, mostly from his department—cops, detectives, lab techs, as well as medical personnel from the ambulance. At that point, Gentry came walking over.

"I'd like to talk to Mr. Gianelli, Detective," he said.

"Of course," Hargrove said, and walked away without another word. He must have been choking on them.

"How did you get here?" I asked.

"I came with two of my Internal Affairs detectives," Gentry said. "They decided Winter had to still be here, after killing Eisman. I wanted to be in on the arrest."

"And so you were."

"Yes." He looked over at the ambulance. "He has a chest wound, and they're not sure he'll make it. I hope he will."

"So you can lock him up."

"Yes," he said. "What about your problem?"

"Gleason's blackmailers are in custody," I said. "I think you'll find the man is the one responsible for the murder in the elevator."

"His name is Leonard Grayson," Gentry said. "Apparently, he worked with the woman, Merlina, and they became romantically involved."

"And decided to make some money by blackmailing Gleason when they realized who he was."

"Yes."

I nodded. "They probably thought it made more sense to warn me off than kill me, and have another body show up."

"And then changed their minds once or twice," Gentry said.

"Until they decided to use me for the payoff—which was probably Winters' idea when he tried to muscle in on their action."

"Once he killed his partner to keep him quiet, I don't think he felt safe enough to come back to Miami," Gentry said. "So he decided to get in on their action."

"I wonder how he found them," I said.

"He's actually always been a very good detective," Gentry said, "just a dirty one, as well."

"Too bad."

"If he makes it, we'll fill in some of the blanks," Gentry said. "If he doesn't, we'll just have to live with them."

"We don't always get all the answers, do we, Chief?"

"No, Mr. Gianelli, we don't." He shook my hand. "Thank you. I believe I can keep Detective Hargrove from coming down on your ass, although he does seem to hate your guts."

"That's one way of putting it," I said, "but thanks."

379

As Gentry walked away, he passed Jerry and Danny, exchanging a nod with them. They walked over to me.

"Are we free to go?" Danny asked.

"Sure, why not?" I asked. "We didn't shoot anybody, did we?"

"Lenny the Blade," Jerry said, shaking his head. "He was too funny to shoot."

"And Merlina still has some questions to answer," Danny said. "I didn't want to kill her."

"We might as well get back to the Sands," I said. "I'll give Gleason a call and tell him we've got his money, and his blackmailers."

"He ain't gonna be happy," Danny said.

"Why not?" Jerry asked.

"He wanted to pay her," Danny said, "and have her go away. Now, if she wants to, she can reveal his secret to the world."

"Only if the cops let her," I said. "And besides, all he has to do is deny, deny, deny."

"You tell him that," Danny said, "and see how he reacts."

"Maybe," I said, after a moment, "I'll have Frank tell him."

Epilogue: 2009

When you watch a video on Youtube, they list all these similar videos along the side, in case you're interested. There are clips of the Rat Pack, alone and together, interviews with Jackie Gleason, Jerry Lewis, Lauren Bacall, anybody who ever had a connection with Frank, Dino or Sammy.

I saw an interview that had been conducted with Jackie and Marilyn Taylor, after they had been married. Jackie looked shrunken and grey, still with the ever-present cigarette in his hand. I didn't watch it.

In fact, I turned my lap top off. I never saw Jackie again after that whole business was finished, and I didn't talk to him. I did call Frank and told him to tell Jackie it was all over and he could have his money back. I figured Jackie would send someone to get it, so I was surprised when that someone turned out to be Frank . . .

***

It was a couple of days later after Chief Gentry had gone back to Miami Beach with a patched-up Detective Winter in tow—and cuffs—Jerry had gone back to Brooklyn, and Danny was away on a case. I got a call at the Silver Queen bar from Frank, asking me to meet him, with Jackie's money.

I had to fetch the money from Jack Entratter's safe, so I decided to have Frank meet me there, as Jack was also out of town.

When Frank walked in, I was seated behind Jack's desk.

"Looks good on you, Pally," he said, sitting across from me. "Maybe one day you'll have this job."

"I don't want it," I told him. "I'm happy doing what I'm doing." I picked the briefcase up off the floor, where I had it next to me, set it on the desk and pushed it across. "There's Jackie's money. Every penny's there, but maybe he'd like you to count it."

"That's okay," Frank said, with a smile as he took it off the desk. "I trust you."

"Is Jackie upset that I didn't just pay the blackmailer off?"

"He was, but I talked him down."

"How?"

"I told him the payoffs would never have stopped, and that they were going up the river for murder, anyway. Anything they said would sound like desperation and all he had to do was deny it."

"And he bought it?"

"Yeah, he bought it."

"Well, good."

"Look, Eddie," Frank said, "I'm, sorry things got so crazy. I know if we had told you the truth from the beginning—"

"Water under the bridge, Frank," I said. "Forget it."

Frank stood up, holding the briefcase in one hand, but he didn't leave.

"Eddie, are we cool?"

"Sure, Frank," I said, "we're cool."

He smiled, and walked out . . .

***

But we weren't cool.

I got myself a small bourbon and sat on the sofa, in front of my now dark laptop. Things were never the same between me and Frank after that. Oh, we talked, interacted, whatnot, but I never felt like we were friends. And maybe the problem was, we never were. I was just a means to an end to be used whenever he needed me.

I didn't feel that way with Dino. I truly believe that Dean Martin and I were friends. Sammy could be called a close acquaintance. It could be said that I knew Joey Bishop and Peter Lawford. I liked Joey, not Peter.

Of Jackie Gleason, all I ever admit to when people ask—and they're always asking, "Did you know him." or "Did you know her?"—was that I met him once.

You see, all my memories of that time when Vegas was "my town" are not good.

On Sale Now!

That Old Dead Magic
A Rat Pack Mystery
Book 12

For more information
visit: www.SpeakingVolumes.us

On Sale Now!

Everybody Kills Somebody Sometime
A Rat Pack Mystery
Book 1

"**FRANK SINATRA** and **DEAN MARTIN** never knew how much trouble they were in until Robert J. Randisi stepped onto the scene. A gem of a read!"
—SUE GRAFTON, author of *S Is for Silence*

For more information
visit: www.SpeakingVolumes.us

CPSIA information can be obtained
at www.ICGtesting.com
Printed in the USA
LVHW052209130720
660608LV00001B/107